Transformations

A thorough or dramatic change in form, appearance, nature or character

James Foley Smathers

ISBN: 0692649026
ISBN-13:978-0692649022

Contents

Book III

This is a work of fiction. All of the characters and events portrayed in this novel are either products of the author's imagination or are used fictitiously, but... JFS

Book I
Chapter 1
The Beginning

SECRET: That which is kept hidden is known as the secret.

At first, the noise floated somewhere in the back of his subconscious; a ringing sound as a distant school bell signifying the end of a class period. With his head wedged up under the Piper Cherokee's dash, the muted sound was far too removed from his task at hand to gain his immediate attention. Eventually, the consistent rhythm and persistence of the rings pushed the thought of the workbench phone into his consciousness. Jackson Andrews stopped tightening the bolt and listened. It was the workbench phone. He quickly slid out from under the dash and dropped down out of his plane.

"Hold on there, I'm coming," he yelled as he trotted across the hanger. "I bet a hundred bucks you hang up before I get there," he chuckled to himself.

It would make little difference to him if the caller hung up. The call would not be for him. He had been scheduled to fly out hours ago, so no one would know that he was still there. Besides, only the mechanics and airport personnel got calls on this phone. However, both hanger mechanics

1

were his friends and were good guys. He would take a message for them. He snatched up the phone in the middle of a ring.

"Hanger B," he said with authority.

"Hello... hello." It was a woman's voice, distant, unsteady. "I am trying to reach Doctor Jack Andrews?" The voice was so faint that he could barely hear it.

"Yes... Yes, this is Jack Andrews speaking," He leaned against the work bench and placed a hand over his left ear and waited.

"Doctor Andrews... this is a... friend... I'm calling to tell you... that... you're..." there was a pause.

"Who is this, please?" Andrews did not recognize the voice. He was becoming impatient with her apparent loss for words.

"It's not important who I am, Doctor..." The voice wavered. "I'm calling... to... I'm calling to tell you that... that you ought to go home right away, sir... your wife is playing games on you..." Abruptly, the voice was replaced by the shrill whine of a dial tone. It drilled as painfully into his inner ear as some cold probing instrument, and for several seconds the sound held him in its spell. Then with one quick deliberate motion, he twisted the receiver away from his ear and slammed it down on the hook.

"Who the hell was that?" he mumbled to the phone as if the black plastic receiver could answer. "Better yet, what the hell was that?" he now said aloud, staring at the receiver. The message was as strange as the voice. Had he heard it right? His wife was playing games? What the hell was that supposed to mean? He had just had lunch downtown with Jill at noon and she was fine.

2

Games! What were games? Was Jill supposed to be having an affair with someone? Obviously it was some kind of joke; and a bad joke at that. It had to have been some sort of crank call. But the voice had sounded strained, emotional, and the urgency was real. Somebody was a hell of an actress he thought. He glanced around the hanger. It was late Friday afternoon and the few people who had been working on planes near him earlier were now gone.

He should call home anyway before taking off, he thought, but looking back at the workbench phone, he noticed that it had no dialer on it, preventing outgoing calls. He set out, walking back to the flight service center. The January sun was setting early and the temperature was dropping rapidly. It would now be dark before he took off for Freeport. As he walked through the service center, Tom Whiten, the Operations Manager, stopped him.

"God Almighty, Doc, I thought that you'd be across the Gulf Stream by now. Did that lady reach you out there at the hanger?"

"What lady, Tom?" Andrews answered with a question.

"She didn't give me her name when she called, Doc. She just said she needed to talk to you and that it was real important. I told her that I thought you had already taken off, but that if she called the hanger B number and let it ring a long time, if anybody answered, they could tell her for sure." Whiten shook his head. "I'm sorry I didn't come looking for you, Doc, but when I saw you a couple hours ago and you said you were leaving right away... I just..."

"Don't worry about it, Tom. I've been trying to put the radio back in my plane and it is one hell of a lot harder than it was taking it out."

3

"Do you need some help?"

"Not anymore, I think I got it together. Say, Tom, I do need to make a phone call before I take off; any chance of my using your office phone?"

"You bet, sir. It's locked now, though, so I'll have to let you in." He led the way down a long corridor to a door marked Manager. "It's supposed to freeze hard tonight, Doc. You don't own any citrus, do you?"

"Nope, we lost all ours years ago." Andrews followed along behind him.

"Thank God I don't have any," Whiten said, shaking his head. "My dad and brother have a little ten acre grove that they are going to fire tonight. My brother is sweating it out. He says tonight could be another bark buster." Whiten was referring to the phenomenon that occurred when the sap in citrus trees froze so quickly that its expansion split the bark of the trees, making loud cracking sounds, each one signifying the death of the citrus tree.

"Hell, I hope not," replied Andrews. "I've got a few friends who still own a lot of groves."

Whiten unlocked the door and turned on a bright overhead light. He quickly moved a stack of papers on his desk to one side. "Make yourself at home, Doc, just turn off the light and be sure this door locks when you come out."

"Will do. I appreciate this, Tom."

"Anytime, sir." Whiten closed the door behind him. When he was alone, Andrews picked up the receiver. He dialed the number for an outside line and punched in his home phone number. He shook his head and smiled. "Go home, your wife is playing games," she had said. Surely this was all some sort of practical joke; maybe it was a test to see how he would respond. Naturally, he would be expected to call home, to make sure everything was alright.

The phone rang once. He would say that he was calling to remind Jill to turn off the water running into the pool. The phone rang a second time. That would make sense because she could never hear it running and he always did. The phone rang a third time. He would also give her the message from the Sears serviceman who had stopped by the house that afternoon. He had meant to include it in the note he had written and left lying on the kitchen counter. The phone rang again. He could also ask her if anyone had been by or called since he left. The phone rang again. No, he wouldn't say that. It would sound too suspicious.

He wouldn't even mention the woman's call. He would just check in, tell Jill that he loved her, and be on his way. The phone rang again. Where in the hell was she? Maybe she went out... Where could she have gone...? "Playing games?" Was she out somewhere, playing games? What a joke. He could try to call the...

 "Hello." It was a woman's voice, but faint and, at first, not familiar. "Hello, Jill, is that you?" Andrews placed a hand over his left ear and strained to hear the distant voice on the other end of the line. "Jill, is everything all right there?"

"Oh, Jack... Yes, of course everything is fine." She sounded sleepy and her voice was stronger now. "Where are you?" she asked, officially now showing some concern. But there was something tentative and hesitating in the sound of her voice.

"I'm still at Herndon Airfield, Honey. I just wanted to check in with you before I took off... I was about to hang up, it took you so long to answer the phone..." He paused intentionally.

"I was... out in the laundry room..." she said softly. He waited. "You know how loud that dryer is now... I just didn't hear the phone." A chill came over him. That was the wrong answer for her to give him. Her voice had become clearer but he was now aware that something was not right. All his confidence vanished. He thought he was making sounds down deep in his throat, but he couldn't hear them. He cleared his throat and pressed a point. "I thought maybe you had gone out or had company there, visiting..." He paused again. There was no response. "Has anybody called or been by since I left?"

"No, no messages," she said gaily. "I just thought that you had to be in Freeport tonight for your seminar."

"I've had a little trouble with the plane; just getting ready to take off now. I'll miss some of the reception tonight, but my lecture isn't scheduled until tomorrow morning.

"Oh, I didn't know... are you leaving now?"

"Yes, I'm about to. I love you, Honey."

"Well, be careful and have a good trip."

"Jill?"

"Yes."

"I love you."

The length of the pause that followed ended any hope that Jack Andrews had that his wife was not playing some sort of game. For although he did not tell his wife that he loved her often; whenever he did, her response was always a quick affirmation of the same. Now, her lack of response strongly suggested to him that someone else could be there with her. A certain someone to whom a soft "I love you" spoken into a telephone at this particular moment would appear grossly hypocritical.

"Jill?"

"Yes, me too," she said quickly. "Bye." The line went dead.

Jack Andrews replaced the receiver and stared at the phone for several minutes. Slowly, he closed his eyes. Something was wrong; terribly wrong. His mind whirled as it sought to uncover an acceptable answer, or a simple explanation. There wasn't one. He could feel his heart pounding and a tight constricting pain in his chest. For several minutes he forced himself to take deep breaths and exhale slowly until the pain eased; then he rose slowly from the chair, crossed the room, turned out the light, and pulled the door shut behind him.

On the way back through the terminal lobby, he waived at the Service Manager. "Thanks for the use of the phone, Tom. I need to run a quick errand before taking off. How about getting someone to check out that radio for me while I'm gone? I just want to be sure that I've hooked it up right."

"Sure thing, Doc." Whiten glanced up from the log book he was writing in and then added, "Is everything all right, sir?"

Andrews stared down at his feet as if considering the question carefully, then the corners of his mouth turned up slowly into a sad smile and he glanced back up at Whiten. "Sure," he said. "I should be back in an hour or so."

It was dark as he crossed the parking lot to his car. The Volvo's leather seats were cold and he shivered as he groped to fit the key into the ignition. The engine roared and he wheeled the car out onto the highway to make the twenty minute trip to his house, dreading what he would find, but now certain that his suspicions were warranted.

He had avoided telling Tom Whiten that he had forgotten something at home, even though the remark would have been truthful. He had forgotten to give Jill the message from the Sears service man. He had stopped by the house earlier that afternoon to work on the clothes dryer, which had been making an unholy racket when Jill used it. Jack had let the guy in and was back in the bedroom packing his bags when the fellow had called through the house for him.

"Sir, be sure to tell your wife," he had said, standing in the kitchen doorway, holding a frayed and unraveled belt in his hand, "that she's going to be without that dryer over the weekend. It was an old drive belt that was making all the noise. I've pulled it out." He held it up for Jack to see. "The problem is, I can't get a new one until Monday. I'd hate for her to do a load of wash and then find out that she had no dryer. Tell her I'm sorry, but I will be here first thing Monday morning."

"I'll be sure she gets the message," Jack had said, and he had meant to include it in the note that he left on the kitchen counter, telling her that he loved her. Now he was making a special trip home to tell her.

****

Chapter 2
Cuckold

Cuckold -The word alludes to the habit of the female cuckoo, who lays her eggs in the nests of other birds, to be hatched by them. 1. A man whose wife is unfaithful; the husband of an adulteress.

Madison Way was typical of many residential neighborhoods in Orlando that, long before the arrival of Disney World, had earned the central Florida city the name "The City Beautiful." The old brick street, maintained at great expense by the city, wound gracefully around a beautiful quiet lake and the large stately oaks that lined both sides of the road were well trimmed and free of Spanish moss. Jack and Jill Andrews had owned their big, spacious house on Madison for fifteen years.

Jill had found the house at a perfect time in their lives. The Andrews were a young couple ready to build a family and Orlando was just beginning to feel the development impact of nearby Disney World. The price of the house, although a bargain at the time, was still more than a young working couple could afford. They had gone into hock over their heads and then worked hard the next five years to get out. During that time, property values had increased immensely, and the appreciation of their home had given the Andrews a mild feeling of wealth.

The years had brought them no children, but Jill had done a magnificent job with the renovation of the house; and with her natural talent for growing things, the Andrews' azaleas had become a well-known local attraction that drew dozens of cars down the out-of-the-way street in February and March.

His house was in total darkness when he arrived. There were no cars in the driveway and both garage doors were down. At first he assumed that Jill must have left shortly after he called, but then, it would not be his wife's nature to return to a dark house. If she had gone out, he was certain that she would have left lights on for her return unless, of course, she wasn't planning to return that evening.

Instinctively, he drove past his own driveway and turned, instead, up into the Kidder's drive two houses past his own. Charlie and Margaret Kidder would be in Colorado for at least another week. He and Jill had been watching their house for them while they were away. He switched off the headlights immediately, but let the engine continue to idle for several minutes while he watched up and down the street. When he turned the engine off, the neighborhood was quiet and peaceful. *Too peaceful*, he thought to himself.

Walking slowly in the grass along the sidewalk and then up his own drive, Andrews made his way quietly to a door on the side of his house. The door entered into a utility room which had been constructed on the side of the Andrews' two-car garage. As the dead bolt lock was keyed to match the front door, he unlocked it with his house key and quickly stepped inside, closing the door behind him. With the door closed, the utility room was pitch black. He could hear the sound of water running through pipes. The feeder valve to the pool was still open. He stood still and listened. He thought he could hear the faint sounds of music. He took a deep breath and held it. Yes, it was music coming from within the house. Jill must be home. It gave him a mild sense of relief.

Slowly, he felt his way across the utility room, past the washing machine and the now belt-less dryer, on towards the always-opened pocket door leading into the garage. Because his car, which normally occupied the left parking space, was out, he was certain that there would be ample room for him to maneuver his way to the kitchen door without knocking down any of the tools that hung on the left wall. His hands found the door casings and, moving through the opening, he stepped with confidence straight out into the blackness of the garage.

A sharp pain in his knee made him grimace. He had collided with some immovable metal object. He reached out slowly in front of him and felt what seemed to be an automobile. It was not Jill`s Jeep Wagoneer; it was far too low to the ground. Once again, he could feel his heart pounding. A strange car was in his parking space! Some mysterious car was parked in the darkness of his garage with him. What was it? More importantly, who was driving it? Feeling his way along the front of the vehicle, he slowly made his way on past it until he felt the front fender of his wife's Wagoneer. He groped past the Jeep and on to the kitchen door, which was closed. Then his hand found the light switch just to the right of the door and, hesitating momentarily with his finger on the switch, he pushed it up.

The bright light made him blink and squint. He had planned to flip the switch on and off quickly, allowing just a flash of light to identify the intruding car, but now he stood transfixed, staring at the familiar vehicle in front of him.

The car, a new model white Jaguar, was particularly beautiful and distinctive parked next to his wife's square

11

and boxy Jeep Wagoneer. While he doubted there was another one similar to it in all of Orlando, the "American Quarter Horse Association" plate on the front bumper and the `Maywood Country Club' sticker in the driver's corner of the windshield confirmed for him in an instant that the car belonged to Anne Cowans.

He closed his eyes and leaned back against the kitchen door, his mind racing once again. He heard them, faintly at first. But they were there, voices hidden in repressed memory that now floated up to his consciousness. They came so fast than he couldn't sort them out or identify them. They flooded over him, holding him spellbound with the realizations they brought with them.

At first there seemed to be many different voices; but then Andrews became aware that they were all the same voice; dull, unimportant statements, but all made by the same person. Each of the statements, spoken at different times, were totally harmless in their own meaning, but when all combined together they produced an alarming connotation. Yes, it was a single voice; the voice of his wife, Jill Andrews, and Jackson Andrews heard it now with amazing clarity.

"Jack, a new couple has moved to town; their names are Phillip and Anne Cowans. He's the new bank president at First National. They are joining the Club and I thought it would be nice if we had them over for dinner this Saturday with the Evans and......"

"Jack, the Kidders have invited us to dinner Friday with the Cowans. Tom and Phillip played football together at Yale. Do you know that Tom Kidder told Maggie that if Yale had been a better team that year, Phillip Cowans would have made All-American...?"

"Jack, what do you think of Anne Cowans...? I mean, do you think she's attractive? Oh, I know she drinks too much... but do you think she's sexy? I can't believe what big tits do to men... What do you think about my getting a boob job?"

"Jack, did you hear the news? Phillip Cowans is running for U.S. Congress. It was on the news tonight. Isn't it exciting? I've volunteered to help three days a week at his campaign headquarters..."

"Jack, how would you compare me to Anne Cowans? Should I have my face lifted now? Anne's had hers done twice... twice, Jack, and she's only forty five..."

"Jack, why don't you want to contribute to Phillip's campaign? He needs the money and we're the only members of the Club that haven't made a formal pledge yet..."

"Jack, I just called to tell you that the networks have already declared Phil the winner; isn't it exciting? I'm going over to their house - why don't you stop by on your way home..."

"I don't understand Anne Cowans, Jack. She has become so reclusive since Phillip's election. She is drinking way too much and I'm so concerned about him ... and her ..."

"Jack, you don't care for Phillip Cowans, do you? Well, he doesn't think you do .. Anyway, they're both good friends of mine and it's a shame that we can't do more things together. We've turned down their invitations to the Super Bowl and the Kentucky Derby and it just seems that you always have some convenient excuse why we can't go with..."

"Jack, do you know that Phillip is thinking about running for the U.S. Senate ... Anne just told me ... Wouldn't that be something if..."

"Jack, I am so upset about Anne Cowan's drinking I don't know what to do ... Phillip has had to put her in Bowling Green Manor to dry out ... She could lose her driver's license now and this may hurt Phil's chances for the Senate ... Jack. Did you hear me? Jack ... Jack?"

Jack Andrews opened his eyes once again and stared at the beautiful white Jaguar shimmering in the bright light in front of him. It was definitely Anne Cowans' car, but as much as he wanted to believe it, Jack was certain that it was not Anne Cowans who had driven it into his garage. He turned off the garage light and turned the kitchen door handle. It opened.

****

Chapter 3
Cuckolding
To make a cuckold of, as a husband, by seducing his wife, or by her becoming an adulteress

The house was dark except for the light from the tiffany lamp at the end of a large leather sofa in the living room. The built-in stereo system was playing music softly throughout the house. An empty Dom Pérignon champagne bottle floated in an ice bucket on a table at the other end of the sofa. . Remnants of an earlier celebration of his departure, no doubt, Andrews thought.

Some photographs were spread on the coffee table in front of the sofa. He picked them up and held them under the lamp's direct light. As he studied the pictures he could feel an immense anger welling up inside of him.

The pictures were high quality and beautiful, and had no doubt been taken during Jill's North Carolina Art Retreat last October. He recognized Mount Pisgah in the background of one print and the backgrounds of the others were various scenic settings around the Biltmore Estate in Asheville, where the conference had taken place.

What gripped his eyes and locked them into an unblinking stare were the two people in the foreground of most of the pictures; two familiar faces that smiled out at him. They were such happy faces at first, but as he shuffled through the prints three and four times, over and over, faster and faster, the smiles became cynical, leering, derisive smirks, directed at him. The two looked as if they were laughing at his stupidity and his pathetic naivety. The faces of his wife and United States Congressman, Phillip Cowans, grinned out off each glossy print at him. Jackson Andrew's world shattered.

Now there was a ringing in his ears and his breath was reduced to short gasps. He steadied himself on the arm of the sofa and forced himself to take several deep breaths as he struggled to quiet his pounding heart. Invisible black waves of unbearable emotions rolled over him. He strove to deal with each of them separately, one at a time; but the emotions all came at once.

The first wave was one of curiosity, spurred by disbelief and desperate analysis. It was a search for answers and reasons, when none were available. And as Andrews worked his way through its maze of wicked questions, the logical answers that evolved filled him with such anxiety that the second wave was upon him immediately.

This second wave was one of pure anger. It broke down on top of him, sweeping over him with such force that his savage rage produced revengeful solutions faster than his conscious mind could cope with them.

A third wave came momentarily, only after much of his energy had been sapped by the rage. This was a wave of terrible sadness and loss. A wave of sorrow filled him with such emptiness and loneliness that it constricted his chest and made him short of breath once again. It was the wave

16

of tears; tears which ran down Jack Andrews face. It was a wave of release.

For ten minutes the waves of emotion held Andrews captive. He stood, stooped and trembling, holding on to the arm of the leather sofa. He was still staring at the pictures, but he was no longer seeing them, and he braced himself against these swelling surges of emotion that rolled over him, in their cycle, one at a time.

As these waves came faster and faster, he no longer had the energy to keep them separated from each other. They merged together; reason, rage, and sorrow all neutralizing each other into a grey nothingness as primary colors mixed together in equal parts. He stood motionless, barely breathing, until at last he was released from the spell. He thought about other things.

He heard voices from out of his past. But these were the familiar voices of friends ... they were talking about United States Congressman, Phillip Cowans.

"Phillip Cowans' political success," Bill Evans, Andrew's handball partner, was saying, "is due to the fact that most of his electorate has never met him. This has to be the case, for it is virtually impossible to know "Big Phil" even a little bit without disliking him immensely. He is a guy who is driving through life with his horn stuck."

They had all laughed. The four men had been taking a rest break from their doubles match when the conversation turned from handball to Congressman Cowans and a problem he had encountered the night before.

Bill and Sue Evans, who lived next door to Phillip and Anne Cowans, had been awakened sometime around two that morning by a woman shouting and a blowing car horn.

"I swear to God," said Billy Evans, "she had driven her car right up into the Cowans' yard, through a flowerbed, over two sprinklers, and just short of touching the house," Evans held his gloved hands several feet apart to illustrate his story. "When I got over there, she was standing next to her car, with its lights shining right into Cowan's living room windows. She was blowing the horn and crying and shouting at the same time ..."

"Had she been drinking?" someone asked.

"Oh yeah, she was loaded."

"What was she shouting?"

"All kinds of crap ... 'I love you, Phillip. You can't leave me now, Phillip ... I won't let you go, Phillip' ... and she kept yelling for him to come out of the house and talk with her."

"Did Cowans come out?"

"Are you kidding?" the second voice said. "Do you mean, did the Congressman come outside and comfort his little drunk bimbo, thereby acknowledging who she was? Not a chance. He didn't do it, did he Billy?"

"No, they never even turned a light on in the house."

"That's got to be pretty tough on Anne," the second voice said. "I mean, she must know - everybody else does - what a womanizing son-of-a-bitch she's married to; but to be directly confronted by it in your own home at two in the morning. That's what I call rough."

"Let me tell you something." Bill Evans shook his head. "You talk about being loaded; well, Anne Cowans is that way every night. I'll bet she never even woke up through the whole ordeal."

"How does that guy get away with that crap?" the first voice asked. "Tom Kidder told me that he thinks the bastard hates women. He just loves to fuck 'em and then when he sees them again, pretend he doesn't have the faintest idea who they are."

"That's right," Higgins asked. "Kidder and Cowans are close friends, aren't they?"

"Not exactly close friends, but they went to Yale together," said the first voice. "Cowans told Kidder a couple of years ago, when Kidder was elected to some high position in the AMA, that they had to stop seeing so much of each other because the congressman was afraid that it would hurt him politically."

"Now there is a good friend to have," said the second voice. "How can that shallow insincere bastard get elected to political office?"

"What are you talking about?" said the first voice. "He's made to order. You can't have feelings and be emotional if you're going to be a successful politician. Walt, what was that story about Cowans and his brother-in-law? Remember, he told him not to come around the house anymore ... ?"

"Oh, you're talking about Anne's brother, the mechanic," Evans smiled sadly. "That took place long before Big Phil was even elected to Congress. Anne and her brother, Kent, were pretty close. He was a mechanic over at Sears and we used to see him come by their house to visit all the time; you know, after he got off work in the afternoons. Anyway, all of a sudden he just stopped coming. I bumped into him one day and asked him why we didn't see him around anymore and he said "Big Phil" suggested that he not come by so often. He said Cowans told him that because 'they

19

had a different circle of friends' that Cowans thought it would be better if they didn't see quite as much of each other socially."

"No shit!" said the second voice. "Did he tell him that in front of Anne?"

"I don't know, but it was right around that time that Anne got into her heavy-duty drinking."

"Well, don't keep us in suspense, Billy, what happened to this girl who drove up in his yard last night?"

"Sue and I took her inside our house, gave her some coffee, and got her to tell us the name of her sister. Sue called her, and she came with a boyfriend and took her home. I was ready to just turn her over to the cops to see how that asshole would handle the press, but Sue talked me out of it, and now I'm glad we didn't. As it turned out, she was a cute little gal and unbelievably young."

"How young was she?"

"Would you believe she was just 19?"

"No kidding ... who was she?"

"She was a student here at the University ... a political science major who had been given the job of chauffeuring Cowans around the campus for a couple of days during some sort of two day political seminar last fall."

"And he nailed her."

"Yep, and where does it all end for a Phillip Cowans?" another voice asked. It was Jackson Andrews' voice. He had spoken for the first time since Billy Evans told his story. His voice was soft and his mood had been serious.

"The White House?" someone asked, and they had all laughed.

Andrews crossed the living room and walked slowly into the dark hallway leading back to the bedrooms. At the end of the hall was the closed door of the master bedroom. He paused momentarily in front of it. His heart was pounding. Until now, everything had been purely circumstantial. was it possible that this whole thing was nothing more than a bizarre set of facts that he had misinterpreted? He sensed the panic of his predicament. He was desperately afraid of what he would discover on the other side of the bedroom door, and yet, he was hopelessly driven to make the discovery. With a slow, deliberate, robot-like motion, he gripped the round metallic knob and turned it until it would go no further. The door was locked.

He experienced a strange sense of relief and frustration. Placing his ear against the door, he listened. He could hear nothing. He tested the guest bedroom door on his right. It opened. He walked slowly through the dark bedroom and groped his way into the blackness of a large closet. Several years ago, Jill had convinced him to install a connecting door between her dressing room and the guest bedroom's large walk-in closet which he was now standing in.

The renovation had been a practical move at the time, for Jill had made the closet an extension of her own dressing room and it was now filled with her summer clothes that were out of season. He could smell her perfume. His hands searched along the smooth back wall until he found the closed narrow connecting door. He turned the handle. It opened.

He crossed Jill's dressing room and stood for several minutes, staring into his own bedroom. Although the soft glowing light from the blazing gas log in the bedroom's fireplace offered little illumination, a bathroom light had been left on, and with the door slightly ajar, a thin sliver of its brightness escaped into the room and fell across the bed. It was as if some fixed theatrical spotlight were directing the one-man audience's attention toward the two main characters on a set.

The audience of one watched and waited. But the two performers, sprawled across the king-size bed, remained mute and motionless. After several minutes, the audience grew restless and eased forward, out onto the set, into the light, and closer to the bed, eyes staring, straining to identify the two performers. Then the audience stopped moving and stood transfixed.

There may be certain times in every individual's life when his or her emotional stability is severely tested. A time when a never-before-imagined stress becomes so consuming and devastating that the person experiencing it becomes totally incapacitated. Now was such a time for Jackson Andrews.

The room was hot and stuffy. The gas log fireplace, which had obviously been turned up to remove a chill in the bedroom, had more than done its job. Lying on the floor beside the bed was Jill's crumpled black negligee and on one of the chairs in front of the fireplace, a man's clothes had been piled hurriedly.

Two empty champagne glasses sat on the night table beside the bed. There, lying on the king-size bed, with the covers unconsciously thrown off to relieve the room's heat, were the nude forms of his wife, Jill Andrews, and her lover, Congressman Phillip "Big Phil" Cowans.

They were both sleeping on their backs, breathing heavily, and the congressman was snoring. Cowans was a huge man; well over six feet tall and weighing close to 250 pounds. Although his powerful physique had earned him the name "Big Phil", to Jack Andrews and many of his friends, Cowans was a man whose giant ego had made him appear smaller than he was.

Now, as he studied the two peaceful sleepers, Jack Andrews was aware of the fact that although they emerged as familiar forms to him, both of these people were total strangers. His brain was racing in an attempt to accept the image of horror that his eyes conveyed to it, but it was as if all of his deductive reasoning powers had vanished. For while his brain received this new information and searched frantically through its circuits for a storage cell in which to place the data, but none would accept it. Not one cell in his entire mass of gray matter would accept this preposterous lie as a truth, and as a result of this constant rejection, his mind raced on, in a whirling search, stretching the fragile boundaries of sanity in a desperate attempt to unload its heavy burden.

Jack Andrews stooped forward to study the giant form of this strange creature lying in his bed, sleeping next to his wife. This was a dangerous Goliath of a man, he thought to himself. This was some demon which possessed strange mystical powers to charm women; to charm them out of their virtues and them away from their convictions; to charm them into doing his bidding. The demon had used his power to destroy Jack Andrews' marriage. With contemptuous disrespect, the demon had violated the sanctity of his home and had shown him no sign of mercy.

For several minutes, Jack Andrews studied the scene before him, and then slowly he turned and walked back into his wife's dressing room and through the narrow door that connected it to the walk-in closet. The door closed quietly behind him. He was moving quickly now; back down the hall, through the kitchen, and out of the house. There was a certain deliberateness about his movements;

an obvious sense of purpose in his actions. Jack Andrews now had the answer to that question he had asked that day on the handball court.

"Where does it all end for Phillip Cowans?" he had asked his friends after Bill Evans had told his story of the distressed young girl crying out in the night. No one had answered his question then and there was no one around to answer it now, but Jack Andrews had the answer ... or, at least, he thought he did.

Outside, the temperature had dropped below freezing, and a bright moon lit up the driveway. He surveyed the street for several seconds and then, staying close to the house so as to remain in the shadows of the large overhanging eves, he made his way around to the lakeside of the house.

When he reached the far corner where the master bedroom was located, he pushed himself between and under two large bushy azaleas planted beneath the windows. The combination of the eves and the healthy plants shadowed out the moonlight, and he was now forced to continue his mission by feeling along the foundation of the house with his hands.

He groveled in the sandy soil for several minutes and then, just when he was considering returning to his car for the little pen flashlight that he kept in the glove compartment, his fingers found it. The hard metal plate that covered the gas meter was partially covered with cypress mulch. He brushed it away and found the metal ring in the center of the plate and, gripping it firmly with his thumb and forefinger, he lifted it up and sat it to one side.

The gas log fireplace had been his idea when they purchased the house fifteen years ago. The dramatic savings gas offered over electricity prompted him to suggest that they make all of their new appliances gas operated, but Jill had been reluctant. While she admitted that gas was quicker and more efficient, she was still afraid of it. They had settled for just a gas hot water heater and the log that was now burning in the bedroom.

He reached down into the cement casing with his right hand and found the valve. Slowly he turned it clockwise, shutting off the gas flow into the house. After it was closed completely, he waited, crouched in the cold shadows, for several minutes. Then, moving quickly, as if reacting to some mysterious impulse, he spun the valve back in the opposite direction to turn the gas back on.

He could imagine what was happening inside the house. The gas log just on the other side of the wall now had no pilot light and he could envision the gas rushing out into the fireplace with no flame to burn it. He placed the metal lid back on the cement casing and, backing slowly out of the bushes, he straightened up. Despite the chilly night air, a drop of perspiration rolled down his cheek. His eyes were filled with tears and a violent nausea swept over him. He walked back around the house, stopping briefly to turn off the water running into the pool. On the way back to his car he paused momentarily in the Kidder's driveway and studied their large two-story house.

 "Jack," Charlie Kidder had told him the morning he and Maggie left for Colorado, "we appreciate you and Jill looking after the house for us while we're away. I showed her where the key is so she can water the plants, but let me show you now, too." Kidder had led him behind a large evergreen bush and pointed to a key hanging on a nail just inside the window casing. "There it is, in case you need to get in."

"Got it," Jack had said. And at the time, it was all a courteous gesture for his neighbor, for he could imagine no set of circumstances requiring him to enter the

Kidder's house. Now however, he had a need to get in. He retrieved the key and opened the front door. He turned on one light in the entrance foyer which illuminated enough of the downstairs that he could quickly make his way to the bar in one corner of the living room. In the unlocked liquor cabinet he found an unopened bottle of Jack Daniels. He turned out the lights, locked the front door, replaced the key, and returned to his car.

Seating himself behind the wheel, he slowly broke the seal and unscrewed the cap on the bottle. He thought briefly about calling Billy Evans and Sam Wadley, his AA buddies. Then he pushed them out of his mind. For over a minute he hesitated, staring at the bottle in the shadowy glow of the streetlight. It had been twelve years since he had taken a drink; twelve years of total abstinence; twelve years of going to meetings, lecturing to large groups, and building back his own self esteem as he helped others to find their way out of the alcohol jungle that surrounded them.

Over the years, he had encouraged hundreds to spring the alcohol trap that held them in its death grip. Rule one had always been to get help when you feel yourself slipping back into the pit. He had been called out hundreds of times to counsel fellow alcoholics.

He took great pride in his ability to help. He understood what he needed to tell them to ease their pain and to get them through the troubled times. He thought now of what he would tell himself tonight if he were asked for council. He would have to be careful what he said. He couldn't say, as he often did, that "It's not as bad as it appears right now. Give it twenty-four hours and see if I'm not right." No, he wouldn't have the heart to tell himself that tonight. The fact was it was no doubt even worse than he was imagining.

The only reason he could feel better in twenty-four hours was because the son-of-a-bitch who had just destroyed his life would be dead, and he would be drunk in Freeport. He sensed tears welling up in his eyes. He shook his head and then slowly, putting the bottle to his lips, he turned it up.

****

Chapter 4
Blindside
The side on which one is least able or disposed to see danger.--Swift

The early winter sunset cast a deceiving warm red glow over the Minneapolis skyline as the big jet glided overhead on its final approach into MSP, the Twin Cities Airport. The clear frigid air accentuated the silver plane's exhaust trail and carried the sound of the giant whining engines far out over the countryside. Robert Warner was coming home.

He sat in a window seat, in the last row of the first class section, watching the shimmering city slip quietly by below. As the plane made a hard banked turn, he could see, off in the distance, the large black sheet of ice that was Lake Minnetonka.

Little snow had fallen this year and he could easily see the clearly defined shoreline, Rorschach-like, with its many meandering coves and bays. For a brief moment he thought he saw the white tile roof of his house on Browns Bay, but the few patches of snow around the edges of the lake made him unsure.

Then, as the plane banked again, he could see the Edina Industrial Park and the large complex of buildings that made up the Warner Chemical complex. The security people would be going on duty right about now. The Friday evening traffic was building on the Interstate directly below him, and yet, from his altitude on this January night, the city radiated a certain peacefulness. Warner reflected on how much he enjoyed Minneapolis and St. Paul, and how good it was to be coming home.

He wondered what Helen would have planned for dinner. He had considered calling his wife from the Dallas airport after he had put Adrian on her plane back to Atlanta, but then he had procrastinated until his flight had been called for boarding.

He would telephone home as soon as he landed. He would ask Helen to meet him at the new restaurant in Wayzata that she loved so much, the one that served the wonderful Walleye. He couldn't remember if they took reservations. Helen would know.

He experienced a slight pang of guilt when he thought about his wife. He had not talked to her since leaving over two weeks ago. He had called the plant on Tuesday to talk to Ken Kiser, the comptroller, but they had only discussed the tax return, and he had hung up without even asking if Helen was in the office. Of course she, on the other hand, had known where he was staying in Dallas, and had not bothered to call to check in with him, so his guilt was somewhat mitigated.

He opened his small notebook to review the past week. Dallas had been a productive trip. With his new gold pen, a gift from Adrian, he checked off the goals he had written for himself on the flight to Texas over a week ago. He had met with the engineers and successfully designed a new container for some of the more volatile products, unbreakable plastic, but glass lined to protect the shelf life. He had also worked up two new ideas for promoting the new lawn spray products and he had acquired the coveted Super Store Account and ... He hesitated before making a check mark by the fourth item, "FTEOOAK". It was his code for "Fuck the eyes out of Adrian Kilmer".

He had to admit: he had done all of the things listed, except fuck the eyes out of Adrian Kilmer. No one could do that; not even a hoard of Huns. He laid his head back against the seat and closed his eyes.

He smiled to himself as he pictured Hun warriors lying scattered over some battleground, all of them rolling on the ground, holding their groins and moaning while Adrian did a little strutting dance off into the sunset, looking for another cute hoard to play with.

She was truly sex crazy and she had proven to him once again that there can always be too much of a good thing. Since their wild and passionate meeting three years ago, he had made dozens of trips back to Atlanta to visit her, but he had never stayed more than a few days.

On most of these weekend marathons, they would hole up in Adrian's apartment while he made frequent phone checks back to his hotel for messages. If he had just been able to remember, before this last trip, how anxious he had always been to come home after those Atlanta excursions; he would never have been so insistent that Adrian spend an entire eight days in Dallas with him.

But Warner's memory had been repressed by his lust. Eight days together turned out to be at least five too many. The fact was, after the third day, he found himself studying the return tickets for the exact time of her departure.

Warner remembered Edward Nelson's sage philosophy concerning the male sex drive. Nelson had been his platoon sergeant when he was a young platoon commander in Vietnam. When their unit shipped out from Camp Pendleton, California on an APA troop carrier, bound for Da Nang, the Navy doctors attached to the regiment became bored with the crossing. In order to stay busy they had aggressively promoted the idea of circumcision among the troops who weren't circumcised. About a dozen of the marines on board had decided to take advantage of the two weeks aboard ship to have the surgery performed. But a problem arose when the ship docked in Okinawa to take on supplies.

On the first night of liberty, one of his newly circumcised troopers, a young lance corporal from Indiana, tore the stitches out of his penis while happily fornicating with a B-Girl in the nearest village. Some of his friends had brought him back aboard ship that night, screaming in pain. Warner, a young 1st Lieutenant at the time, had been horrified to see the terrible trauma that this young man had inflicted on himself. He had returned to his office from sickbay feeling queasy, and relayed the story to his platoon sergeant, Edward T. Nelson.

"Hell fire, Sir," Nelson had said after hearing the details. "That son-of-a-bitch was just as any other male with a hardon. He was crazy. Plum-ass crazy! The male of any species, when it comes to pussy, is plum-ass crazy. Horses will kick down stall doors, dogs will chew through metal fences, all the males in the animal kingdom will kill each other in a minute over a female ... if they're in love ..." He had let his voice trail off theatrically.

"But man is supposed to be a higher-developed creature," Warner had suggested. "We are not supposed to act as if we're horses and dogs. In fact, Teddy Roosevelt said that until a man gains control of his carnal urges, he can accomplish nothing; and hell, TR became President of the United States!"

"With all due respect, sir, if Teddy Roosevelt had total control of his carnal urges, he must have been one jack-offing son-of-a-bitch." They had all laughed, including the two clerks in the office, before Warner had said, "Who knows, Sergeant, maybe he was."

E.T. Nelson was truly an "Old Corps" philosopher and poet. He was loved by the troops because he was in touch with them and honestly understood their weaknesses.

"What's the first thing you're going to do when you get home, Sergeant?" Warner had asked the platoon sergeant as their thirteen-month Vietnam tour together was ending.

"I had better not talk too much about that, sir," Nelson had replied with a wily grin. "Let me just say that the second thing I am going to do when I get home is put down my sea bag."

"Did you ever notice, Lieutenant," Nelson added, "how sex is the one thing you can get further behind on and catch up the quickest of anything there is?"

This last week had been a perfect example of that, for Robert Warner. He had made elaborate plans for what he was going to do with Adrian when he got her to Dallas. "We're going to swing from the chandeliers, baby, if there are any out there," he had told her over the phone. And when she argued with him about taking off a whole week from her job, he had insisted that she could do it if she wanted to.

It had taken her less than two days to break his appetite. They had arrived in Dallas Friday evening on different flights, less than an hour apart, and he had worked his hand well up under her dress during their cab ride downtown. Friday night and most of Saturday were a blur in his memory, but he could distinctly remember the turning point in their long week together. It occurred last Sunday, in the early afternoon, as they were finishing a wonderful brunch at the hotel. They had together consumed two bottles of Moët & Chandon and he was contemplating going back up to the room for a long afternoon nap.

Adrian had been sitting quietly across the table, staring at him while he expounded on the differences between Coho and Chinook salmon. Her beautiful auburn hair fell on her shoulders and her green eyes fixed intently on what he was saying. Then, with a casual movement, she reached across the table and laid a pair of black lace panties in front of him. Quickly, he snatched them off the white linen table cloth and, looking around the dining room, nervously he leaned forward and whispered, "Where did these come from?"

"Right off my body, baby. I'm airing it out for you."

He smiled and shook his head. She leaned over the table towards him. "Let's go back up to the room, Robby, and I'll show you a new little trick I just thought of." She smiled confidently and Warner instantly saw that the tide was turning.

"Adrian, I've got to make some phone calls ..." he said, and then, realizing that it was Sunday, he quickly added, "I've ... got to call these people at home today before they go to a meeting tomorrow."

"That's all right, Robby," she cooed. "Your talking on the phone doesn't distract me at all, and you know that."

He did know that, and at that instant, Robert Warner also sensed that he was on the ropes. For the rest of the week, he had conducted a retrograde movement to salvage his ego. His excuses included a bad back, which had bothered him earlier, but which now caused him excruciating pain whenever he thought about accommodating her. Also, the tensions of his business were at hand, demanding that he be given some space in which to move about.

Adrian had understood and, except for the flying finale that morning, just before their departure from the hotel, she had restrained herself and accepted his two measly sessions of lovemaking a day. Now, after being away for over two weeks, Robert Warner was returning home with his own carnal urges so under control that even the thought of sex was painful to him. He wondered how Adrian Kilmer and Teddy Roosevelt would have gotten along together. He opened his eyes and stared back down at the notebook lying in his lap. With his new gold pen, he slowly scratched several lines through the letters FTEOOAK.

The big jet's wheels hit the runway hard and the jolt brought him abruptly back to the present. He watched a blue line of taxiway lights streak by the window. It was still early evening, just a few minutes past five. He would drive to the plant first and call Helen from there. Maybe he should take Helen on a trip somewhere; the Islands ... or Europe ... he would talk to her about it. Their life together had become so empty since Danny's death.

After the motorcycle accident four years ago, they had both lost their ability to communicate and function normally. The loss of their only child left them devastated and bitter. Because Helen had vehemently opposed giving their 16-year-old son a motorcycle, and Warner had overridden her objections, he bore the brunt of guilt for Danny's death. Despite that guilt, he had recovered quicker than his wife. He had grieved openly, crying frequently and talking to anybody that would listen. Helen was a more private person; she kept her grief quietly to herself and could not seem to work her way through the

34

crisis. Non-communicative and alone in her sorrow, she had immersed herself totally into the cloudy world of alcohol.

"Mr. Warner, you do understand that your wife has a serious drinking problem, don't you?" The doctor had made it sound as if it was his fault. Hell, he had lost a son, too.

"No, I don't understand that," he had responded. "Sure, she drinks, but she's always in control, and I certainly don't believe she has, as you call it, a serious drinking problem."

"Your wife drinks more than you think she does," the doctor had said, looking back down at the charts in his hand. "These blood tests show that. I'll tell you what you can to do when you get a chance. Look through her closets and drawers and see if you don't find some bottles that you are not even aware of."

"What do you mean, bottles I am not aware of?" Warner was offended. "We have a liquor cabinet in our house, for god sake. She can get all she wants right there, so why would she hide bottles in her closet?"

"Maybe she doesn't," the doctor had said. "But it certainly won't hurt for you to make an inspection just to see. If she took it out of the liquor cabinet, you would know how much she is drinking. All I ask is that you look around. If you don't find anything, we won't worry about it; but if you do, then we know we have a serious problem on our hands."

His search had been alarmingly revealing. Helen's closet was awash with vodka. He found four fifths hidden in a drawer under some sweaters and an opened, half empty bottle sitting upright in a hatbox on the top shelf of her closet. The most disconcerting evidence, however, were the six half pints, hidden in toes of two pairs of tennis shoes and a pair of riding boots. Helen entered the hospital without argument. To Warner, it was as though she had been looking for help all along and was now relieved to have her problem out in the open. Her recovery was considered to be model rehabilitation, and because of her exemplary performance and attitude, the hospital staff suggested that she be released early.

She had come home from the hospital a new person. Her main interests now were her health and their business, and about both of these, she became fanatical. At home she was involved in nutrition studies or exercise classes every day and at work she was aggressively delving into every facet of their business. At first, his wife had taken Warner aback with her new found energy and drive. In some respects, he was even envious of her.

Helen had spent long hours at the plant, working on the production lines and in the shipping department. She came to know all of the employees on a first name basis, and at company parties and picnics that she planned, she got to know their families. She established a nutritional workshop and an employee exercise class. She was genuinely interested in their wellbeing and the employees loved her. In a relatively short period of time, Helen Warner had developed a relationship with the employees of Warner Chemical that Robert Warner, the founder of the company, had never had.

At first Warner had urged his wife not to become so emotionally involved with the employees. Reiterating his old Marine Corps training, he had pointed out to her that an obvious short-coming of a too-friendly employer/employee relationship was a loss of command presence for the boss. "If a time of crisis comes, you won't be perceived as their leader," he explained to her.

Helen had listened politely, but continued her close fraternization anyway, and when it became obvious that the plant was operating with more efficiency and less absenteeism than ever before, Warner said no more.

Of all her contributions, Helen's involvement within the sales department had been the most dramatic. She had recommended a broker rebate program that paid incentives directly to individuals making the sales, instead of to their employers. The results of this program had been phenomenal, literally doubling the company's sales within a two-year period.

Even though he did it reluctantly, Warner had to give his wife some of the credit for Warner Chemical's tremendous financial success in recent years. Most of the stories were written about their relatively new, upstart, Minneapolis-based company. They had featured his wife and her contributions to the industry. Although Robert Warner was aware that women wrote many of these pieces, and they particularly enjoyed featuring other woman in their articles, he nevertheless experienced some uncomfortable jealousy over his wife's new notoriety.

Despite working closer together within their business, Rob and Helen Warner had never been able to replace the magic that had once existed in their relationship as husband and wife. To Warner, it was as though this feeling had passed on with their son, never to return. As far as he could tell, Helen did not seem the least bit concerned about its loss. In fact, neither one had attempted to rekindle the flame. Both accepted their new relationship with a certain complacency and comfort that would perhaps make change unlikely. It was a strange paradox in which the couple had grown closer together within their business, but further apart in their personal relationship at home.

To Robert Warner, however, this situation had allowed him a certain amount of guilt-free philandering; for as Helen had lost interest in sex with him, he had developed his own outlets - one of which was the most formidable Miss Adrian Kilmer.

Inside the terminal, while waiting for his luggage to slide down the blinking carousel, he decided to take advantage of the delay and call Helen. He found a private corner pay phone and dialed his home number. A recorded message was on the line even before the phone rang once.

"I'm sorry, the number you have reached, 473-6272, is no longer in service... I'm sorry, the number you have reached..."

He hung up the phone and quickly dialed the number again; once more the message was repeated. "What has the damn phone company done now?" he mumbled to himself. Surely Helen had paid the phone bill. She was too much of a perfectionist to overlook any bill, particularly one that would carry such a penalty for non-payment. Also, he thought, the message would have said "temporarily disconnected" instead of "no longer in service." He dialed information.

"Directory service," said a live, much friendlier voice.

"Hello, operator." He struggled to not show his irritation. "I've got a little problem I hope you can help me with. I'm out here at the airport, I've been out of town for several weeks, and I just called my home and a recording tells me that the number is no longer in service. Now, I know your company doesn't often make mistakes, but this time, you have."

"What is the number you are calling, sir?"

"473-6272"

"Thank you." Instantly, she was back on the line.

"Sir, that number, 473-6272, was disconnected at the owner's request last Tuesday."

"At the owner's request?" he said incredulously. "Hell, I am the owner, and I made no such request."

"I'm sorry, sir, that's all I can tell you. However, I am certain that we would not have made the disconnection without authorization from someone on the account."

"Is there a new number listed?" He didn't understand.

"No sir, it was a disconnect order, not a change order."

"It wasn't because we have not paid the bill, was it?"

"No sir, my screen shows it was a disconnect request."

"Thank you, operator." He broke off the connection and dialed the plant number. He let the phone ring for several minutes while he considered how a mix-up such as this could occur. "Disconnected last Tuesday," the operator had said. Helen must be spastic if she had been without a phone at the house for four days. He imagined her wrath towards the telephone company and he smiled and shook his head.

He gave up on the plant number and picked up his one leather suitcase and the empty aluminum sample case at the luggage carousel and took the elevator down to the parking garage underneath the terminal. In the elevator, he retrieved the parking ticket from a back section of his wallet. He had written Section D, Floor 1, Row G, Space #37 across the back of the ticket when he had parked his car 14 days ago.

In comparison to the long-term parking areas out away from the terminal, the covered space underneath the terminal was expensive; three times the cost to park overnight. Nevertheless, Warner had always considered it well worth the price. The fact that you only had to carry your luggage a few hundred feet and not worry about the weather made all the difference - that, plus the fact he had always imagined the security to be infinitely better in parking areas within the terminal itself. He had read stories about professional car thieves taking entire engines out of cars while they were parked in long term airport parking.

He walked down Row G, looking for his silver Mercedes. There was a van parked in space number 37. He retrieved the ticket from his inside coat pocket and checked his figures once again. He glanced up and down Row G. The only Mercedes he saw was an older tan model. He must have written down the wrong row. But he could distinctly remember Row G and his equating it, at the time of his departure, with the word 'gone.' He walked diagonally now, through the rows, checking all of the spaces numbered 37. His car was nowhere to be seen. His heart sank as he wandered aimlessly through the rows of cars, looking for his misplaced vehicle. He could find it nowhere and it was only after walking through the entire D section that he came to accept the realization that his beautiful new car had been stolen.

"Son-of-a-bitch," he said quietly to himself. "Welcome home, Warner, welcome home."

The woman in the parking office did not appear the least bit sympathetic to his plight. She chewed her gum at a high rate of speed as her eyes darted between the computer monitor and his parking ticket lying on her desk.

"What kind of car was it?" she asked.

"It was a 280 SL Mercedes. This year's! Brand new! Silver! I parked it in here for the extra security. How in the hell could someone just drive it out of here without that ticket?"

She leaned back in her chair and reached for a clipboard that was hanging on a hook behind her desk. "It happens all time," she said turning through the clipboard sheets. "People lose their tickets, we charge them our two-week minimum, and they can drive out of here."

"Do you mean to tell me that you let somebody steal my car by just paying a two week parking charge?" His anger was beginning to show in the tone of his voice.

"Let me ask you a question, Mister." The gum chewer was not the least bit intimidated. "Suppose you had lost this ticket you just gave me, your car is sitting out there, but you don't have a parking ticket. What should we do for you?"

"Yes, but I can prove who I am! I can show you that I own the car!" He was shouting now, and the woman continued her search through the clipboard sheets.

"That's what these sheets are for," she said, glancing back up at him. "Before anybody drives a car out of here without a ticket, we make a copy of their driver's license and the car's registration. These are just the release sheets for people who have lost their parking ticket in the last thirty days." She was flipping through the sheets rapidly now, and then something caught her eye and she stopped. "Did you say your name was Warner?"

"Yes. Warner spelled with an A."

"Do you remember your tag number, Mr. Warner?" There was now a certain smugness about her that annoyed him.

"HS 4140... Minnesota," he growled.

Although she attempted to hide it, he saw her quick little smile of satisfaction. "Your car was picked up last Thursday, Mr. Warner, by your wife. Is this woman your wife?" She turned the board around abruptly and slid it over in front of him.

The sheet was a photocopy of a Minnesota car registration and driver's license. The registration described his Mercedes, listing him as the owner and his address as 1001 West Forest Road. The driver's license belonged to Mrs. Helen A. Warner, who lived at the same address. He stared at the sheet for several seconds. The November renewal date on the license was less than two months old, and he had not had an occasion to see his wife's new license until now.

What struck him as odd was the license photograph itself. It was an excellent likeness of Helen, except he had never seen this expression before. To him, the pretty face that smiled up at him off the photocopy reflected a certain smugness. The smile was forced and condescending and it startled him.

Now his anger and frustration were replaced by a slight twinge of nervous fear. Something strange and sinister had happened while he was in Dallas last week. There was no doubt that a conspiracy had been formed against him. He had no idea of what was going on, who was involved, or exactly what they were doing to him, but instantly he sensed that time was of the essence and that he must act quickly to protect himself.

"Is that your wife, sir?" the parking attendant was now concerned that perhaps it wasn't.

"Yes, that's her," he said softly. "Where can I catch a cab?"

****

Chapter 5
The Homecoming

Forest Road was typical of many of the attractive residential areas that ringed the Twin City area. The neat, well cared for homes sat along the shoreline of the big lake; some of them positioned amazingly close to its rocky banks. As the cab traveled west on Forest, the acre lots with their comfortable homes soon gave way to large rolling estates with extraordinary sprawling compounds that were just barely visible from the road.

Giant trees, many of them ancient elms vaccinated and medicated against the dreaded Dutch disease, rimmed the road and intersecting driveways. There were no names; just numbers on mailboxes, for these were some of the beautiful homes of the Roanes, Middletons, Hutchens, and other fine old Minnesota families who had amassed tremendous wealth over the years and, in most cases, generously given much of it back into the communities in which they lived.

Five years ago, Robert Warner had purchased property as far west on Forest Road as one could go before the road turned away from the lake shore. He and Helen had purchased the property on the lake that was known in the area as The Old Brown Estate. It consisted of twelve acres of beautiful rolling woods on which an old line Minneapolis family named Brown had constructed their summer home more than eighty years earlier. The house was charming and well maintained, but dated, and despite his wife's objections, Warner had it torn down.

It had been one of their most violent arguments. Helen insisted that the old home's charm was irreplaceable and that it could be renovated. Warner had argued that the old construction was inefficient. That because the house had initially been constructed as a summer home for the Browns, who came out from the city each summer, it was not suitable for Minnesota winters. They were both right. But in the final analysis, there was another factor that would have made Robert Warner raze the old house, even if it had been well insulated and suitable for winter living. It was his ego.

The battle to buy the property had been fierce. Another potential buyer had entered a bidding war against the Warners and the price had risen substantially above the asking price before Robert Warner was able to close the deal.

The Warners' recent rise to wealth had been well publicized in the Minneapolis newspapers, and the general feeling among the east lake residents was that this purchase proved once again that new money was not necessarily wise money.

The tearing down of the old Brown home did little to enhance Warner's image among his neighbors. As he had told his wife in one of their many spirited arguments on the subject, he was not about to pay millions of dollars for a house and have people call it somebody else's home.

"I am not going to be introduced to people as the man who lives in the Browns' old house or on the Brown Estate. It is going to be our home and it is going to be known as the Warner Estate," he had said with great determination.

Without saying any more to Helen and before anyone else was aware of what was happening, the Browns' house had been torn down in less than three days. It was the major requirement in the demolition contract.

"I don't want to see any trace of the building four days after you start," Warner had told the contractor, and it was as if the old home had disappeared into thin air. There had been some talk, that spring, of a possible injunction by a historical group who wanted to preserve the old home as a landmark. But Warner had moved so quickly that the old house was gone and a new one was under construction before anyone was aware of it.

Perhaps the most distressing thing to those who had been interested in saving the old house was the fact that Warner did not build his new home on the old site. Instead, he selected a new site set several hundred yards back from the lake. Warner told those who asked about this new location that environmental setbacks had required him to build further away from the lake, but most of his neighbors thought that there was another reason for the repositioning.

Unlike the Browns' old home, which had been hidden from the road by the rolling hills leading back to it, the new Warner house sat on top of the highest of these hills, a massive brick Tudor structure positioned for the entire world to see; or at least, for all those who drove down West Forest Road to see. If someone who saw the giant structure was impressed with it, there was no doubt who the proud owner was; for there on the wall, next to the massive stone column entrance, large bronze letters proclaimed this fine expensive looking structure to be the home of "R. L. Warner."

Lack of acceptance into his new neighborhood infuriated Warner. Once the demolition on the old house had occurred, both he and Helen could feel the resentment and hostility. After the new house was completed and the situation failed to improve, Robert Warner made an overt attempt to buy acceptance into the community. He offered money to any community activity that would publicize his gift, and he now went out of his way to introduce himself to his neighbors. He would walk up to anyone that he recognized as a Forest Road resident and invite them to come by and see his new home.

No one ever came and Warner could never understand why. He was a wealthy man and he had attempted to be friendly to all of his neighbors along West Forest Road.

"These people are all from old money, Rob," Helen had told him one day when he was complaining about the snooty neighbors. 'They are not the least bit impressed with wealth; not anybody's wealth, much less some kooky chemist who makes fertilizers and insecticides. We are known in the social circles out here as `those bug spray people at the end of the road.'"

Helen handled this lack of acceptance well. She continued to work with her garden club in town and pursued her volunteer work with the Minneapolis Art Council when she had time. The fact that she was so oblivious to a situation that tormented Warner only made his reaction worse. He became totally hostile towards the neighbors.

He would blow great long warning blasts on his car horn, whenever he saw one of them driving out of their driveway or picking up their mail. Always, as he passed by, he would glare at them as if they had somehow imposed upon him by just being there. Most of the neighbors ignored these gestures, but there were a few who would glare back at him as he sped by.

Tonight, Robert Warner glared out at the darkness and thought about those memories. He rode along in silence in the cab which wound its way down the same tree-lined road, taking him home.

"Up here on the left, at the stone gate." He spoke his first words to the driver since leaving the airport.

"Yes sir." The young man glanced at him in the rearview mirror and slowed the car. He was listening to a basketball game on the radio and had enjoyed his passenger's need for solitude. Warner glanced at the meter, which had just clicked past $34.20. Including the tip, it was going to be a forty-dollar cab ride. He had given Adrian most of his cash in Dallas to help pay her airport parking and the vet boarding for her poodle. He still had the four twenties in his money clip that he had saved for his own car parking. So he was going to come out ahead after all, he thought to himself, if he just discounted the fact that he no longer had his car.

As the cab swung into the driveway between the big stone columns, the lights flashed across something at the base of the column on the right.

"What was that?" he asked in a loud voice that startled his driver.

"Sir?" the driver slowed the cab and glanced into his outside mirrors.

"There was a sign or something. Back up a minute."

"Yes sir, I didn't see it." The young man slowly brought the car to a halt. Slipping it into reverse, he backed between the two stone columns and out into the road. As the headlights lit up the entrance gate once again, Warner saw what had caught his eye. It was a small metal sign, attached to a metal rod, driven into the frozen ground at the base of the stone column. It was certainly unobtrusive and neat by industry standards, which is why his driver had not noticed it; yet it was effective, and for Robert Warner it was frightening.

It was a small 1 by 2 foot sign with a blue background and two lines of neat white letters. The top line was one word, "Available" and the second line, "Rita Ross Realty," was a name that had become synonymous, in recent years, with luxury home sales in the Twin City area. Rita Ross was also Helen's good friend. For some time he stared at the sign, until the cab driver glanced nervously at the oncoming headlights off in the distance.

"Looks as it is some sort of `for sale' sign to me, Sir," he offered after Warner's long silence.

"Yeah, that's what it is," Warner answered. "Drive on up to the house."

The house was dark except for a light that burned in the upstairs front bedroom. He and Helen had developed the habit of leaving that light on when they were away from the house. It could be seen easily from the road and gave the appearance that someone was home, without allowing an intruder to see into the downstairs.

The cab came to a halt under the covered entrance and Warner got out. "Let me just turn some lights on out here and I will settle up with you," he spoke back into the cab as he held the back door open.

"Yes, sir," said the young man as Robert Warner made his way up to the front door. For several moments, he fumbled with his keys in the frigid night air. Using the reflection of the cab's headlights, he selected the right key and inserted it into the front door lock. The key would not turn. He struggled with it again and again, frantically jiggling and pulling on the door, but it would not work. With sagging shoulders, he resigned himself to the fact that the lock had been changed and that he was now locked out of his own house. He returned to the cab and opened the back door again. The cabby was intent on his basketball game.

"I've got a little problem here. My key doesn't seem to work, but I know how to get in around on the side. You don't happen to have a flashlight, do you?" His voice had lost some of its authority.

"Yes sir, but I don't know how good the batteries are." The young man reached under his seat and pulled out a long black cylinder. He smiled at Warner's startled look. "I think of it more as a club for protection than a flashlight." He flicked it on and the lamp emitted a bright stream of light. "Not bad." He acted surprised and handed it to Warner. "Here you go, help yourself."

Robert Warner took the flashlight and made his way carefully over the frozen ground around the side of the house and onto a large stone terrace which was covered with snow and surrounded the house on three sides. He found the key he had hidden on the edge of a planter just outside the dining room door, but that lock had been changed also. As he worked with the key, desperately trying to make it work, the beam from the flashlight momentarily shown through the narrow window on the left side of the door and penetrated the dark dining room.

Warner froze and slowly pointed the flashlight back to the window. The room was empty. The beautiful long dining

50

room table and the twelve matching chairs that they had bought at Sotheby's were gone. He shuffled through the snow, around the porch, to the living room windows and probed the darkness with the powerful beam of light. It was empty. Not a stick of furniture and not one painting or mirror remained on the walls. Gone also was the Steinway Grand Piano and all of the beautiful Oriental rugs that he had been so proud of. Just the bare oak floors remained. The house was totally empty.

A tremendous dejection swept over him. He stumbled unconsciously back off the porch, slipping on the frozen ground and falling headfirst into a planter bed that was filled with dried plants and snow. His right knee struck one of the large stones that formed a border around the bed and the pain made him cry out. For several seconds he lay there in the cold snow and then, with tremendous effort, he struggled to pull himself back up on his feet. Limping gingerly, he made his way slowly around to the front of the house again, and opening the back door of the cab, he fell inside.

"I... I need... a ride back... towards town." He was breathing hard and unconsciously waving the flashlight, which was still on. His passenger's new appearance startled the young cab driver. The well-groomed, arrogant man he had picked up at the airport had become disheveled, snow covered, and stammering. The man was obviously distressed and the driver wondered if he was about to have a heart attack or stroke victim on his hands.

"Are you all right, sir?" he asked his passenger. There was no response.

"Look, mister, if you live here, I can get you in your house. You just say the word."

Warner shook his head and handed him the flashlight.

"No point... my wife has ... taken out all of the furniture."

"You mean she did that without telling you?" the driver was bewildered.

"Yes... without telling me." Warner pulled the door shut. "Take me to... Edina," he said so softly the cabby barely heard him.

"Edina?"

There was no answer.

"Yes sir, Edina, you got it." As he eased the cab back out of the driveway, the driver turned down the volume of his ball game and picked up his 2-way radio. After a brief conversation with the dispatcher about his present location and where he was going, he hooked the mike back on the dash. He wanted to talk some more with his passenger. The man's situation had now become quite interesting to him, but as the cab passed under a street light, and he caught a glimpse of the man's face in his rear view mirror, he changed his mind. In fact, the hostile look on the man's face made him uneasy and he quickly turned back up the volume of the ball game.

Robert Warner sat in silence, staring through the cab's dirty side window at the dark countryside. Although furious at the things that had been done to him, he was also fearful of what he did not know. What else had his wife done while he was away? And what were his options as far as controlling the damage to their relationship? Obviously, his indiscretions with Adrian had been discovered. Helen must have somehow found out about his Dallas trip. So now, he must find her and explain things to her. He would tell her he was sorry and set the record straight.

The whole thing was so strange and unreal to Warner. His wife was considered, by all her friends and acquaintances, to be a sweet and gentle woman who had firm convictions and empathy for the underprivileged. It was impossible for him to imagine her scheming and planning the scenario in which he was now involved. No, there was no way she would or could have done these things by herself; she had to have had help.

Someone else, not his wife, must have orchestrated this attack on him. It was not Helen's nature to be hostile and vindictive. Taking his car from the airport parking terminal, disconnecting the phone, moving abruptly out of their home and immediately putting it up for sale; these could not possibly be his wife's ideas ... or could they? He thought about the strange face that he had seen on the photocopy of her driver's license at the airport, and another wave of apprehension passed over him.

During the eighteen years they had been married, Warner could remember only a few major arguments or confrontations he'd had with his wife. Most of these had concerned their son, Dan. Because he was an only child, Helen had been far too protective of the boy, never letting him out of her sight until he was twelve years old. Because there was no babysitter competent enough to care for him, except for her mother, who lived in Connecticut, their activities had become limited.

When Danny became interested in sports and wanted his parents' permission to play football, Helen had refused to sign the required parental permission slip the boy brought home from school. When his father had come to his defense and eventually signed the waiver form himself, Helen had flown into a rage. It was the first time Robert Warner had ever seen his wife show such hostility and the

53

thought of that particular incident now made him rather uncomfortable.

Although he saw at the time that it was her fear for the safety of her only child that drove her to attack him, nevertheless, Warner had been astonished by Helen's aggressiveness. As a lioness defending her cub, she had attacked him with uncharacteristic ferocity.

"If you are so unconcerned and carefree about the safety of our only son," she had told him, "then I will take him to Connecticut and live with my mother." It had been a time of major crisis in their marriage, but the boy wanted to play so badly that Helen had reluctantly consented.

Dan played well and she quickly saw how much he loved the game and how important it was to him. When, later that year, he decided that he wanted to play hockey, also, she could not bring herself to sign the permission slip, but offered little protest when Rob signed again.

Now, as he thought back to those times of trauma and remembered Helen's reactions, Warner could feel a certain anxiety creep over him. Maybe under the right circumstances his wife did possess a killer instinct; a subtle, invisible instinct, that could be triggered by just the right set of circumstances. Adrian Kilmer could have helped to provide the right set of circumstances.

Robert Warner laid his head back against the headrest and closed his eyes. He had been married for twenty years to a beautiful and brilliant woman. He wouldn't argue with that premise. Although Helen had attended University of Michigan on a swimming scholarship and majored in finance, her general knowledge was astounding. A voracious reader, she had great retention for what she read and she was interested in all subjects. Her involvement in their business after Dan's death had

54

proven her ability to deal with people and to solve problems.

While Warner had continued his work with the research and development engineers, Helen had taken over the sales force and propelled the company through the terrifying $100 million dollar annual sales barrier. Helen had pushed the marketing beyond the capabilities of the plant and when a logistical crisis had occurred because of their inability to produce product fast enough to fill the orders that poured in, she had worked out sub-contracts with one of the world's largest chemical companies to lease plant space from them. There they could continue to meet production using Warner employees and still protect their proprietary interests.

After their son Dan's death, their sex life together had become a mechanical routine, with Helen giving perfunctorily whenever Robert asked. But her "sense of duty" attitude that prevailed in these passionless sessions eventually took its toll on his enthusiasm and he drifted into a period of subconscious impotency with his wife. Eventually Robert accepted this sexual passiveness on the part of his wife and had utilized it to alleviate any guilt resulting from his other relationships. These had been numerous at first, until Adrian came along. With her, Robert had established a whole new standard for what he had considered to be a normal sex life. He had enjoyed the relationship immensely as long as their times together had been limited.

The cab quickly gained speed as it headed up the onramp, out onto the interstate, and into the heavy Friday evening traffic. He wondered how Helen could have found out about Adrian. He had been so careful. He had always called Adrian collect from pay phones. In addition, they had agreed never to write anything to each other for fear of it being discovered by someone else. When he had given

Adrian money for her phone and other expenses, he always paid her in cash. The one thing that he was certain of was that there was no written record or evidence of his relationship with Adrian Kilmer.

He thought about his only daring indiscretion with Adrian. It had occurred last August. Adrian had told him she was flying to Chicago for a three-day buying trip and had invited him to meet her there. He had previously scheduled a business planning meeting during the same time, and had to decline. It was on one of those rare mornings, when he arrived late at his office, that he found a message on his desk telling him that Mr. A.J. Kilmer would be at the Minneapolis Airport that day from 2:00 P.M. until 4:30 P.M. "Mr. Kilmer's secretary called to ask if it were at all possible for to you please try to meet him there to discuss your business. He will be in the Delta VIP room."

Unlike most of his other messages written to him by Mary Webster, his secretary, this one had been written in Helen's handwriting, and he had quickly decided that it was not something he could just ignore. He stepped next door into his wife's office.

"When did Mr. Kilmer's secretary call?" he had asked casually, holding the message out to remind her of what he was talking about.

"Just a few minutes ago," Helen said without looking up from her work. "She said if you could not meet with him today, that he would be back in a week or two. Who is A.J. Kilmer, anyway?" She was only mildly curious.

"He's a patent attorney that I wanted to discuss some of our new products with." He had been a little uncertain of exactly who Mr. A.J. Kilmer should be, but thought it relatively safe assigning him to the technical world of research and development. This was his primary area of responsibility, and one in which his wife seldom got involved.

This explanation apparently satisfied Helen, who had other things on her mind that morning and gave the impression that she was no longer interested. The incident had shaken him, however, and his primary purpose in going to the airport that afternoon was to tell Adrian that it was cute little games such as this one that would eventually end their relationship.

At the airport, she met him in a crowd of people, shaking his hand formally and smiling sweetly. "It's so nice of you to meet with me, Mr. Warner. There are not many people flying from Chicago to Atlanta with a layover in Minneapolis, but then there are not many people who make layovers as I layover." She had smiled again, picked up her briefcase, and with great official flair, she had led him across the corridor to a door marked "meeting room."

"I have reserved this conference room until 4 o'clock," she whispered as she motioned him into a rather spacious meeting room. Adrian had closed the door behind them, turned a bolt lock, and immediately unbuttoned her blouse. He had been initially horrified with the idea that she intended for him to make love to her in an airport conference room, but once she had demonstrated the effectiveness of the door lock and shown him her paid receipt for the room, he relaxed.

"Why are you so uptight, Robbie?" she had cooed as she kissed him and rubbed his body. "We've got to loosen you up before we can harden you up." She giggled, and Warner had eventually forgotten his surroundings and made love to her on the soft pile carpet in one corner of the room.

Before putting her on her flight to Atlanta, however, Warner had extracted a promise from her that she would not come back to Minneapolis again. "We have a great relationship, Adrian," he had told her, "Why risk it?"

Helen was still at her desk when he returned to the office around six o'clock that evening. "How did your airport meeting with Mr. Kilmer work out?" she had asked without looking up at him.

"Fine..." he answered. "I think his firm will be able to do some work for us." He had then walked quickly out of her office and into the rest room to check his appearance.

Robert Warner had noticed in the past that when he spent time with Adrian Kilmer, trying to feed her insatiable appetite, he had always left these sessions feeling totally drained and vulnerable. And while he enjoyed the feeling of total sexual satisfaction, Adrian was extracting a deeper price from him; for after a session of lovemaking with her, he was the one who sometimes felt used and even abused. At these times, when he imagined himself lackadaisical and used up, he was sure others could see it.

He sometimes thought that any stranger could look at him and tell immediately that he had been a victim of an Adrian Kilmer attack. It was as though she had branded his forehead with bright red letters that said "fucked flat."

When he thought it through, he was sure it was just guilt that made him so momentarily shy. Whatever the reason, these were the times when he wanted to be by himself.

Helen could have suspected him right at that moment, although her actions gave no indication that she did so. If anything, she was even more aloof than usual, and he had decided then that if Helen was aware, she didn't care. She had shown little interest in him other than as a business partner. Warner thought it obvious, that since Dan's death, the business had been the only glue holding the fragile and shattered pieces of their marriage together.

He directed the cab off the interstate and into the entrance of an attractive industrial park. Warner Chemical Corporation's plant and storage facilities had evolved in just ten years, from a small 5,000 square foot rented warehouse to a sprawling 200,000 square foot mass of buildings gathered around the railroad siding at the back of the park.

As always, the bright security lighting made this particular section of the park stand out at night as if it were a neighborhood ball park. He and Helen had decided several years ago, after attending a seminar on plant security, to spend the money required to install stadium-type lighting around the chemical plant. The bright iodized lamps were economical and they had totally eliminated the vandalism of the past and reduced the company's insurance premiums dramatically.

Tonight, however, as the cab drew near the drive leading into the plant, Robert Warner immediately noticed that something was different. In his two week absence, a ten foot high chainlinked fence had been constructed around the facility. Across the driveway leading into the company compound was a giant gate on rolling wheels, and standing out in front of the gate was a security guard bundled up in a heavy uniform coat and hat that gave him the appearance of a Russian soldier. The man was a stranger to Warner, who quickly rolled down the rear window and called out to him.

"Good evening, I'm Robert Warner. How about opening the gate and letting us drive on back to the offices?"

The guard's stern expression never changed. "I'm sorry, sir, no one is allowed in."

"No, you don't understand. I'm the owner. I own this place. You want to see my driver's license?" He fumbled for his wallet.

"No sir, I have been given orders to let no one in, and particularly not to let you in, Mr. Warner."

Warner was dumfounded. He attempted to think of something to say, but no words came to him. He opened the door and got out of the cab, glancing at the cab driver, whose attention had once again been diverted from his basketball game.

"What the hell are you talking about? I own this Goddamn business. You weren't given orders to keep me out of here!" Warner was losing control.

"Yes sir, I was." The guard was unimpressed, and certainly not intimidated.

"Whom do you work for?"

"Evans Security, sir."

"Who gave you orders to keep me out of my own business?"

"Captain Harlan, sir."

"Who's that?"

"He's my boss, sir."

"And he told you specifically to keep me, Robert Warner, off of my own property, is that right?"

"Yes sir. I just take orders. I was told that you would try to come into the facility because you would not know about the new owners."

Warner was about to speak, but the words, "new owners", broke his train of thought completely. He shook his head in little tiny motions resembling a shiver.

"What new owners?" Warner leaned close to the guard's face as if trying to peer through a disguise. "I said, 'what new owners?'"

"That's all I know, sir. There are new owners here now, and you are not one of them. I can give you Captain Harlan's phone number, sir. He authorized me to do that and he is expecting your call." The guard held out a card in his gloved hand. Robert Warner took it and backed away slowly, looking to his left and then to his right at the new shiny fence that surrounded his plant.

"I must be dreaming... I've got to be dreaming this shit." He shook his head in disbelief as he slowly returned to the back seat of the taxi.

The cab driver was now concerned about his fare. In less than two hours, he had seen the confident business executive he had picked up at the airport melt away before his eyes. The newly transformed personality riding in the back of his cab was nervous and emotionally distraught; a man who now had diminished in size. He was a man whose voice had become higher and whose gaze was darting and uncertain. He acted frightened and definitely unstable.

"Where to, sir?" the cabby asked, looking up at his rear view mirror. He didn't understand what was going on entirely, but he now sympathized with his passenger. He gave the impression of an allright guy who had apparently just returned from a business trip to find that his wife had locked him out his own home and business.

"Just drop me off at this Executive Park Hotel up here on the corner. Maybe you had better wait until I make sure they have a room for me."

"You bet, sir. The way things are going for you tonight, it could burn down before we get there." The driver smiled but noticed, in his mirror, that his passenger didn't. His basketball game was over now. He had turned down his radio so that it was barely audible.

"What do you think is going on, sir? Is your wife doing all this shit to you?" There was no response from the back seat and the driver could see his passenger staring blankly out the rear window. They rode on in silence.

At the hotel, the driver called in his position while Warner went inside to check on an available room. In less than a minute he had returned for his bags and paid his $65.00 fare. Warner gave the young man his last four twenty dollar bills. "Keep the change, son."

"Thank you much, sir. I hope everything works out okay for you."

"Oh, don't worry about that," Warner said softly. "It will. I am sure that it will." Warner picked up his two bags and, still favoring his injured knee, limped up the three steps and into the hotel entrance.

Inside the hotel lobby, Robert Warner gave the clerk at the registration desk his American Express card and registered himself and the name of his company. Once in his room, Warner picked up the phone and dialed the number on the Evans Security card the guard had given him. After several rings, he got a recorded message requesting his name and number. He hung up.

"Captain Harlan is expecting your call," the guard had said. *And a chicken has lips*, he thought to himself.

His hotel room was large and smartly furnished. He relieved himself in the john and splashed some cold water on his face in an attempt to clear away the haze that was now engulfing him.

He hesitated in the bathroom, eyeing the commode, as a wave of nausea past over him. Then he slowly limped back into the bedroom and sat on the bed. He retrieved a phone directory from the bedside table's only drawer and found the number for the residence of Rita Ross. He dialed it several times, each time getting a busy signal. That was good; at least she was home. He would call her back in a few minutes.

Now he found the number for F. W. Carter on Palmer Drive. Florence Carter was a well-known Minneapolis artist. She was a beautiful and gracious woman in her seventies, and one of his wife's closest friends. She had been a great supporter of Helen's during those tough years after Dan's death, and Warner was sure that if his wife was not there now, Flo would know where he could get in touch with her.

"Hello," her voice was low and friendly.

"Hello, is this Flo?" he asked uncertainly.

"Yes it is. Who's this?"

"Robert Warner, Flo. I just got home from Dallas and Helen is not home. I was wondering if she could be over there at your place." He spoke slowly trying to hide the excitement and anger that was churning inside him.

"Oh, hello, Robert. I thought Helen was with you. Weren't the two of you going somewhere south, maybe Florida to get out of this cold weather?" Her voice was friendly and sincere.

"Did she say she was going to Florida?" His voice cracked with astonishment.

"Well, honey, I thought she did."

"When did you see her last?"

"She came by last Monday or Tuesday morning. Let's see now, it was Tuesday because I was going to that watercolor show downtown. Anyway, she told me that she wouldn't see me for a couple of weeks because she was going south... Now, I just assumed you were going together... Oh dear... I hope nothing has happened."

"How did she seem, Flo? What was her mood when you saw her... did she seem unhappy?"

"No, darling, in fact she was extremely happy. Two of my young male art students had come to the house early and they were here when she came. I introduced Helen to them and they both thought she was just charming and one of the most beautiful people they had ever met. But I dislike this, Rob. It's unlike Helen to take off without telling you where she can be reached." The gaiety in her voice had been replaced by a frightened tone, and Warner believed her concern was genuine.

"Well, don't worry, Flo; I am sure she is all right. We just got our communication wires crossed."

"Have you called the authorities, Robert?"

"Called the authorities? No, I haven't."

"Yes, the police. Wouldn't it be a good idea to report this to them right away?"

Warner was startled by the question. He had no intention of talking to the police, but then, Florence Carter didn't know all the facts. If he had told her of all Helen's manipulations while he had been away, Flo would have known immediately that it was he, Robert L. Warner, who needed help and sympathy, not his wife. The fact was, the way he was beginning to feel about Helen, she was the one who should be calling the police, for protection. He quickly decided to end the conversation on a positive note.

"Well... I suppose it wouldn't hurt," he said quietly, to appear agreeable. "But, Flo, we don't want to get the press involved if we don't have to. You know what I mean, don't you? There may be a simple explanation for all of this. Flo, please don't mention this to anyone until I can look into it further, all right?" There was a long pause.

"All right, Robert, but I just can't believe Helen would leave town without telling you where she was going. Helen just wouldn't do that." She was genuinely distressed now, and her voice sounded as if she was on the verge of tears. "Will you call me as soon as you find out where she is... even if it's late?"

"Yes, of course. I'll call you as soon as I know something."

"Thank you, dear. Goodnight, Robert."

"Goodnight, Flo." He hung up, regretting the call.

He dialed Rita Ross's number again, and after several rings, he found himself listening to another recorded message. This time it was Rita Ross telling him how much his call meant to her and for him to please leave a message so she could return the call.

He hung up the phone before the message finished and turned on the radio by the bed. His favorite march, John Philip Sousa's 'Stars and Stripes Forever,' was playing. "Be kind to your web-footed friends, for a duck may be somebody's mother," he mumbled the words to himself. Warner turned the volume up and limped gingerly over to the window and drew the drapes open.

Outside, large soft flakes of snow were dancing downward in the bright parking lot lights. They floated toward the ground as pieces of oversized, thick confetti. Cars on the interstate were now moving through the white swirl at a snail's pace, and for a brief moment it seemed to Warner as though he was watching a ticker tape parade. He thought he saw his Mercedes go by; silver, sleek, and beautiful. Could that have been it, with Helen driving? Sousa's march blared on, "They live in the deep of the swamp, where the weather is damp." It was an impressive tickertape parade indeed. It was a ticker tape parade honoring his wife, Helen, for her ingenious plan to embarrass and humiliate him. "Now you may think that this is the end, well it is..." But the music roared on, building towards its splendiferous climax.

As he stood there in the hotel room, transfixed by the scene from his window, a terrible feeling of helplessness swept over him. From a military strategist's viewpoint, he may have already been defeated before he had even a chance to fight. He had certainly been taken by surprise. The enemy had lured him to sleep, infiltrated his positions, and then captured him without ever firing a shot. He had already been taken prisoner. He was now just an emasculated victim; a lone spectator watching a parade honoring his victorious conqueror.

What was the total plan? What else did the future hold in store for him? How much of it was he aware of now; or was he only seeing the tip of an iceberg? He stood, motionless, at the window for several minutes. Sousa ended. A deep resonate baritone voice talked about a program called "classics by request" and gave a number to call. A quiet, soothing harp was playing something by Debussy. A loud laugh from the room next door brought him back to reality.

He checked his watch. It was after 8:00 P.M. He needed to discuss this situation with his lawyer immediately. He limped back over to the bed and, looking through the phone directory once again, he found the number of Douglas A. Hawkins.

"Hello." A woman's voice answered the phone.

"Hello, Joan?"

"Yes."

"Joan, this is Robert Warner. I hate to bother you at home on the weekend, but it is important. Is Doug there? "

"Sure, Rob, it's no bother. We're just watching television."

Within a few seconds, Doug Hawkins was on the line. "What's up, Robert? How were things in Big D - or are you still down there?"

"No, I'm back here in town, Doug, but I've got some big problems."

"I'm listening."

He related the story of the events since his arrival at the airport: the disconnected phone, the missing car, his house, empty of furniture, with Rita Ross's sign in front of it, and his plant, fenced off with a guard at the gate - a guard who conveyed a story about a recent sale of the property and who said he had specific instructions to keep Warner from entering. It all sounded so ridiculous that he fully expected to be interrupted by the sound of Hawkins' laughter, but the lawyer listened quietly until he had finished.

"Where are you now, Rob? Do you want to spend the night with us?"

"No thanks, I've checked into the Executive Park Hotel. This is a Hertz outlet, so I can rent a car here in the morning. I know you usually work on Saturday mornings and what I want to do, Doug, is to meet you in your office tomorrow as early as possible."

"Well, the trouble is, Rob, I've got a University Club Annual Board Meeting downtown first thing in the morning, but it shouldn't take too long. Why don't you just meet me out there at the club around noon?"

There was a knock at Warner's door. "Doug, hold on for just a second; there's someone at the door."

Opening his door, Warner immediately recognized the desk clerk who had registered him.

"I hate to bother you, sir, but this American Express card number you gave me has been cancelled. I wonder if you have a new number."

"What do you mean, cancelled? I just got that card a month ago; the expiration date is over a year from now."

"I know that, sir, but when we called the company for confirmation, they told us not to accept it and that it had been cancelled. That's all I know, sir." The tall, thin, effeminate man was most assuredly not trying to make trouble, and Warner got his wallet from his coat pocket and handed the clerk his Gold Visa card.

"Put the room charge on this. I'll come on down there in a minute to pick it up."

With a "Thank you, sir," the clerk was gone, closing the door behind him. Warner picked up the phone.

"Doug, she has cancelled my American Express. Shit! Can you believe that? The crazy bitch has cancelled my American Express account."

"What are you talking about?"

"That was the desk clerk at the door. He said that my American Express is no good. I can't use it to pay for my room."

"Do you have any money, Rob?" Hawkins sounded concerned.

"No, I used my last cash to pay my cab driver. I'm all right, I just gave him my bank card and..."

"Rob, is that a company card also?

"No, it will be all right. It's a personal card."

"Rob, is it a joint card? Is Helen on it with you?" Hawkins was trying to make a point.

"Yes, she has the card too; but she wouldn't cancel that also, do you think...?" His voice trailed off as he answered his own question. "Well, if she has, I'll give them a personal check."

"Rob, let me ask you: who's going to take a personal check from a guy whose credit cards have all just been cancelled? Hell, I don't know, maybe they will; give it a try, and if you need some help call me back; otherwise I'll see you in my office in the morning, all right?"

"All right..."

Robert Warner hung up the phone and closed his eyes. What was happening to him? He kept going back to his dream wish. *Please, please, let this be a dream. Please let me wake up.* He opened his eyes and glanced around the hotel room. It was not a dream.

He picked up his wallet, put his suit jacket back on, and was reaching for the door when the phone rang.

"Hello, sir, this is the front desk. I hate to report to you that your Visa card has been cancelled, also." There was a certain sadness in the voice, but it was overshadowed by what Warner understood to be concern.

"I'll be right down," Robert Warner said, and hung up.

The lobby was busy when Warner stepped off the elevator. He waited patiently at one corner of the registration desk as the clerk checked in an elderly couple who had an endless list of questions to be answered.

Warner removed all of the credit cards from his wallet and spread them on the counter in front of him.

"Take your pick," he said to the clerk when the man came over to him. "She may have cancelled them all, but we won't know that until we try them."

The clerk handed Warner his cancelled Visa card and studied the cards on the counter for several seconds. "We can accept your Diners or Carte Blanche and, in fact, the hotel has an arrangement with Shell Oil to use that card also; so whichever one you want to give me will be all right."

Warner handed the clerk his Diners and Carte Blanche cards and watched him move to a desk at one end of the registration area. There, the young man studied a sheet attached to a bulletin board above the desk, then picked up a phone and dialed a number. For some time, Warner watched the clerk turning the cards over in his hands, and then he was reading the numbers off to someone on the other end of the line. After several seconds, Warner saw him nod as if in agreement with something said. He thanked the party on the other end of the line before hanging up. He repeated the whole process again with the second card before returning to the counter, shaking his head.

"Mr. Warner, I'm afraid these have both been cancelled also. Shall I try your Shell card?" He picked the card up from the counter before Warner could answer and returned to the desk. As Warner watched him look up the authorization number on the wall chart, a feeling of helplessness came over him. For the last three hours, he had sensed that the layers of his identity were being peeled away from him. It was as though all of his worldly possessions had been auctioned away for nothing.

To Robert Warner, it was as though he had returned from Dallas to find himself in a different world. The plane had somehow returned him to a different Minneapolis. This was not his home town, but only one that was similar. It was a Rod Serling Twilight Zone script where everything was the same, but not quite the same.

Who was behind this? he wondered. Who was doing this to him? What had happened while he was in Dallas? As he pondered these questions, he still found it difficult to believe that Helen was the major force behind the plot. The scheme was too hostile; too cruel and diabolical to be the work of his wife. Helen would never have been so vindictive towards him, and besides, it was all too well organized and orchestrated to have been the work of his wife alone.

An important question to be answered immediately was who? Who was in on the coup? And, most importantly right now, he needed to find out who were his real friends. The clerk set the Shell card back down on the counter in front of him and shook his head. "Sorry, Sir."

"Will you take a personal check?"

The clerk flinched as if Warner had struck him. "We would prefer not to." He endeavored to smile, but couldn't.

"May I use your phone to make a local call?" Warner pointed to the phone on the counter in front of him.

"That's a house phone there, sir. If you come down here to this end, I'll hand you one of our desk phones." The young man walked to the far end of the registration area and quickly set a phone up on the counter.

Once again Robert Warner dialed Doug Hawkins's number. The phone rang only once before Hawkins answered.

"Hello."

"Doug, it's me again; the bad penny."

"Yeah, Rob, What's up?"

"Helen has cancelled all my credit cards."

"All of them?"

"Even my gas card... The bitch has gone crazy... hasn't she? I mean, she just can't do this legally, can she?"

The long pause on the other end of the line made Warner swallow air. "Well hell; tell me, Doug. Can she do this shit to me or not?"

"It appears to me, old buddy, that she has already done it to you. The thing for us to do now is to relax and take it easy and try to figure out how much of it we can correct." Doug Hawkins's calm, relaxed voice did little to soothe Warner's temper.

"Come on, Hawkins!" Warner was becoming frantic. "You don't understand what I'm trying to tell you. I have been set up! I have been blindsided by the fucking phantom! I mean, I come back from a business trip and what do I find? My car has been taken from the airport; my house is locked up with no furniture in it and a frigging for sale sign in the front yard; my business, my plant, the one I founded with my own two hands, has got a prison fence around it and some daffy guard's on the gate with specific orders to keep me out. And now I find out that all my credit cards have been cancelled. This goddamn hotel is getting ready to throw me out into the street; and you say just relax and take it easy..." Warner's voice, which had been a hoarse whisper, had risen to a shout, and at once he was aware that other guests in the lobby were staring in his direction.

"Look, Rob," Hawkins broke in, "things are never quite as bad as they seem. Let me speak to whoever is in charge there." Warner handed the phone to the clerk, who spoke briefly and made notes on a sheet of paper before handing the receiver back to Warner and nodding his head up and down several times, signifying that everything would be all right.

"Rob, I just gave him my American Express number and my phone number so he can call me if he needs to. I told him to give you anything you wanted and I will check you out in the morning when I pick you up."

"What time are you coming?"

"I am going to pick you up before my meeting, so be ready at eight."

"Doug, what do you think has happened…? I mean, what do you think Helen has done to me?"

"Rob, I think it's just as you said; you have been set up royally, my boy. But, don't worry, we will figure all this out in the morning. In the meantime, get a good night's sleep; you're going to need it. See you at 8 o'clock sharp."

Robert Warner went back to his room and returned to the window. The snow had stopped falling and the traffic on the interstate had thinned considerably. Helen's ticker tape parade was over. He hoped that was the case, for he wasn't sure he could stand much more trauma. He closed the drapes and slowly and clumsily removed his clothes. Clad in just his undershorts, he laid on the bed without turning down the covers. He turned out the light on the table by the bed. There, in the dark, staring at the ceiling, Robert Warner thought about his life and waited for morning to come.

****

Chapter 6
The Epiphany
A sudden, intuitive perception of or insight into the reality or essential meaning of something

Jack Andrews lurched forward as he opened the car door and vomited into the gutter. For a brief moment, he hung inverted, his head touching the pavement while traces of the whiskey-laced spittle burned into his sinuses. Only his strong right hand gripping the wheel kept him from falling out of the car. He remained still for several seconds, making low painful sounding noises, and then he heaved again. The violent retching continued for a minute before it subsided, leaving him dangling motionless, suspended in the cold night air as if he were some lifeless rubber manikin.

Then, with a great groan, he pulled himself back up into the car and closed the door. He sat bolt upright now; ramrod stiff, as if attempting to regain some of his lost dignity.

"Too fast," he mumbled to himself. He drank the whiskey much too fast. It always amazed Andrews, how the human body could change its chemistry so dramatically. There was a time in his life when he could have gulped down a half-fifth of some cheap rotgut with one big long pull and not even belched. But now, his new body, the one developed through his own health fanaticism, couldn't even handle a few swallows of Tennessee's best sipping whiskey. Andrews could feel his thought processes slowing down. The un-regurgitated alcohol was being absorbed into his bloodstream and for the moment its numbing effects were delicious. He craved the relief it offered. The alcohol allowed his mind to drift away from the horrors of reality and into a vague and hazy dream world. Facts were unchanged, truth was still truth, and emotions were still emotions, but now the whiskey coating softened the hard sharp edges and made them all more bearable, at least for the moment.

He gripped the door handle again as another wave of nausea swept over him. It quickly passed and he rested his head back against the seat.

"I can't do anymore..." he whispered to himself. "Nothing's left." He felt along the car seat for the cap to the Jack Daniels bottle. He couldn't find it and his interest quickly shifted back to his physical condition. "You can't even handle a few sips of good whiskey, Andrews." He spoke so loudly that his voice startled him. He gawked at the darkness outside the car.

His old drinking buddies would say that he had absolutely ruined himself. Of course, most of them couldn't say anything, because they were dead. There were exceptions. Evans and Wadley were two of them. They had both dried out and taken the cure with him years ago. They were the friends that he had briefly considered calling before opening the bottle in his lap; two other reformed drunks who would have rushed to his aid immediately.

Of course, his call would have stunned them. Jack Andrews had never been a backslider; not once in over twelve years. From the time he admitted and accepted his alcoholism, he had been clean. "One of the most inspiring examples of how a drunk can take control of his life," that's how he had been introduced at the AA National Convention two years ago. The featured speaker on the program, he had stirred his audience that night with his story of determination and dedication.

"Alcoholics Anonymous can work for you," he had told his listeners then, and repeated in a loud voice now. "But only to the extent that you work for it. You take out of your relationship with this organization exactly what you put into it. Giving is, in fact, receiving. And, my friends and fellow members, it is only when one of us understands this truth, that he or she can take control of his or her life with complete confidence." His audience had responded with a long standing ovation.

"I'll drink to that," he said now, holding the bottle up before his imagined gathering. He peered around in the darkness for someone to toast with him. "Where are Evans and Wadley?" he asked, staring out into the night. "I called those bastards," he said softly. He hung his head in thought for several seconds. "No, shit no, I didn't call them." He laid his head back on the headrest. "You dumb sumbitch Andrews, you didn't even call them," he shouted out. He closed his eyes mumbling to himself, "Evans and Wadley, great guys... great goddamn guys..." He felt along on the floor of the car, continuing his search for something but no longer remembering what it was.

If he had called Evans and Wadley, they would be there; of that, he was certain. Both would have come to his aid and no doubt they would have talked him out of drinking again, for they were both as good at counseling as he was. Of course, they would have also prevented him from killing his wife and her lover, and Andrews was aware that this was the real reason he had not called them.

At the time he had opened the bottle in his lap, drinking had not been so important to Jack Andrews. The murder had been his obsession. He desperately needed to escape the grief and sorrow that was consuming him. He had to find a way to ease the unbearable pain growing within him. Destroying those directly responsible should offer a chance of relief. The whiskey was just a crutch. It helped him rationalize his flawed reasoning; it allowed him to overlook the obvious wrongness of what he was doing.

He gave up on finding the cap and instead took another nip from the bottle. He glanced at the Volvo's clock in the dash. It had been a half hour since he had left the two nude forms sleeping next to each other on the king-size bed and manipulated the gas valve to exterminate them - twenty-three minutes, to be exact.

Because he had estimated that it would take thirty minutes to complete total asphyxiation, he now assumed that it could be over with. It was a deed performed; a feat accomplished. He had murdered his wife and her lover.

"How does it feel?" he mumbled out loud. "Hey asshole, I say, how does it feel to be a murderer?" There was no immediate answer, and once again his head drooped and his mind wandered. For several minutes there was no movement and the car was quiet except for the occasional clicks of the clock; the last of which startled Andrews back to reality, and he jerked his head up.

"A Volvo has a damn good little clock," he mumbled out loud. They were a quartz movement, made in Sweden with the car. This one had never lost a minute during the three years he had owned the car. "Damn good little clock," he said again softly.

"Why? Why did she do it?" he cried out to the clock. "Why, Jill, why, why, why?" Again, tears streamed down his already-

78

streaked face and for several minutes he sobbed softly, with his head bowed. Then, with a new wave of remorse welling up inside him, his body trembled and shook convulsively as it strove to rid itself of a great, overwhelming sorrow. A long slow series of groans and primitive animal moans rolled up from out of his chest and throat. As these sounds grew louder, reverberating around within the enclosed car, Jack Andrews could feel all semblance of emotional stability slipping away from him. The sadness and remorse had progressed on beyond his control. It was an all-consuming, possessive grief that offered no options for escape.

In his groggy, inebriated state of mind, the murder had been committed. It was over with; a past fact; a dreadful deed that now offered him no relief for his having committed it. More shocking at this moment was the realization that he was not grieving over his wife's infidelity; he was no longer weeping for the loss of her character and honor. Instead, he was experiencing this new terrible sadness because of the loss of her life. He grieved for the loss of Jill as his wife, and he grieved for her loss as a companion, and he grieved for her loss as a loving, living person.

Also, to some extent, he grieved for himself. Dr. Jackson Andrews was now a murderer. He was a man who had abruptly lost all confidence and self-esteem. He was a man who had even lost his identity. Jack Andrews, the murderer, would no longer be the loving husband, the patient, kind and tolerant man who was known for his gentleness and understanding.

Even through the whiskey-induced fog that shrouded his thoughts, Jack Andrews could see that Jill's death had done nothing to change her image; it would only change his. Tomorrow she would be his poor dead wife and he would be her living murderer. Instantly, he saw that he should not let this happen. He could not let her die.

He stumbled out of the car and, walking quickly but with a noticeable stagger, made his way back up the street and into the shadows of his house. Despite the closed bedroom doors, he could smell the gas as he rushed down the hallway. Inside the bedroom, the fumes were so overwhelming that he was sure that he was too late to save anyone. A wall switch controlled the overhead, indirect lights. He flicked it on. The two nude forms were positioned on the bed exactly where he had last seen them, only now they were listless and still. With great effort he gathered Jill's limp body in his arms and, struggling through the narrow closet, he made his way back into the guest room. He gently laid the lifeless form on the big four-poster bed. Jill's skin had a bluish tint to it. He quickly checked her pulse. He could feel one; it was weak and sporadic and she was breathing in short little gasps, but she was alive. He sought to organize his thoughts. The gas; he had to stop the gas!

He staggered to the window and threw it open, letting the cold night air flood into the room. He sucked in several lungs full of it himself and then hurried back into the master bedroom to turn off the inside valve to the gas log. When the flow of gas had ceased, Andrews crossed the room and pulled open the drapes in front of the sliding glass doors that opened out onto a porch on the lake side of the house. He removed the metal security pin and undid the latch.

He hesitated. The gas fumes made him weak and dizzy. He struggled to logically reason exactly what his next step should be. He glanced back at the large form of Phillip Cowans, lying face up, sprawled across the bed, with his head thrown back and his mouth opened as grotesquely as a beached bass. He appeared to be dead. Andrews went to the bed and felt for a pulse. The big man was still alive, but

80

barely. A few more minutes of breathing the heavy gas fumes would finish the job.

Jack Andrews stood transfixed and stared at his dying nemesis. To him, the unconscious body in front of him was no longer that of a man. It was not even the form of a human being. It was, instead, the body of some dangerous, evil creature; a wicked and vile monster that had come into his home and fouled his life forever. How could he possibly save it, when he desperately wanted to watch it die and have it be forgotten?

He studied the body for several minutes as he pondered his options. The congressman was a powerfully built man, with massive chest and shoulders and a thick neck. His arms and legs were well muscled. And to Jack Andrews, he represented a certain amount of danger. It was as though he had sedated and captured some sort of wild gorilla and must now decide what to do with it before it awakened.

For the first time, Andrews allowed himself to study the creature's genitals, *The real tools of his trade*, he thought to himself. Their size corresponded with the rest of its body. In any male locker room, the big man would have been classified as a stud. Andrews couldn't help but think of all the stories he had heard about big men who had little, tiny dicks and little guys who had peckers that hung down to their knees. The congressman sadly disproved that theory. His large penis and testicles made him appear to be a bull of a man. Even gasping for life, he was the consummate male specimen, and Andrews quickly decided that all those stories he had heard so often about penis size were the creations of little guys with short legs.

Death would be an easy way out for Phillip Cowans, now. He would never have to wake up and deal with the reality of what he had done. He could slip peacefully away from this world without being held accountable by his

81

constituents; without being ravaged by a hostile press. In death the Congressman might even be eulogized as a great statesman, remembered for his positive contributions and his likable traits, whatever they were.

No, under the circumstances, death was too easy a way out for Phillip Cowans, and at once Jack Andrews saw that he must not let the congressman take it. He crossed the room to the sliding glass doors and shoved them open. The cold air rushed by him into the room and he inhaled deeply five or six times in an effort to clear his own head. Then he walked back to the nude form lying on his bed and studied it further.

He remembered his old friend, Peter Clause, and his theory for handling sex offenders.

 "For god's sake, don't put them in prison. That will just cost the tax payers money and accomplish nothing. They will still be questionable offenders when they are released. The government should take their sex drive away from them permanently; and the only way to effectively do that is by castration." A group of interns had been drinking coffee during a lunch break at The Kessler Animal Hospital and were talking about a particularly heinous crime that had just occurred in the Tampa Bay area. A man had repeatedly raped a pregnant woman, causing her to abort her baby. Clause had been describing the facts of the case to the others gathered around the table, and he had move on to his own solution for handling cases of this sort.

"Castration would be adequate, in most instances," he elaborated. "But I think a fair punishment in this case would be to put this son-of-a-bitch's pecker on an anvil and let me hit it just one time with a ten pound sledgehammer. That should slow his sex drive down dramatically, and require him to squat to pee for the rest of his life." Clause's remarks brought laughter from some of the interns, but only a smile from Andrews; for after having lived with Peter Clause for seven years, Jack saw that his friend was serious.

At that point and time in his life, and despite his five years of service in the Marine Corps as a fighter pilot, Jack Andrews was considered by Clause and his other friends, who attended Auburn's College of Veterinary Medicine, as pretty much of a liberal thinker. He had argued back to Clause that forced sterilization, while admittedly effective, had been a tool of Hitler's Third Reich, and was certainly not an acceptable idea in America. He had argued that point with some mild support from the others at the table until Clause had smiled condescendingly at all of them and held up his hands to make a point.

"Fellows, the rights of our society take precedence over the rights of any individual. For example, the use of torture to extract information is abhorrent to all of us, but suppose a terrorist had hidden an atomic bomb in some unknown major city and it was set to go off in several hours unless it was defused? Imagine we have captured the terrorist who did it. Would you read him his rights - one of which is to remain silent - and let him make a call to his lawyer while a million people are annihilated, or would you do everything in your power to find out where the bomb was? I would hope that you would do everything in your power to extract the information - everything, including torturing the bastard." Peter quickly continued on before anyone could answer his hypothetical question.

"Andrews, I know what you would do. You would say, *torture that no good son-of-a-bitch*. And do you know what? You would be fully justified in saying that. Why? Because any terrorist's rights are totally overshadowed by the rights of society."

"Now, as far as castration is concerned, you and I both know that there has never been an animal castrated that didn't become a lot nicer critter to be around. Whether it's a roving tom cat, a bad dog, or a mean bull, if you clip him, it makes him a lot easier to get along with. In fact, most of these bad actors become lovable, don't they? Stop and think about that for a minute. I think that the castration of sex offenders would not only benefit society tremendously, but it could also be a blessing to the offender himself, by just making him a lot nicer critter to be around."

Peter Clause had been a convincing proponent of his causes back then, over twenty years ago, and there was little question in Andrew's mind what Peter Clause's solution to his present situation would be. He enjoyed thinking about it. The Clause solution would be neat, tidy, and professionally done. "Perhaps some of my best work," Clause would always say. It would solve a great many problems for a great many people. Still in his inebriated state, Jack Andrews saw that the Clause solution could also be the Andrews' solution. He could do it himself, but he would have to move quickly while there was still time.

He stopped in the guest room once again to check on Jill. Her pulse was stronger now, and her breathing steady. The room was freezing. He closed the windows, leaving them only slightly ajar, and then pulled the covers up over his wife's nude body. He took a large, heavy quilted comforter from the closet's top shelf and spread it over her for additional warmth. Then he paused to study the woman's face on the pillow.

He saw in the face only the slightest resemblance to the beautiful young girl he had met that day in New York when he was shopping at Saks. She was smiling at him, asking if she could be of service. He was looking for a birthday gift for his mother and had spent over an hour talking to her before he had amassed enough courage to ask her to have dinner with him. Her name was Jill Coleman. She was vibrant, fun-loving, full of life, and her face showed it all. Jack had fallen in love immediately with that wonderful face and the beautiful person to whom it belonged. Where had Jill Coleman gone? What had happened to her? The face on the pillow was now only a vague likeness.

He saw in this face on the pillow a much greater likeness of Jill Andrews, a distraught young woman, broken-hearted by the discovery that she would never bear children - a woman anguished and tormented by an invisible internal biological clock that relentlessly drove her on towards a goal she could never achieve.

And now he saw, in the blue-tinted face on the pillow, the sadness of a woman somehow lured away from all of her own values; a wife pulled away from an adoring husband's love by some strange, unexplained force that had now destroyed her world. As a moth is drawn into the flame that burns it, Jill had so little control over what was happening to her. The tears that filled his eyes once again forced him to look away from her.

Now the realization of where he was and what he needed to do came back to him. Indeed, he had serious business to take care of and little time left in which to do it. He walked down the hall, out of the house, and back down the street to his car. He retrieved the car keys from the ignition and fumbled with the trunk lock for several seconds before opening it.

He studied the two medical bags sitting alongside his suitcase on the floor of the deep trunk. One contained papers and files; the other his instruments; but even under the trunk's bright lights he could not tell them apart. He stared at them for several seconds before grasping the handles of one and turning it over on its side. The gold letters printed just below the handle were worn but were still readable: Jackson L. Andrews, D.V.M. A silver chain through the handle held an identification tag. On one side of the tag was printed his name and address and on the other side were large blue letters reading Faculty Member - Auburn University School of Veterinary Medicine. Andrews had the right case. He lifted it out of the trunk and gently closed the lid.

Walking quickly back towards his house, carrying the bag, Jack Andrews retraced his steps of a few minutes before; only now he walked straight, with no trace of a stagger.

****

Chapter 7
The Background

By the time they entered Auburn University's School of Veterinary Medicine together, Jack Andrews and Peter Clause had become inseparable. Fate had paired the two together as roommates when they were going through jet training at the Naval Air Base in Pensacola, Florida.

Unlike Andrews, who was a third generation Floridian, with relatives all over the state, Clause had no family. He had grown up in South Florida in a foster home and his drive and determination had earned him an academic scholarship. Andrews liked his roommate immediately and the two had continued to share various living quarters together during most of their aviation training. Both pilots were assigned to fly F-4 Phantoms, and both were sent to Vietnam as soon as they completed carrier training. When both Andrews and Clause were discharged from the service, both men had decided to pursue careers in veterinary medicine. They had applied to Auburn University simultaneously and celebrated their acceptance together with a rousing grain alcohol (stolen from the carrier's sick bay) party, that left them and most of their guests incapacitated for several days.

Both students worked hard at Auburn. They were enthusiastic, eager to learn, and anxious to experiment. Clause's 4.0 grade average was considered one of the highest overall standings in the school's history and Andrews' 3.7 average ranked him third in their graduating class. After graduation, the two continued to move in unison as they both accepted an invitation from Dr. Newton Kessler to complete their internships at his Kessler Animal Hospital in St. Petersburg, Florida.

Known historically as a city for retirement, St. Petersburg has one of the highest percentages of elderly inhabitants of any city in the United States. Because most middle-age and elderly people are childless at home, their pets receive the same attention and concern that their children once did and in effect become the focal point of their lives.

It was not surprising that a large number of small animal practices flourished throughout the area. The largest of these was the Kessler Animal Hospital. Founded by Newton Kessler, this hospital employed over 15 veterinarians and was one of the largest of its kind in Florida.

Newton Kessler, a fastidious, immaculately dressed little man with a great mane of well-coffered white hair and a pencil-thin mustache, worked around the clock overseeing the hospital procedures and constantly recruiting to maintain his large staff of doctors. This he accomplished by hiring young new interns who required a minimum salary, but would only stay for their short intern period before moving on to greener pastures. Their greener pastures had to be at least 100 miles away, however, because of the no-competition clause that Dr. Kessler required all of his employees to sign.

Also, the clinic was operated with Newton Kessler's flair for the dramatic. The furnishings, the staff's uniforms, and the entire presentation to the public was more oriented to that of a hospital for humans than one for animals. This included, of course, a billing and pricing system which was based on the Kessler floating scale concept of charging whatever the market will bear.

While Doctor K, as he was known to both his staff and patients, spent a great deal of his time touring the country recruiting new interns to fill the vacancies on his constantly diminishing staff, he was also extremely active within the hospital and was constantly lecturing to his staff on ways to improve their attitudes and performances.

"Boys," he told Andrews and Clause upon their arrival in St. Petersburg, "I assume you two have learned a great deal about veterinary medicine at Auburn. It's a fine University, but now I am going to teach you what counts in this business; and that is how to handle the public."

Newton Kessler was a painfully thin, nervous little man who had several facial tics that occasionally possessed his countenance to such an extent that it was impossible for a listener to concentrate on what he was saying. One of these nervous gestures, always with him, was his constant chin lift or thrust, a gesture which made it appear that some invisible collar was too tight about his neck and was perhaps pinching the sensitive skin on his throat. A second gesture that occurred during most of Newton Kessler's waking moments was a mouth gesture in which the Doctor would stretch his lips out across his face, as if making an exaggerated smile without showing any teeth.

These two gestures worked synergistically in that anyone meeting Newton Kessler for the first time would come away from the encounter certain that the doctor had a great many more ticks than just the two. There was, in fact, a third nervous disorder that occurred only when the Doctor was excited or irritated. This involved an upward twitching of his eyebrows, and on rare occasions when one could observe Doctor K under the influence of all three facial spasms, "it was indeed," as Peter Clause would say, "a sight to behold."

Even though they had personally met him at Auburn a year earlier, when he was on campus recruiting, Clause and Andrews had not noticed the extent of Dr. K's nervous disorders. It wasn't until Newton Kessler gave them his standard "welcome aboard" speech the first day of their arrival in St. Pete that they quickly became aware of what a nervous little fellow their new boss was.

He had them seated in his office while he stood behind his desk, occasionally pacing back and forth and talking in machine gun-like bursts.

"Boys, most of the people who come into our little hospital here love their animals. I mean. they love them more than anything else in the world. More than they love their spouses... more than they love their kids. Their animals are the major focal points in their lives. I don't care what breed it is, or how old and ugly it is; they will dote on it and spoil it until you absolutely won't believe it. Now, you may find this to be somewhat disgusting - personally, I do too. The point is not whether you approve or disapprove, gentlemen; the point is that you understand how the system works..." Here Doctor K paused for effect, making two quick lip stretches followed by a chin thrust.

"Now, once you understand how the system works, men, you'll quickly figure out how to win the hearts and minds of your patients." Lip stretch. "That's right, boys. I said "patients", and I don't mean cats and dogs, either. Your patients are the people who bring those cats and dogs in here. Don't ever lose sight of that. Cats and dogs don't call up and make appointments. Cats and dogs don't drive their car out here to keep those appointments, and cats and dogs can't write checks and pay you for your services." Two lip stretches, one chin thrust.

"Now, we don't want to go overboard on this. I mean, we never lose sight of in whose ass we are supposed to stick the thermometer, although I have sometimes wondered about that myself." Doctor K paused again for effect, but kept a straight face and made another chin thrust. "We administer first aid to the animals that come in here and then we treat their owners, who are our real patients. How do we treat them? We listen." Lip stretch.

"We listen to them talk about their trials and their tribulations, and we tell them how great their animals look and what a wonderful job they are doing of caring for them. And I tell them all how lucky their pets are to have such wonderful owners. It is pure psychoanalysis, gentlemen, and it works. An animal that comes in here may or may not leave feeling better, but if you do your job, it's for damn sure its owner will feel better, and that is when he or she becomes your patient." Doctor K worked in two more quick lip stretches and asked, "Do either of you understand what I am saying?" Andrews and Clause's nods were answered by a single chin thrust.

"Good, good." Doctor K said. "Now, there are some other things we do here that more or less go along with this type of thinking. Since our patients treat their pets as family, we call all pets by their names. I don't care if it's Sweet Pea Baby and we talk to them constantly while we work with them. It doesn't do shit for the animal, but it puts the patient at ease. We pay the animal constant compliments, as if it could understand us. And I don't care if it's an old Chihuahua with the mange; we will talk about how beautiful its eyes are. We find some point about each animal that is positive and we talk about it, and we appreciate it. This is important." Lip stretch, chin thrust, two more lip stretches.

"Also, follow-up is important. We make at least one follow-up call after each office visit for any procedure, and if it was a surgical procedure, we make two calls. We enter the time and date of the calls on our patient's file card. Our girls are good at watching this and they will stay on your ass until you make the calls. So don't let us down on this, fellas. I'm telling you right up front. Don't let me down." Quick chin thrust.

"Also, we encourage all of our clients to put our 24-hour emergency line sticker on their phones at home. Gentlemen, it's hard enough to get patients in this business. When we get one in here, we don't want to lose him to anybody. We sell services, gentlemen: uncompromising service. We charge for it, oh yes, but because it's better than anybody else's, we can justify it." Slow chin thrust.

"We have a minimum charge for every procedure that we do, but if we do an exceptional job, we charge extra. How do you know when you have performed an exceptional job? The patient will tell you. Remember that, fellows: the patient will tell you." Lip stretch, chin thrust.

"Let me give you an example of how my uncle charged for his services." Doctor K paused again and studied them both, as if trying to decide whether they were qualified to hear what he was about to tell them.

"My Uncle George was an optometrist who made more money than any two optometrists in the business. I asked him one day, how he did it. Do you know what he told me? 'Charge what the market will bear, Newton, charge what the market will bear.' When I asked him, 'Uncle George, how do you know what the market will bear?' he said, 'Let me give you an example, Newton. After I make a pair of glasses for someone and they are happy with them, they

92

generally ask how much they owe me. And I get real close to them, so I can study their faces, and I say $25.00. And if I don't see them flinch, I quickly add, 'for the frames.' And then I say, 'and for the lenses... its $15.00,' and if they don't flinch, I quickly add, 'a piece... ' That means that a pair of my glasses costs somewhere between $25.00 and $55.00, depending on what the market will bear." Both young interns burst into laughter and Newton Kessler froze, a lip stretch into a permanent smile and followed up with an approving final chin thrust.

Because he had been a thespian at heart, Peter Clause caught on immediately to the Newton Kessler system of practicing drama and veterinarian medicine simultaneously. And it was only with the exception of his misdiagnosis of Fifi, the cat, that his otherwise-perfect tenure of internship at the hospital was spoiled.

The misdiagnosis, which occurred during that first week in residency, was only known by Clause and his best friend Jack Andrews, so it had little bearing on his reputation at the hospital and was, in effect, only Peter's cross to bear.

That first week on the job, both of them had felt the pressure to perform well. Fresh out of vet school, they could feel the eyes of the staff watching their every move. Peter had confided to Jack about his misdiagnosis.

"Did you see the couple who came with a coffin to claim the body of their cat today?" He initiated the conversation as they were drinking a beer together after five sets of night tennis.

"No, I don't think so." Jack was busy wrapping a new handle on his racket.

"She was a big fat woman, her husband was tall and thin, and they were wearing black."

Andrews stopped his taping and glanced up.

"No shit, Jack, they were dressed in black. And they had this custom-made coffin for their cat. It even had her name, Fifi, on it."

"What had happened to the cat?"

"It had swallowed a small fly fishhook and it went all the way into the stomach before it caught."

"Is that the surgery you were doing two days ago?"

"Yeah. I took it out, no problems, but you know, the question was whether the cat could survive the anesthetic."

"Was it old?"

"It was fifteen, sixteen."

"Wow. That's old for major surgery."

"Hey, what else are you going to do? I mean, you or I would have put it to sleep immediately. I explained all this to the couple. I told them that the cat had little chance of surviving and that it would be expensive, but she said if there was any chance at all, to go ahead and perform the operation."

"So it never came out from under the anesthetic?"

"Listen to this, Jack. First, the woman wanted to spend the night with the cat. I had to get Doctor K to talk to her. He gave her his bullshit about being on call twenty-four hours a day and she decided she would go home. Anyway, I come in the next morning and there was the cat, feet up in its cage. I checked it out, did some reflex tests - there was no body temperature, and the son-of-a-bitch was dead. I go inside and call the woman. She goes to pieces over the phone, but she tells me to keep the body and she will come by later in the morning and pick it up. I go on with work and pretty much forget about it until about 4:00, when the black orderly...... what's his name?"

"Warren."

"Yeah. Warren comes to me and says there is a man and lady up at the front who wants to pick up a dead cat and he can't find one. So I go up to receiving and here they both are, dressed in black, with this little coffin. I put on my most somber face and take the coffin from them and asked them to wait for just one minute. Then I go back to the cage and there is the fucking cat, standing up looking at me, meowing."

"No shit." Jack stopped his taping again. "What did you do?"

Peter Clause glanced down and shook his head. "I just kind of went nuts, Jack. I mean ... I totally lost it. Here I was a brand new doctor right out of vet school, everybody's watching me to see if I'm any good at all, and I can't even tell if an animal is alive or dead."

"Peter, what did you do?" Jack couldn't hide the concern in his voice.

"I put on a pair of handling gloves and then I quickly strangled the cat and put her in the coffin."

"I don't believe you!"

"Believe me, Jack, I did it. Nobody saw me. Nobody saw the cat alive after I diagnosed it dead. Everybody was looking for a dead cat, and I produced one."

"Good God Almighty Peter, if you believe in Doctor K's theatrical veterinary practice, there are all kinds of things you could have done. Newton would have told them he had given the cat a shot of hormones and brought it back to life, and then charged double for it. What the hell happened to you?"

"I just panicked. It was as if that cat was challenging my professional ability. I didn't look at it any other way. If the cat were alive, it meant that I was so stupid I couldn't even tell if an animal was dead. I am sorry I did it now, but I had no control whatsoever at the time that I did it."

The following week Peter had a chance to make amends; an elderly woman brought her parakeet into the hospital for an examination. The bird, a scraggly light grey color, was so old that the owner could not remember exactly when she came by it. It had become so feeble that, according to the lady, it could no longer hop up on the perch in its cage. Peter asked her to leave it with him for a day or two so he could watch it, but while he was examining it on the day she was to pick it up, the bird died in his hand.

Peter quickly gave it to Warren and sent him to a nearby pet store with money and instructions to purchase a replacement.

"Get one the exact same size and color as Warren, take your time, and just make sure it matches."

Warren was back in less than an hour with a reasonable replica of the original, and Dr. Clause was able to give the woman her bird, totally restored through nutritional therapy with only slight personality changes. Peter paid for the new bird himself and there was no charge to the patient, who was thrilled.

"He may act a little differently," Peter confided to her. "But one thing is for sure: he has to feel better, because he is acting years younger than he did when you brought him in here." Jack scoffed at his friend's tactics, calling them dishonest. Peter said it was some of his best work, and Doctor K called it a wonderful and kind gesture and beamed at Peter's creative genius.

The Kessler philosophy did not always work so smoothly. One day a kind-hearted woman with a station wagon full of children brought a stray cat into the clinic that had been struck by a car in front of her house. The cat's pelvis and left leg had been crushed, and as it had no other injuries, it had been running around in tight circles in the street when the woman wrapped it up in a towel and brought it in. Since the animal had no owner, the sensible thing to have done would have been to put it to sleep immediately. But it was too good of an opportunity for Newton Kessler to demonstrate his technique to his interns.

Once the woman, who lived in a well-to-do neighborhood, had given him her name, address and phone number, the wheels were set into motion. Doctor K told her that the hospital staff would do whatever was necessary to take care of the poor unfortunate animal, and she was invited to check by the following day for a progress report.

It was, indeed, an ideal situation for Doctor K to allow some of his brilliant young interns to perform reconstructive surgery. Andrews and Clause were selected to do the procedure and the two of them worked all afternoon, piecing and pinning the cat's pelvis and leg together; a major surgery procedure producing well over seven hundred dollars of billing.

The following morning a tall, well-dressed gentleman entered the clinic and asked to speak to Doctor Kessler.

"My name is Sullivan, Doctor Kessler. George Sullivan. I'm a lawyer in Tampa and the husband of the Mrs. Sullivan, who brought an injured cat in here yesterday."

"Mrs. Sullivan ... oh yes, that was the poor animal that had been struck by a car, wasn't it?"

"That's the one. I want to settle up with you." The man's abrupt unemotional tone, his introduction of himself as a lawyer, and his use of the words "settle up" sent an immediate warning signal to Newton Kessler.

"Oh, of course Mr. Sullivan," Doctor K beamed, and made a quick chin thrust. "It's a pleasure to meet you, sir." He turned away quickly. "Carol," the doctor said, looking through the receptionist's window. "Would you ask Doctors Andrews and Clause to come to the front for a minute, please." He turned back to his new patient, giving him two quick lip stretches followed by another chin thrust.

"Mr. Sullivan, I just wanted you to meet the two surgeons who saved your cat's life. They operated on him until late last night, and did an incredible job. They had to rebuild his entire pelvic area, and of course the bones in his left leg were shattered into powder. The doctors tell me, however, that they think he's going to be as good as new. Isn't that remarkable?" Here Newton Kessler paused for a reaction, but there was none. Mr. Sullivan stared at him impassively. Dr. K spotted Andrews and Clause coming up the hall. "Here they are now, so I'll let them give you a firsthand prognosis." Newton Kessler smiled at his two interns. "Gentlemen, this is Mr. Sullivan. His wife is the lady who brought in the cat that you two operated on late yesterday. The one with the crushed pelvis and leg," he added as if they had operated on so many they may not remember. "I wanted you to give him a firsthand report."

"That won't be necessary," said the man, holding up his hands. "Just tell me how much you charge to gas an animal?"

"I beg your pardon?" The question had caught Newton Kessler completely off guard, as was reflected by his first eyebrow twitch.

"How much do you charge to gas an animal - you know, to put one to sleep?" The man was serious and Doctor K's face was fast becoming a contorted mass of twitches, stretches, thrusts.

"We charge $20.00, Mr. Sullivan, but I can assure you, sir, that there is no need to..."

"Fair enough," said the man, taking a twenty dollar bill from a silver money clip and slapping it down on the counter with authority. "My wife says she informed you that the cat was not ours. If it had been ours, we would have put it to sleep immediately, so here's twenty dollars to gas that cat. This is the only money that you are ever going get from me, Dr. Kessler ... so my advice to you is to gas that cat." He turned and walked quickly out of the clinic, leaving behind a stunned and twitching Newton Kessler.

After a long silence, Doctor K realized that all activity in the front office had ceased. He shrugged his shoulders and stared at his two interns. "You heard the man, fellows; gas that cat," he said, and walked off down the hall.

But Clause and Andrews could not bring themselves to throw away what they both considered to be "some of their best work." They decided to keep the cat in their apartment to see if it would fully recover. He did so after several months, and by this time they had given him the name "Pins" and he had become a part of their little family.

The intern year with the Kessler Animal Hospital passed quickly, and while Peter had thrived under the tutelage of Doctor K, Jack had grown tired of making the effort required to deal with the public. The facade of the Kessler operation had an air of hucksterism about it that made him uncomfortable. He decided to direct his practice to larger animals. And so while Peter Clause was offered the rare opportunity to become a partner with Newton Kessler in the hospital, Jack had applied for and was accepted for the position of veterinarian for the Aqueduct Race Track in New York.

It was a position that Andrews always believed he had acquired because of the flowery, exaggerated letter of recommendation that Doctor K had written on his behalf. Nevertheless, he was grateful. His separation from Peter had been somber. After living together for eight years, the two had little to say, except for a promise to stay in touch. Jack had packed his Corvette with everything it would hold and had given the rest of his personal effects, including his expensive Fisher stereo, to Peter. As he drove out of the driveway, Peter was standing there with a sad smile on his face. The cat, Pins, was draped around his neck much as a fox fur. They had waved goodbye and Jack had roared off in a cloud of blue smoke.

That is how Jack Andrews had always remembered his best friend Peter Clause. They had never seen each other after that. They had spoken by telephone at least once a month for a year before Peter had been killed. He had been coming back from a weekend fishing trip with friends down in Stuart. The young girl who hit him head on was drunk, pregnant, and unmarried. Apparently, in a fit of depression and despair, she had decided to take her own life by driving head on into the first car she met when she entered the interstate, going in the wrong direction.

Peter's car had been the second one she met; the first one having driven totally off the road in order to avoid her. Predictably, Clause had assumed that the car coming towards him at a high rate of speed had entered the wrong lane by mistake, and instead of leaving the road to get out of its way, he had blinked his lights and blown his horn frantically to warn its driver. At the last minute, she had swerved directly into his path, and they were both killed instantly.

After Peter Clause's death, Jack begin to drink more than just socially. Although he wasn't aware of it initially, Jill had pointed it out to him. He had met her on the first floor of Saks Department Store, where she was working as a sales girl. When they found that they couldn't keep their hands off each other for longer than a few minutes at a time, they decided to live together. She had come to Florida with him for Peter's funeral and was as stunned as he was to discover that he had become his dead friend's sole heir.

Peter Clause's estate included his stock in the Kessler Hospital, which had been valued and insured in the Hospital's key man buy/sell agreement for $500,000; and his house on Treasure Island, which was valued at little more than the $200,000 mortgage Peter owed on it. However, after a home mortgage insurance policy paid off the house loan and a settlement was made on the new Corvette that Peter had been driving, the value of the estate swelled to $800,000. The money was of little consolation to Jack Andrews, who grieved so over the loss of his best friend that he eventually lapsed into a deep period of depression.

He and Jill had loaded up all of Peter's personal effects, including Pins the cat, and returned to New York. Peter's death had reminded Jack Andrews that time was forever fleeting. Life should be lived with urgency on a daily basis. He asked Jill to marry him and she accepted. The ceremony was held in a small 200-year-old church in Jill's hometown of Saratoga. Only their parents and a few friends were in attendance. After a brief honeymoon in Lake Placid, Jack reported back to Aqueduct and threw himself into his work in a desperate attempt to take his mind off the loss of his best friend.

It didn't work. After several months he gave notice to track management that he wanted to return to Florida. Because of his association with Aqueduct, he was offered a position by the American Trotter Association to serve as the veterinarian at their winter training track in Orlando. He accepted. The ghost of Peter Clause had called him back to Florida.

Between his position in Orlando and the rapidly growing thoroughbred industry in nearby Ocala, Andrews' business flourished. He soon became known as the Florida expert on thoroughbred insemination. Because of a basic belief that he had not earned his inherited wealth from Peter Clause, he had invested the money in tax-free bonds with instruction to his broker to reinvest the income. He and Jill were happy in their relationship with each other. She had adjusted to the idea that she would never bear children, and while he was excited about the idea of adopting, she was hesitant. It would be a major change in their lifestyle and she wasn't sure she was ready to make it immediately. Jack understood. He was certain that his wife had not entirely given up hope of conceiving on her own.

A new dark shadow was slowly creeping across their sunny existence, however. As always, it progressed slowly, never seen or acknowledged by its victims until it was too late. It was alcoholism, and it enslaved Jack Andrews, causing him to lose it all.

He had fallen into the habit of meeting the same group of friends for drinks each afternoon after work and soon he found himself going out of his way to have lunch at the club so he could have a martini or two. The martini lunches exacerbated the problem dramatically, and within a short period of time, Jack Andrews could no longer deny that he had a problem.

Jill asked him to quit drinking entirely just to prove that he could do it, but Jack Andrews quickly found out that an alcoholic can't quit drinking for anybody but himself. He can't stop because his wife asks him to do so. He can't stop because the rest of his family or his pastor asks him to do so. Nor can he stop because a judge orders him to do so. Jack discovered that he could only stop drinking when he decided to quit for himself. And as with most alcoholics, he had to sink close to the bottom of his existence before making the required personal commitment.

Even after Jill left him, he continued to drink. Even after the accident, in which he totaled his car and subsequently lost his license, he continued to drink. It wasn't until his friend, Malcolm Briggs, struck and killed a child while he was riding with him that Jack Andrews saw he had to change.

Malcolm Briggs was a third-generation cattle rancher from Central Florida. He was loud and boisterous, but basically a generous and good-natured fellow. Several years earlier, he had purchased a large horse ranch in Ocala and, using Jack Andrew's knowledge and contacts within the industry, Malcolm had initiated a selective thoroughbred breeding program that had already produced two major winners at the track.

The Brigg's Farm thoroughbreds were quickly making a name for themselves and Malcolm Briggs gave most of the credit to his good friend Jack Andrews. So, when Andrews' license was suspended for driving while intoxicated, Malcolm Briggs quickly volunteered to become his chauffeur.

"Hell, Jack," Malcolm had pointed out to him as they were having a couple of drinks one afternoon. "You are working on my horses most of the time anyway." It was true that Andrews did spend much of his time working for Briggs' Farms, and so a deal was made. The relationship had worked well for several weeks, with Malcolm willing to take his doctor friend wherever he wished to go. But then, one day in late September, as the two men were returning from a trip to Ocala, it happened.

They had spent the morning at the Briggs Farm and had stopped for lunch at the Brahma Restaurant, a downtown Ocala landmark. They were both well on their way into their third martini when Jack decided to call his office. He discovered that a champion trotter mare was about to foal early and was apparently having complications. He was needed in Orlando immediately.

In later years he would remember little about the accident. Malcolm was driving fast and talking about rodeo riders. They had just entered the city limits of Leesburg when the small white football with two black circles on each end of it bounced out into the street in front of them. It came from between two parked cars on the right side of the street and it rolled to a stop on the road's yellow centerline.

"Watch out, Malcolm!" he had remembered shouting, but he didn't mean watch out for the ball; he meant to watch out for someone or something to come after it. Some little fellow in a red shirt and blue baseball cap, whose

104

concentration was so totally directed towards retrieving that white and black ball that he wasn't even aware of where he was. Malcolm, also concentrating on the ball, had swerved in close to the cars on the right to avoid it and was so confident that he had more than enough room to miss it that he had hardly slowed the car.

During the investigation and the short segment of the trial that followed, Malcolm Briggs swore that he never did see the child that ran in front of him. He just felt his car hit something and heard his friend Jack Andrews scream. The reenactment of the accident at the trial and the sober objective assessment of his own gross negligence and guilt were too much for Malcolm Briggs. After the second day of his trial for manslaughter, a dejected and depressed Malcolm Briggs put a pistol to his head and killed himself. The next day Jack Andrews joined Alcoholics Anonymous and commenced his new life of abstinence.

****

Chapter 8
Minor Surgery
Surgery involving little risk to the life of the patient; *specifically*: an operation on the superficial structures of the body or a manipulative procedure that does not involve a serious risk

Dr. Jackson L. Andrews worked quickly and professionally. He rubbed the entire genital area with an alcohol disinfectant and then carefully administered several injections around the base of the scrotum. The first shot of Xylocaine was to deaden the entire area. The second injection of Epinephrine a few seconds later would constrict the blood vessels and reduce the amount of bleeding.

While waiting for the drugs to totally take effect, Andrews went into the bathroom and scrubbed his hands and arms with an antiseptic soap he had removed from his bag, along with a pair of surgical gloves. He retrieved a new safety razor from the medicine cabinet and, wetting a new wash cloth with hot water, he grabbed a large clean bath towel out of the linen closet and returned to the bed.

He folded the towel once and then, with a great deal of effort, he rolled the big man over on his side. Placing the towel under the congressman's buttock, he rolled him back over onto it.

Next, he washed and lathered the big man's privates with the same antiseptic soap he had used on his own hands. Then, slowly and painstakingly, he shaved Cowans' entire scrotum area and once again applied a liberal quantity of the antiseptic. Now he organized the necessary instruments next to the two empty Champagne glasses on the night table beside the bed. Carefully he dipped each instrument into the antiseptic solution and then pulling on the pair of surgical gloves. He was ready to begin.

With a scalpel he made a small incision about half way down Cowans' scrotum. A few drops of blood fell on the towel as he attempted to work one of the big man's testicles out through his incision. It would not fit. Andrews carefully enlarged the incision and was now able to push one through the opening. Using a heavyweight degradable suture thread, he tightly tied off the spermatic cord attached to the testicle. Then, using his sharp snips, he severed the cord just below his knot. There were several more drops of blood, which he quickly blotted up. He laid the severed testicle on the bath towel and repeated the procedure with the second one.

When both had been removed, he pinched the loose skin of the scrotum together and, using his tightest stitching, he closed the incision. He repeated the antiseptic treatment and then, folding Phillip Cowans' severed parts up in the towel, he placed it into his bag along with his instruments. Jack Andrews assessed his work. Clean and neat; just a small amount of bleeding. As Peter Clause would have said," Maybe some of my best work," he whispered softly to himself.

Now a shiver ran through his body and he became aware of how cold the room had become. He pulled the covers up over his patient and hurriedly closed the sliding glass doors. Once again, he checked the big man's pulse. It was stronger and his breathing was returning to normal.

Andrews backed away from the bed and studied the resting form of Congressman Phillip Cowans for several minutes. He was no longer a creature to be hated. He was no longer a fierce apelike form to be feared. There would be no more love-sick girls crying out their despair in the middle of the night; no more broken hearted, compromised wives made to look foolish when their sudden interest in politics was dashed with an intentional snub by their carnal hero. And there would be no more despondent husbands, cuckold and disadvantaged by a roving and handsome womanizer.

Andrews pulled the covers up closer to the congressman's chin. The womanizing creature was now gone from the scene. It had been vanquished by the scalpel and replaced with a quiet, peacefully sleeping patient who was now convalescing from some minor surgery; a patient who would, without a doubt, survive this ordeal and go on to prosper; a patient who would lead a comfortable and productive life and a patient who, if Peter Clause's theory was correct, was going to be "a lot nicer critter to be around."

****

Chapter 9
Damages
Problems that are caused by a mistake, wrong action, etc. bad or harmful effects on a situation, a person's reputation, etc.

Sunrise that Saturday morning in Minneapolis was nothing more than a gradual graying of the darkness. The heavy snowfall from the evening before had covered the entire city with a soft, deep blanket of white. While cars on side streets glided slowly between the massive six-foot banks of ice and snow, traffic out on the plowed-cleaned highways sped along at a normal pace. Robert Warner was always amazed at how quickly the Twin Cities dispatched large amounts of snow from its major road systems. He rode slouched down on the passenger's side of Douglas Hawkins's big Lincoln Town Car. Other than the faint sound of a classical radio station, the two men rode along in silence.

As a matter of convenience this morning, Warner was accompanying his lawyer friend into the city on business. The two men had spoken little to each other since Hawkins' attempt at early morning humor had failed. He had called Warner's room on a house phone upon his arrival at the hotel.

"Hello, Mr. Warner," he had said, using a semi-British accent.

"Yes." Warner had been fooled.

"Mr. Warner, this is Emerson at the desk, sir. I regret to inform you that the American Express number your friend left to cover your room expense was summarily cancelled by your wife during the night. I know this is an imposition, sir, but I'm afraid we will have to ask you to get your ass out of the hotel immediately."

"Not funny, Doug!" Warner shouted before slamming down the phone. The two men shook hands in the lobby, but Warner had not returned Hawkins' smile, and they had been driving in silence for ten minutes.

Robert Warner felt terrible. He had found it impossible to sleep the night before. And because of his fatigue, frazzled nerves, and shaking hands, he had cut himself badly while shaving that morning. He still wore the little pennant of toilet tissue that he had pressed against his chin to stop the bleeding. Because he had returned from his week in Dallas without clean clothes, he still wore the rumpled grey suit and wrinkled blue shirt from the day before. Warner's greatest discomfort, however, came from his injured knee, which had swollen to such an extent during the night that he could no longer bend it.

"Hey, Rob, have you heard the story about the teacher giving a lesson to her first grade class on word association?" Doug Hawkins was determined to lighten the mood. Warner did not respond.

"She said, 'all right now, boys and girls, we are going to go around the room, and when I say a noun, you say back to me an adjective that you think best describes my word. O.K. Betty ... ocean?' and Betty said `deep.' And the teacher

110

said, 'that's good, Betty. And now, Katherine, it is your turn ... sky?' and Katherine said 'Blue.' Then the teacher said, 'that's good, Katherine, and now Johnny ... baby?' and Johnny said, 'Beautiful.' The teacher was impressed with the boy's sensitivity. 'Well, I think it is just wonderful, Johnny, that you think a baby is beautiful.'

'But I don't think a baby is beautiful,' said Johnny.

'Then why did you say beautiful?' asked the teacher.

'Because,' said Johnny, 'the other night at dinner, my big sister told my father she was going to have a baby and my Dad said, 'Beautiful ... fucking beautiful!''

Hawkins threw back his head and laughed while Warner smiled ever so slightly.

"Come on, Robert, cheer up. We are going to straighten this mess out. She just got the jump on us."

"I still can't believe this is Helen's idea." Warner stared blankly out the car window. "It's too vindictive, too hostile."

"Let me tell you something, Robert, my boy: all women can be vindictive and hostile. When it comes to real cruelty, bet on the women every time." Hawkins turned the radio off. "Remember our golf buddy, Sam Whitney?"

Warner nodded.

"Well, if you remember, when he and Alice separated, she just took the children and relocated to Chicago without any warning. She filed for divorce and wouldn't let Sam see the kids for months. It was driving him crazy. Then one day, out of the blue, she calls him up and says, 'The kids want to see you, and I am planning to go out of town this weekend, so why don't you come to Chicago and spend some time with them.'"

"Well, of course, Sam was delighted, so he flies to Chicago, checks into a hotel, and spends the weekend with his kids. But when he comes back home Sunday, guess what he finds out that Alice had done with her weekend out of town? She had flown here from Chicago, met a moving company at Sam's house on Saturday, opened it up with her keys, and removed all of the furnishings. She cleaned it out entirely! Poor Sam comes home after spending the weekend with his kids in Chicago and the house is empty, just as yours is now. The only things Alice left him were his gun collection and his clothes."

"I'm not sure Helen left my clothes." Warner had been listening attentively. "But it does sound as though she could have been talking to Alice Whitney. What have you done for Sam?"

"What do you mean, what have we done for him?"

"Well, did you get his furniture back?"

"No, but I think we are going to work out a deal to allow him to keep his clothes and some of the guns," Hawkins smiled.

"No, seriously, Doug, what have you done for him?" Warner was uncomfortable with the similarities between Sam Whitney's situation and his own.

"Seriously? I've advised him not to go to Chicago anymore, without changing the locks on his doors. I don't think we are going to get any of the furniture back, but I think Sam will get to keep the house, which of course has been in his family for a hundred years anyway. The point is, Robert,

112

whoever said that women are the fairer sex didn't know what the hell they were talking about."

"Hey, I agree with that; in fact, that was said by a woman as part of an overall propaganda program to keep men off guard." Warner spoke softly, as if talking to himself. His spirits had improved upon hearing of someone else's tribulations. "Misery loves company," he said softly as he shook his head.

Doug Hawkins glanced over at him, smiled knowingly, and continued on with the conversation.

"Can you imagine how an army of women would function?" he asked Warner. "The one thing we know for sure is that they would not spend a lot of time worrying about their prisoners. The fact is, they would take no prisoners."

Warner nodded his head in agreement.

"Just stop and think, Rob. Of the recent wars fought in the world, the losers were countries ruled by men who stupidly underestimated the ability of their women adversaries. Pakistan found out that Mrs. Gandhi was a long way removed from Mahatma Gandhi. The Jews whip the Arabs about every three to five years, but the only time they did it in seven days, Golda Meir was calling the shots. Then look at those clowns in Argentina who thought Maggie Thatcher would just sit back and let them take over the Falkland Islands without a fight.

"It seems to me that history has offered man a valuable lesson which he has, for the most part, chosen to ignore, and that is: don't piss a woman off."

The two men rode on in silence for several minutes before Hawkins spoke again. "Rob, what do you think you did to piss Helen off?"

Warner was taken aback by the question, but he had already decided to tell his friend all the facts, as he understood them, even though he was uncomfortable doing so.

"I've had a girlfriend for the last couple of years. She lives in Atlanta, but she was with me last week in Dallas, and Helen must have found out."

Hawkins was unaffected by the confession. His eyes squinted as though he were in deep thought, and his silence made Warner uneasy. "What do you think my first step ought to be?" he asked.

Hawkins glanced over at him. "Rob, when we get to the club, I'm going to put you in one of the office suites that are available for members and their guests. This annual board meeting I have to attend won't last much more than two hours, and what I want you do while I'm in there is to call all your good friends."

"My good friends?" Warner acted startled.

"Yeah, just your best friends. If you have any doubt as to whether they would be loyal to you or to Helen, don't call them." Hawkins slowed the car and changed lanes. He glanced back at Warner's troubled expression. "Call just the ones you know you can count on. See if you can find out what's been going on. Can you handle that assignment?"

"Right," mumbled Warner, staring blankly out the window again.

"Also," Hawkins had another idea, "since all your banking is at the Commerce Bank, you could try to catch Walter Brooks at home. I'm sure he'll know if Helen closed out your accounts at the bank."

"What do you think I should tell him?" Warner was becoming unsure of himself and this new insecurity startled the lawyer.

"Hell, just tell him the truth. Maybe if she hasn't transferred the money out of the bank yet, we can prevent her from doing so. It's for sure that Brooks will side with you if he knows Helen intends to move the company's banking business elsewhere."

They were downtown now, and Hawkins swung the big car off the street and into a parking garage adjacent to the Downtown Club, an elegant old brick building which sat on the edge of a large park. The parking attendant stepped out of his booth and, upon seeing the sticker on the windshield, waved them through.

"The fact is ,Rob, you should ask Brooks to meet us at the bank in about two hours."

"Today is Saturday."

"So..."

"So, I don't think Walter Brooks wants to go to the bank during the week, much less on a weekend." Warner sounded as though he was uncomfortable with the idea of meeting the banker.

Hawkins stared across the car at his client. It was hard to believe how passive his friend had become.

"Rob, if he is about to lose one of his biggest accounts, Walter Brooks will come to the bank whenever you ask him to. Believe me, he will. This way you would be able to sign a stop payment order or whatever he will want you to do to justify his not paying funds out next week." Hawkins parked the Lincoln in a vacant space near the elevators and patted his friend on the knee. "The one thing you don't want to do is call any more of Helen's friends. No more calls to Rita Ross and Florence Carter. Call your friends, instead. What's the name of your secretary?"

"Mary... Mary Webster."

"Yeah, call Mary Webster. See what she can tell you. Also, call anybody at the plant that you feel would be closer to you than to Helen."

Once again, Warner had a strange expression on his face.

"What's the matter?" the lawyer asked.

"I'll have to think about that for a minute."

"Why, isn't there anybody in your organization that you are closer to than your wife?"

"Yes, I think so." Warner said with great uncertainty.

"Good then, call them." Hawkins turned the car engine off and the two men got out.

"Rob?"

"What?"

"You've got some toilet paper stuck on your chin."

"Yeah... I know."

"Rob?" Doug asked again.

"Yeah."

"Don't tell anybody, except Walter Brooks, about what has happened to you. Just ask questions and take notes. We will kick ass later, all right?"

"All right, I won't tell anybody."

****

Chapter 10
Analyzation
Proof of a mathematical proposition by assuming the result and deducing a valid
statement by a series of reversible steps

The temporary office suites that the Downtown Club
maintained for its members' use were spacious and
elegant. Robert Warner picked out one with a corner view
of the park. Although the view this morning was limited to
just a vast openness of white, the snow's reflected light
illuminated the room, making it brighter and more
cheerful than the others.

Warner made himself at home, opening his briefcase and
spreading its contents out on top of the beautiful
rosewood desk. He found a yellow legal pad in the desk
drawer along with several well-sharpened pencils.
Quickly, he jotted down a list of names he would need to
call. "His good friends, his best friends," Hawkins had
called them; people who would be loyal to him. The list
was short.

His first call was to the company's comptroller, Ken Kiser.
No one answered. Mary Webster, his secretary, was the
second name on the list. Warner found her home number
in the directory and dialed it carefully. He patiently let the
phone ring for two minutes before hanging up.

Then, following Hawkins's advice, he made the next call to Walter Brooks, President of the Minneapolis Commerce Bank. The phone was answered by Mrs. Brooks, a friendly and cheerful person, who informed Warner that her husband was playing in a bridge tournament.

"I don't expect him back home until late this afternoon, unless, of course, they lose in the first round this morning. Is there some message I could give him, Mr. Warner?"

Yeah, thought Warner to himself, *tell him my wife is trying to ruin me financially and I desperately need his help.*

"Yes, Mrs. Brooks, would you tell him that I have some urgent business to discuss with him before Monday morning." Warner made an effort to keep his voice relaxed and confident.

"Of course, can he call you at home, Mr. Warner?" She was most obliging and sounded sincerely interested in his problem.

"No, I'm going to be moving around quite today, so it would be better if I just try to call him back later..." He reconsidered. "But, let me leave a number for now, just in case he should come home early. I will be at the Downtown Club for most of the morning." Warner read the seven digit number off the desk phone and then thanked the friendly woman. He thought of the old saying his father had told him, "If you ever want to meet a nice woman, follow a son-of-a-bitch home." He smiled to himself. There was no doubt that some people would think that statement typified Robert L. Warner just as well as Walter Brooks.

He dialed Mary Webster's number once again. This time someone answered immediately.

"Hello."

"Hello, Mary?"

"No, this is her sister, Irene. Mary's not home... may I take a message for her?" The voice was questioning.

"Irene, this is Robert Warner. Will Mary be home soon?"

"Oh hello, Mr. Warner." She was obviously surprised. "No sir, she is still in Madison."

"Madison?" Warner was puzzled.

"Yes sir, she did as you suggested; she went to Wisconsin for a couple of weeks to visit her daughter and that new grandbaby. I just came by to feed the cat and water her plants."

"For a couple of *weeks*?" Warner failed to hide his astonishment.

"Yes sir, but I thought it was all your idea."

"Well... I've... been... out of town."

"That's what Mary said... she said that you were in Texas, or someplace out west, and you just called in last week and told your wife that you thought Mary should take some extra time off to be with her new granddaughter. She was thrilled to pieces by your doing that, Mr. Warner."

Warner had no response.

"Now, if you need to talk with Mary, I can give you my niece's number and you can call her there."

"Please, if you wouldn't mind... I just want to ask her a few questions." Warner was recovering his composure. "I was just checking in to see how everything was going... is the baby doing well?"

"Oh yes sir, she is doing just great. They've named her Laura Anne. Isn't that beautiful? "

"Yes, it's pretty... Ah... Irene, what day did Mary go to Madison? Do you remember?" Warner was trying to put the pieces of the puzzle together.

"She left Wednesday morning. I took her to the airport. Here's the number, Mr. Warner." She read the number to him several times as he wrote it down on his pad.

"Well, thank you again, Mr. Warner, for being so nice to Mary. Our family appreciates you; we all think she's lucky to have you for her boss."

"Yes, of course. Thank you, Irene ... goodbye."

"Goodbye," she said.

Warner hung up the phone and unconsciously dialed Ken Kiser's home number once again. Hawkins had made him feel uneasy about whom he should call, but he had already decided that if his long time accountant, Ken Kiser, didn't qualify, no one did.

He had called Ken at the plant from Dallas last Tuesday. They had discussed the company's year-end statement and tax return. He attempted to remember the conversation. Ken had been relaxed and jovial. In fact, he had made a comment about Warner developing a Texas accent. Surely, he could not be part of this conspiracy.

"Hello." Warner recognized the voice immediately.

"Hello, Ken, this is Robert Warner," he said excitedly.

"Hello, chief."

"Ken, what the hell is going on?"

"Beats me, boss, but I told my wife when they fired me yesterday that I was sure that you didn't know anything about it."

"Fired you? Ken, who fired you? Was it Helen?"

"No sir, I never saw her. It was some guy named Henderson, who said he was the new plant manager. He told me that the business had been sold and that the new management no longer had a need for my services. He was real nice about it. He just asked me to clean out my desk and get off the premises immediately, and he gave me a severance check for $9,000."

"What did you do?"

"Well, I told him that I wasn't going anywhere until I talked to you, and then in the next minute there were these two security guards in my office who said they were to escort me to my car."

"Ken, did you notice what bank your check was drawn on?"

"It's an ADP payroll check as we use. Only it was drawn on a First National Bank account downtown. Have you been to the plant yet, boss?"

"Yeah, I went by there last night, but the guard on the gate wouldn't let me in."

"You're putting me on."

122

"Nope, I wish I were. But it's a fact. He said there was new ownership."

"Did you see the new fence?"

"Yeah, when did that go up?"

"Believe it or not, they didn't start putting those posts in concrete footers until Thursday and when I went to work Friday morning, the damn thing was finished. They worked all through the night. It was unbelievable."

"Ken, how could anyone buy Warner Chemical when Helen and I jointly own 100% of the stock?"

"I don't know sir, but the word is that Mrs. Warner held a stockholders meeting while you were out of town and voted to sell the plant and all of the assets. I don't think she could sell the corporation without your approval."

"What the hell are you talking about, Ken? She can't sell the corporate assets without my approval..." There was a long pause. The accountant said nothing and Warner continued. "What I can't figure out is who would participate in the purchase? Who would be the buyer in a contested sale? I mean, it's crazy."

"Nobody seems to know exactly who the buyer is, sir. In fact, whoever it is apparently doesn't want to change anything. I think I am the only employee who was laid off."

"Well, you're not laid off as far as I'm concerned, Ken. And as soon as I straighten this mess out you will be back at work, believe me."

"Well, good luck chief. I hope you can work it out." His accountant did not sound too optimistic, and his lack of enthusiasm made Warner uncomfortable.

"Yes, well, I'll be back in touch shortly."

"Goodbye, sir."

"Goodbye." Warner hung up the phone and jotted some notes on the legal pad. He fought hard to overcome the urge to rush out of the room and find Hawkins, wherever he could be, and tell him of this latest development. His wife had sold his business. He was sure that she couldn't do it legally, but she had nevertheless done it anyway. How could this be happening to him? It had been his idea to make Helen president of their company two years ago. It was part of the overall promotional program that he had developed to attract more attention to the company to enhance a possible public stock offering. But even as president of the company, she couldn't convey assets of the corporation without a corporate resolution of some kind, and that would require the stockholders approval. How could this have been done without his knowledge? He was certain that it could not have been done, and he needed to talk to Hawkins.

Now, Warner dialed Adrian Kilmer's number in Atlanta. For years, because he frequently called Adrian collect, Warner had paid her phone bill. Now, however, in light of the recent developments, it had little consequences.

"Hello." Adrian sounded sleepy but came to life immediately as she accepted the charges. "Oh my God, Robby, I'm so glad you called. I've been going crazy trying to figure out how to contact you." Her voice was full of excitement.

"Why? What's the matter?"

"Well, when I got home from Dallas yesterday ... there were all these boxes stacked up in my garage."

"What kind of boxes?"

"UPS boxes Robby; UPS packages. You know how I get samples for my business here at the house all the time. I just leave my garage door unlocked and the UPS driver always puts them inside if I'm not home. Anyway, I got home last night, and there were five huge boxes stacked up in the garage and ... well, they had your return address on them and I just assumed you had sent me some major present ... but when I opened them up, they were full of your clothes."

"My clothes?" The pencil's soft lead point broke as he pressed it into the legal pad.

"Yes, aren't you missing your clothes?" Adrian was surprised at his disbelief.

"Well, I'm locked out of my house, so I didn't know ..." Warner could feel the knot tightening again in his stomach.

"Jesus, Robby ... locked out of your house ... Helen must have found out about us ... huh?" Warner stared blankly out the window into the blinding whiteness of the snow and said nothing.

"Robby, what are you going to do? Have you talked to her about it?" Adrian was whispering.

"No ... I can't find her. I think she's left town."

"Do you want me to send these boxes back to you? I could address them to your business."

"No! Don't send them to the office." Warner shouted. "I'm having some trouble getting in there right now, also. Just wait until Monday, Adrian, and I'll have a better idea of what's going on."

"Robby, are you all right?"

"Shit no, I'm not all right! You wouldn't believe the things Helen has done to me ... but it's a long story. Listen, Adrian, I've got to call some other people right now, but I will call you back this evening and we can talk ... okay?"

"Okay."

After he hung up the phone, Robert Warner could feel the surge of adrenalin taking over his body. It propelled him up out of his chair and made him pace back and forth within the office. If Adrian had already received his clothes, they must have been sent to Atlanta well over a week ago. Perhaps, even the day after he'd left for Dallas. Helen had been busy; extremely busy, indeed.

Something else that was becoming painfully obvious to him was the fact that this plan he now found himself caught up in was much too intricate and involved to have been conceived on the spur of the moment.

This was not just the spontaneous reaction of a jealous wife. On the contrary, this was a scheme that must have required weeks or even months of preparation. How long, he wondered, had his wife plotted against him? How long had she been living with him, all the while scheming? How long had she been patiently playing the role of wife and business partner, all the while arranging to strike this savage blow that now had him so completely traumatized, he had lost his ability to reason.

Oh, it was a masterful plan indeed, Warner thought to himself. There was perhaps only one flaw in Helen's calculations. She may have underestimated his reaction to such an attack. He had experienced the fear and bewilderment that accompanied the instant loss of identity and self-esteem. But his fear had now turned into humiliation. And it was a humiliation greater than one of just being made to look foolish. It was the total humiliation of being helplessly controlled and manipulated by outside forces.

It was here, with the imposed humiliation, that he felt his wife had gone too far. Robert L. Warner was too proud and much too vain and egotistical to handle the massive amounts of shame to which he now found himself subjected. He had always been aware of his anger, from the moment he discovered his car missing at the airport, but now it was out of control and he found himself seething with a rage that made him irrational. A cornered, frightened animal, when it has no other defense, will attack; and for the first time in his life, Robert Warner was thinking about killing somebody.

The phone on the desk rang, startling him back to reality. He walked over and picked it up.

"Hello," he snarled.

"Hello, Mr. Warner?"

"Yes."

"Walter Brooks here, Mr. Warner. What's on your mind?"

****

Chapter 11
Accounting
An instance of applied accounting or of the settling or presenting of accounts

The Minneapolis Commerce Bank had employed Walter Brooks for twenty years before making him President of the bank. It was a position he had held for over five years. He was a short, pudgy man with a severely receding hairline and a thin-lipped mouth that few people had ever seen smile. His years of dealing with those, asking for favors, had taken its toll on any humility he may have once possessed. Although his arrogance and pomposity had cost the bank many clients during his five-year tenure as president, Walter Brooks remained unaware of such things. He did this by not asking questions to which he would not want to know the answers.

Warner Chemical had been one of those larger commercial accounts that had just walked out of his bank one day last week, without comment. Despite the fact that he was friendlier with Robert Warner than most of his bank's customers, he had nevertheless procrastinated against contacting him for fear of finding out that perhaps he, Walter Brooks, could have been part of the explanation.

Today he was discussing the situation with Robert Warner under terms he much preferred. Warner had contacted him, and even though it meant coming into his office on a Saturday afternoon, he was much more comfortable being the requested than the requester; particularly if there was any chance of getting one of the bank's largest commercial accounts back in good order. He scowled at the open file folder on his desk for some time before looking up at the two men seated across from him.

"You're right, Mr. Warner, she closed them all out last week; but they are all one-signature, joint accounts and I can't see where she did anything improper."

Robert Warner sat quietly, nodding his head in tiny little movements signifying that he understood. His rumpled clothes and disheveled hair gave him an unusual unkempt appearance. The banker noticed the deep circles under the man's eyes and thought how much he had aged since he had last seen him. He was obviously extremely tired and though he leaned forward in his chair as if he were preparing to speak, he said nothing. The lawyer spoke instead.

"Can you provide Mr. Warner with copies of last month's transactions, so we can get an idea of the cash flow, how much money was involved, and where it could have gone since the account has been closed? For instance, did Mrs. Warner open another account here in the bank?" Doug Hawkins was aware that the banker would not be required by law to answer his question and that any answer would be a courtesy gesture on the part of the pudgy little man.

"No, I am sorry to say she did not. There was a large deposit made into the Warner Chemical Account two weeks ago for $20,200,000 and it looks as if that it was a cashier's check from Chase Bank and the reference note on the check just says "purchase of assets." But last Monday,

129

all these funds left our bank. The nearest I can tell, your wife came in last Monday and went to her ... your ... safe deposit box, which we now know is empty. Then, she had a cashier's check made payable to her for the total of $23,324,034. That was the exact balance in the account at the time and in effect closed your company account with us."

"Do you usually pay out on million dollar checks without some sort of verification?" Hawkins was leaning forward with his elbows on the banker's desk.

"Normally, no, but Fay Wilson, who runs the clearing office upstairs, has a note in the file that says that your wife called her last week to ask about closing out the account and they discussed what the current balance was and what the exact amount of the check should be, so there were no questions on it when it came through, and it was paid."

The lawyer was making notes in a little black notebook while Robert Warner continued the short jerky bobbing of his head.

"How about my personal checking account, the one that she does not sign on; how did she get that money?" Warner's voice was tired.

"All we can tell you about that, Mr. Warner, is that someone drew the $300.00 daily maximum out of that account every day for nine straight days. Whoever did that had to have your cash card and know what your personal identity number was."

"PIN?" the lawyer asked as he turned towards his client. "Did Helen know your personal identity number, Rob?"

"Hell, I guess she did." There was a long pause before Doug Hawkins asked another question.

"That large deposit check that was drawn on Chase Bank for the purchase of Warner's assets - is there no other note or reference on the deposit?"

"Well, it appears that Chase was facilitating the purchase of Warner Chemical's assets for another chemical company called Helena. They didn't hide that fact, and you can see on our copy of the check, there at the bottom, that they referenced the buyer right next to their account number." The banker handed the photocopy of the check to Doug Hawkins, who laid it on the desktop in front of Warner.

Robert Warner stared at the slip of paper, moving his head in owl-like circles as if trying to bring it into better focus. The lawyer picked up the check copy again and studied it closely for several seconds before turning to his client. "Robert," he asked, "who is Helena Chemical Corporation?"

"I've never heard of them," Warner said, shaking his head.

"Beautiful," whispered Doug Hawkins softly. "Fucking beautiful."

****

Book II
Chapter 12
Rebirth
A period of new life, growth, or activity

The day was brilliant. The high-pressure area that shifted from the mainland down into the Bahamas over the weekend brought with it cooler temperatures and a bright, clear sky.

The tiny land mass that was Walkers Cay rose up out of the shimmering, turquoise water, appearing as a ship's forecastle. To the pilot of the red and white single engine plane banking hard into a final approach turn, the 69-acre island had always resembled a small stationary aircraft carrier.

Jackson Andrews eased the throttle back and added more flaps while concentrating on the tip of the little airstrip. Dredged out into the water and sea-walled with rock and shell, the short, narrow runway resembled a disfigured diving board protruding off the north end of the island. The broken pockmarked pavement, treacherous and unforgiving, rushed up to meet him. Only his night-time carrier landings off the coast of Vietnam, were scarier to Andrews. He remembered when the Marine Corps wired up all the F-4 Phantom pilots in his squadron to determine the amount of stress they were under when they went in over the target. To everyone's surprise (except the pilots), the most stressful part of the flight was their return to their carriers at night. The ship would be tactical, running without any lights whatsoever, and as a pilot approached, it became a moving big black hole in the ocean, devoid of any moon or star light reflection off the water. The Phantom just dropped down into the black hole forever and the darkness came up around the aircraft, filling the pilot's peripheral vision with blackness just before the jarring contact with the up-rushing deck.

Andrews, as had many pilots landing at Walkers, sensed the pressure to set the plane down as quickly as possible. His initial fly-over the little island had confirmed his hunch that there would be little activity at the resort this time of year. Less than a dozen boats were moored in the marina, and only two aircraft were parked on the apron near the hotel. It would be a perfect place for him to drop out of sight for a few days and review his options. He pushed the plane's nose down a fraction more and cut the throttle further.

Walkers Cay was the northernmost island in the Bahamas chain. Perched on the edge of the continental shelf where a fishing boat could be in deep water within minutes, the small island was famous with divers and sports fisherman alike.

For the past ten years, Jack and Jill Andrews had spent much of their summers here. They usually lived aboard Sam Wadley's big Hatteras or, on occasion, in the island's only hotel. An accomplished diver, Andrews was extremely knowledgeable about the local waters and he recognized the reefs and large coral heads that darkened the blue water around the little island. He had never seen Walkers in January, however, and was fascinated with how the crisp clear air accentuated the blueness of the water. It was truly a beautiful sight.

He pulled the yoke back and flared the Cherokee out, right over the seawall. The wheels touched down less than 100 feet from the start of the runway and Andrews pulled the throttle all the way back. With his toes, he felt above the rudder pedals for the brakes. The little plane slowed as it bounced along the bumpy runway, past the generator plant and the unkempt tennis court, towards the hotel at the other end of the airstrip.

At once, Jack Andrews felt safe. He loved Walkers Cay. It had always been a home away from home to him, and now, seemingly deserted in the off-season, it offered him the comfortable sensation of seclusion.

Only Billy Evans and Sam Wadley were aware he was here. He had called Billy the day before, on Saturday afternoon, right after completing his lecture at the Freeport seminar. They had talked for an hour, with Andrews telling his friend all the details he could remember about his Friday night trauma. It had been a much-needed catharsis for him. Billy had listened in silence while Andrews poured out his confession.

"I called Sam first, Billy," he explained after he had talked to his friend for over fifty minutes. "Only because Sam is my lawyer and I think I need some good legal advice. No one was home, so you've had to listen to all this shit."

"Come on, Jack," Billy sounded offended. "As you have said many times yourself, 'good friends are those who listen, don't judge, and do what they can to help out. Any friend will help you move, but only a great friend will help you move a body.'"

Andrews smiled at his friend's turning his own words back on him. Although Billy Evans sounded calm and collected, Andrews could sense a certain tension in his voice, particularly after he described the surgical procedure he had performed on Phillip Cowans. There had been a long pause, after which Billy had asked him for his phone number there at the hotel.

"Jackie boy, you just take it easy and relax. I need a little time to check this thing out. I'll get together with Sam and we'll get right back to you ..." Another pause. "You sure you wouldn't want to have some company down there?"

"No ... Don't worry about me drinking again, Billy." Andrews saw immediately what his friend was concerned about. It was the AA instinct.

"Believe me, and tell that to Sam when you talk to him. Tell him not to worry, I got the drinking back under control."

He had hung up and reluctantly reported back to the seminar to participate in a one-hour panel discussion on thoroughbred breeding techniques, after which he had gone back to his hotel room and collapsed into bed before dark.

The next day was Sunday. He had read through all the newspapers at the hotel, half expecting to see headlines reading "U.S. Congressman hospitalized" with a picture of Big Phillip and a story about his admission to an Orlando hospital, but there had been nothing. The main story in all the papers was the Friday night freeze and all the damage it had done to the citrus crop.

After the Sunday breakfast meeting, the seminar was officially over. Andrews had checked out at the desk, returned to his room to finish packing his bags, and was just about to call for a cab to take him to the airport, when the phone rang. It was Sam Wadley.

"My god, you *are* at this number. I thought Billy was hallucinating," Wadley said, trying to be light.

"Hi, Sam. You mean you had *hoped* Billy was hallucinating?" Andrews had said, sheepishly.

"I'm going to tell it to you as it is, Jack. If you did to Phillip Cowans what you told Billy you did to him, it's the best kept secret in town."

"Well, I'm afraid I did it, Sam. Am I in big trouble?"

"Damn if I know. If Cowans says you did it, I think you're in big trouble." The lawyer paused, as if collecting his thoughts. "You know, we can't fall back on a crime of passion defense, Jack. Now, maybe if you were an ophthalmologist or a dermatologist, we could, but hell, you're a horse veterinarian. You did what you do best. And Billy says that you did a first-rate job." He paused again, and when Andrews remained silent, he continued.

"Have you talked to Jill since you left?" Sam asked.

"No, she thinks I'm coming home tomorrow."

"But you're not, right?"

"No. I'm checking out of the hotel here this morning, but I'm not coming back to Orlando just yet."

"Good! Here is where we are right now, Jack Boy. I just went by your house. I rang the doorbell forever and got Jill to answer the door. She was in a bathrobe and was a terrible sight; I mean, death warmed over terrible. She gave me all this crap about not feeling well and that you were in Freeport until Monday. I asked if I could borrow your hedge clippers, as I often do, and she let me into the garage. Just her jeep was in there, and of course there was no sign of anybody else. Your house still smells of gas, though; otherwise I would have thought you dreamed this whole thing up." He paused again. Andrews remained silent.

"Billy thinks one of us should fly down there to be with you."

"No, Sam, I'm all right, believe me. The whiskey made me sick; sicker than a dog. I had the dry heaves in my plane all the way down here to Freeport and I still have an unsettled stomach. I went to bed last night before dark ... believe me, Sam; I'm okay in that respect. I'm about to lose everything else in my life, but I'm not going to take a drink. I promise."

"All right, I believe you. Bill is going to stop by Cowans' house this afternoon, unannounced. I guess you know that the freeze Friday night knocked the hell out of all our citrus. Billy has volunteered to lobby the politicians for some state and federal aid. He's going to try to catch Cowans at home this afternoon to talk about the freeze damage, but he wants to look him in the eye; see if he can get a feel for how he's thinking. I am going to try to go with him." The lawyer paused. "Billy thinks Cowans' Senate campaign will keep him from going public with this shit, and I agree. The son-of-a-bitch will just let the whole thing blow over. He's got to, or otherwise it's the end of his political career."

"Wishful thinking, Sam, but I sure hope that you are right. Listen, I didn't tell Billy yesterday because I wasn't sure, but I am going to fly out of here this morning and spend a couple of days up at Walkers. I'll be in the hotel there after 1:00 PM and I'll check in with you at your office tomorrow.

Tell Billy to stay calm and not to worry about me slipping off the wagon again."

"One day at a time, right, Jack?"

"Right, but you know what, Sam?"

"What?"

"I'm a lucky guy to have you and Billy as friends. Wow, I'm a lucky man indeed ..." Andrews' voice choked a little and he paused momentarily. "I appreciate your support, Sam. You're a hell of a good friend."

"You just want your fucking hedge clippers back."

"I'll call you Monday."

"Jack?"

"Yes."

"This, too, shall pass."

"So long, Sam."

After he hung up the phone, he stretched back out on the bed and stared at the ceiling. "This too shall pass, huh," he whispered. "But oh, how it all hurts now." With tears welling up in his eyes he rolled over onto his stomach and buried his face into a pillow. He had struggled to not think about Jill, to force any thoughts of her out of his mind, but now he gave in to reminiscing. He lay still for thirty minutes, grieving over his life and his lost relationship with his wife. He could dwell on it no longer, and a little surge of energy gave him the strength to gather up his luggage and catch a cab to the airport. That had been three hours ago. Now he had just landed at his favorite place in the world to relax and think. He could feel the relief ease over him at once.

He turned the Cherokee right off the runway and, lining it up with the two other aircraft that were tied down on the side apron, he killed the engine. No sooner had he tied down the plane and gathered his suitcase and medical bag out of the back seat than a golf cart, pulling a trailer behind it, drove alongside his plane. The driver, a huge black man wearing khaki pants and a light blue polo shirt, flashed a wide smile at him.

"Yes sa, Mister Jack! I say dat was you when you flew over and waggled your wings. I bet Eddie five dollar. Fool didn't believe me. How long you gonna stay with us?" The man extended a huge paw and Andrews shook it.

"Just a few days, Cookie." Andrews threw his luggage into the trailer. "You think they have room for me up at the hotel? I didn't make a reservation."

"For you sa, dey always gots room. Anyway, this time in January is slow. We don't have mo den 12 peoples here right now."

"That will suit me just fine, Cookie." Andrews seated himself in the cart next to the big man and patted him affectionately on the back. "You're looking well, Cookie; did you have a good Christmas?"

"Yes sa." The driver patted his stomach. "I hads too good a Christmas." He turned the cart in a tight circle and drove across the asphalt parking lot toward a little barn-red house with a small white sign over the door that read "Customs."

"Is anyone in there?" Andrews asked, squinting to look through the small front windows.

"Naw sa, Ronnie Lee is coming down from the hotel."

"Ronnie Lee?" Andrews laughed. "So he's a customs agent now?"

"Yes sa, Mr. Hardwick got him the job two months ago. He gots a uniform and he don't do nothing around here any mo 'cept looks important." The big man shook his head.

Andrews laughed as he remembered Ronnie Lee as the effeminate resort employee that had no obvious job on the island. Unlike Cookie and Eddie, who worked as guides for fishing or dive trips, or the other Bahamian employees who worked in the hotel, Ronnie Lee had no duties or responsibilities, but more or less acted as hotel manager Earl Hardwick's, errand boy. Their relationship had raised more than a few eyebrows and earned Ronnie Lee the title of "Miss Walkers Cay" from Sam Wadley. Also, Andrews had always sensed that Ronnie Lee was perhaps more educated than most of the other Bahamians on the island.

"Well hell, Cookie, I never thought that Ronnie Lee did much of anything around here anyway, except look pretty and try to run the fuel dock without getting his hands dirty."

The big man flashed his wide smile again. "Well, Ronnie Lee don't even do that no mo. He just be important now." There was the sound of someone coming down the path above them and both men fell silent.

Ronnie Lee did look impressive in his customs uniform. His tall, slim figure stood even more erect than usual. He sashayed up to the golf cart, smiling at Cookie and then at Andrews.

"Hello there, Ronnie Lee," Andrews spoke with enthusiasm. "Congratulations on your new job."

"Why thank you, Doctor Andrews," the tall man said, smiling. "Do you want to bring your bags and come inside?" He opened the door of the little customs house with his key and glided through it, with Andrews following him. Cookie retrieved Jack's suitcase and medical bag from the trailer.

"Let's see what we have here," Ronnie Lee said, placing both of his hands on the outside of Jack's suitcase and closing his eyes as if he could sense what the bag contained through his extraordinary sensory perception. "No drugs that I can feel," he smiled at Andrews.

"No, Ronnie Lee," Jack smiled back. "The drugs are over here in this bag." He pointed to his medical bag. "Do you need some?"

"Oh my God, do I!" Ronnie Lee threw his head back and laughed out loud. "What have you got that will make me younger and prettier?"

Andrews shook his head. "I'm afraid you want too much for $9.95, Ronnie Lee, but I do have a drug that will make you not care about being younger and prettier if you wanted some."

"No, I don't think so; I will just keep on hoping for a miracle." Ronnie Lee pushed the suitcase and medical bag back toward Andrews. "Welcome to beautiful Walkers Cay, Mister Jack. We love having you with us and hope that you enjoy your stay."

****

Chapter 13
The Lay of the land
The general state/condition of affairs under consideration; the facts of a situation:

When he returned to the cart, Jack shook his head and smiled at Cookie. "That Ronnie Lee was never on my wavelength, but I think this new customs inspector job may have just pushed him around the bend; what do you think, Cookie?" Andrews punched the big man's shoulder affectionately as the two rode the golf cart up the winding concrete sidewalk that led a twisting course through the thick sea grape vegetation for several hundred yards to the hotel.

Cookie shook his head. "We be better off with no customs inspector."

"How's business, Cookie; any tournament fishing going on right now?" Jack was wondering who he could meet in the hotel who could recognize him.

"We only has about 12 guests in the hotel right now, Mister Jack. Let me think, we got four men from Texas that have been diving with Eddie for two days and we have two couples from New York who are snorkeling right around our reefs. We have dat lady from Minnesota who is here by herself - well she has a little dog with her, but all she do is swim in de pool all day. We only have one couple from Florida dat I know." The black man smiled and shook his head slowly. "You ain't gonna see dem; dey newlyweds, been here fo days and ain't come out of der room da whole time." The black man threw back his head and laughed and then had a thought. "Mister Jack, yo friend Mister Bart, the fish spotter, he here right now. He be happy to see you."

"Bart's here now?" Jack said in surprise. "I didn't see his plane.'

"Yes sa, Mister Bart's got him a new plane. That two engine blue plane down dere is his." Cookie grinned, proud to break the news.

"Wow!" said Jack. "Bart's driving a Beech Baron now; his business must be good!" Bart Keener was a professional bill fish spotter. He had been a Marine Corps chopper pilot in Vietnam and now made his flying services available to the highest bidder following the bill fishing tournaments up and down the Atlantic and Caribbean.

Flying in Vietnam had welded Andrews and Keener's friendship together long before the two ever shook hands for the first time. Jack had flown with Bart several times, when the pilot was working fishing tournaments. At first Andrews thought he could help his friend spot one of the big marlin; but it never happened. On the occasion when Jack would see the shadowed image of a big fish, he would realize that his pilot had already seen it and was guiding the plane right for it. Bart Keener's eyes and instincts were amazing. Jack would look forward to catching up with him.

"So, it's been real slow here, huh, Cookie?"

"Yes Sa, it was better on de weekend; we had a few mo boats in de marina, but most of dem left dis morning."

143

"Well, slow sounds real good to me, Cookie," Andrews smiled at his friend. "I'm here for some peace and quiet."

The big man frowned at the term "peace and quiet". "We gonna fish, right, Mister Jack?"

"Right, Cookie; set it up for tomorrow. Let's go early in the morning."

"Yes sa, it already set up." He threw back his head and laughed.

The golf cart came to a stop under a large porte-cochere in front of the hotel and as Cookie gathered the two bags out of the trailer, Jack Andrews sprang up the five stairs to the entrance of the lobby.

Andrews' lawyer and friend, Sam Wadley, always said that the Walkers Cay Hotel reminded him of the movie set for Casablanca. "All they need in here is a piano for me to play," he said one night to a group staying on his boat. They were all sitting in the hotel bar drinking coffee after dinner. "Then you could ask me to 'Play it again Sam' and I could give you my rendition of 'As Time Goes By.'"

The group had laughed and agreed. The sprawling two-story building had been constructed on a high limestone hill on the island's southern end. A long wing of rooms ran from the pool area out along a ridge to the tip of the island that gave each room on both sides wonderful views of the water. The plantings were tropical; hibiscus, bougainvillea, and lots of fiddle leaf fig and sea grape. The interiors were nautical, with the walls of the lobby, bar, and dining rooms covered with beautiful trophy fish mounts of all kinds.

Andrews didn't recognize the attractive woman working behind the desk in the hotel's small office, but before he could speak, Cookie launched into an introduction.

"Miss Kate, I want you to meet my main man. You know de man Eddie and me is always talking about; de man who caught dat big tiger shark in a whaler by his self out here at de first marker; de man who stayed here with us during de hurricane? Dis him! Dis is de man ... dis is Doc Andrews, Mister Jack!" The enthusiasm in Cookie's voice was genuine and Andrews was touched by the big man's affection for him.

The woman smiled and got up from her desk. "Nice to meet you, we have heard a lot about 'Mister Jack'." She extended her hand and Andrews took it. "I'm Kate Judson, the new manager." Her blue eyes sparkled and she spoke with what sounded to Andrews like an Australian accent.

"Well I hope you've been here long enough to know not to pay attention to anything Cookie and Eddie say." Her hard squeeze of his hand distracted him for a minute. "I just took a chance and flew in here without a reservation. I was hoping I could get a single room for a couple of days?"

"You may have a room for as long as you care to stay with us." She smiled again, warmly.

"Would you prefer a room on the sunrise side or the sunset side?" She pushed a registration card across the counter.

"Sunset, please," he said as he picked up the desk pen and began to write. "Cookie says business is generally pretty slow this time in January."

"Yes, after the holidays we never do much business until after the 20th of the month. Mr. Hardwick calls it `The

January Jitters.' The season is supposed to start, but it doesn't."

"Is Mr. Hardwick around?" Andrews glanced up from his writing.

"No, he isn't. I don't know if you have heard that Earl has some major health problems and in fact he just recently bought a home in Ft. Lauderdale and has retired from most of the duties here at the resort. I guess you could say I'm training to eventually take his place... " she smiled and then added, "Of course, I am sure that no one could ever take Earl's place."

"I'm afraid that's not quite true, Kate; you're far more attractive than Earl Hardwick ever was. Have there been any other staff changes? Is Eddie still here, and is Chef Walter still in the kitchen?"

"Oh yes, they are all here, along with Sally and Anna; so I'm sure you will feel very much at home, as usual.

"What kind of health problems does Earl have?"

"He just recently had open heart surgery and is convalescing at home in Lauderdale. He calls and checks in with us every day, though."

"Well, give him my best the next time you talk to him. Tell him I said to push through that rehab and get well."

"I will do that, and I am sure he will appreciate it." She smiled sweetly and Andrews went back to filling out his registration card. *Sharp woman*, he thought to himself.

He glanced up from the card. "Do you have any Florida folks staying here now?" He needed to confirm Cookie's information.

"Only a pair of newlyweds from Orlando," she said, smiling. "We haven't seen a whole lot of them, though, have we, Cookie?"

"No ma'am, dey had me book de boat to take dem fishing two times and I ain't seen dem yet." The big man stared down at his belly and shook his head.

Andrews slapped his friend on the back. "Well, Cookie, you've got a live one now, it's you and me first thing in the morning. Who knows, there's been no moon this week, so we could just get ourselves a trophy fish."

"Yes sa, we leave at eight in de morning?" he asked, smiling.

"Eight o'clock it is."

"I'll put de bags in your room, Mister Jack." Cookie picked up the key Kate Judson had laid on the counter and, grabbing up the suitcase and medical bag he had carried in from the golf cart, he headed across the lobby and out onto the pool deck area. Andrews smiled at Kate Judson.

"Hope you enjoy your stay with us," she smiled back.

"I always do," he said with a grin. "I always do ..."

****

Chapter 14

Grasping At Straws

To "grasp at straws" has, since at least the 18th century, meant "to make a desperate and a certainly futile effort to save oneself"

Robert Warner wondered if he could be having a serious heart attack. There was a sharp pain in his chest and his left arm felt numb - or was he just imagining that it felt numb? He peeled a five-dollar bill off his money clip to tip the doorman, who had hailed the cab for him earlier when he had made a trip to Dayton's Department Store to pick up some clothes. The man was now holding the door open for him to move through, with his armload of packages.

Warner was still living in his hotel room compliments of his attorney, Doug Hawkins, who had also given him a credit card and $1,000 in cash. "You're a lifesaver, Doug," Robert had told his lawyer. "I don't think that I will need this much cash, as I hope to get my credit cards straightened out right away."

"Don't worry, Rob," Doug had said with a smile. "I gave you a grand so I wouldn't forget it. My office will bill you for it."

They were to meet for a Sunday brunch in his hotel dining room and Warner was running late. All day Saturday and into the night, Doug Hawkins had been in his office, working on Robert Warner's case. He had attempted to put the pieces together and review the file copies that Walter Brooks had made for them at their morning meeting at his bank. The documents included a copy of Rob's notarized Power of Attorney to Helen which allowed the Warner Chemical Resolution to sell the company's assets to Helena Chemical. The resolution had been prepared by Grant, Davidson and Carter, a St. Paul blue ribbon law firm. It was ironclad and included a detailed 54-page list of all the assets to be sold, including legal descriptions of the real estate, plant, and equipment.

There was also a corporate resolution from the Helena Chemical Board of Directors authorizing the purchase of the assets from Warner Chemical for $20,000,000 and approving a loan from Chase Bank of New York for $12,000,000 to do so. There was a public relations piece on the background of the buyer, Helena Chemical Corporation. It apparently had been chartered a year earlier and included over 300 stockholders (most all were Warner Chemical Employees) including Helen Warner, who still owned forty percent of Helena's shares.

Hawkins was struck by the brilliance of the plan. Helen's $4 million stock purchase of her 40 percent ownership in Helena Chemical had provided the seed capital to finance the entire transaction. Company employees were offered the opportunity to purchase the remaining 60 percent of the shares, which they apparently did immediately. Once that capitalization was in place, Helena Chemical then obtained the $12 million dollar loan to finance the $20 million purchase and provide $2,000,000 worth of working capital for the venture. Helen Warner had arranged the sale of Warner Chemical's entire asset base for $20,000.000 and invested $4,000,000 of the sales proceeds in the new venture. The transfer apparently had been seamless, with the new company, Helena Chemical, using the assets and employees of the old company and never missing an operational beat. In addition, Helena Chemical was now operating with an invigorated workforce of owners. "Touch Black, No Backs," Doug had said softly to himself when he made the discovery. The best he could hope for was to get his client, Robert Warner, half of that sales price.

Hawkins had decided that, under the circumstances, Rob's best defense would be a strong offense. His wife had not only stolen half of his business from him and apparently sold it to herself, but she had also confiscated all of their other joint assets and removed them from his access. At the least, Warner was entitled to half the value of the business and all their joint property. As soon as they could locate Mrs. Helen Warner, they intended to file a suit against her to reclaim it.

Doug had come to the hotel Sunday morning to meet his client for breakfast and was sitting at a corner table in the dining room, drinking coffee and reading over his notes, when Robert Warner approached him and sat down. They ordered and then Hawkins reviewed all the facts as he understood them. Warner sat in silence, listening to his friend.

"Helena Chemical is owned by my employees?" he asked in disbelief. 'What does that mean?"

"It means that it is going to be much harder to nullify the sale, with over 300 stockholders involved," Hawkins answered back. "Your wife is no longer the controlling stock holder, and we know that Helena Chemical borrowed $12 million from Chase to make this deal happen. I would assume that since your wife only purchased 40 percent of Helena for $4 million, that your employees have purchased at least $6 million for their 60 percent control of the company. "

"That's the way this thing was planned and that is exactly how it was carried out. Can you think of anything I may have left out?" he asked his client after speaking for a good twenty minutes.

"She shipped all my clothes to my lady friend down in Atlanta," Warner said, looking off into space. "I've been to Dayton's this morning so I can put on a clean shirt and underwear."

Hawkins stared at his client for a few seconds before he spoke. "Well, at least you are going to get your personal effects back. I was going to ask you what you thought could have happened to all those silk suits and alligator shoes of yours. That's good news, Rob." The lawyer pointed to the documents that had been pushed aside for dishes. "This thing is too well done, and I think any judge is going to see that you have been set up for at least a year. Your wife didn't do this to you in a fit of rage. This thing was set up just a little too perfectly. Believe me; we are going to get half of whatever the bottom number is."

"Half of the bottom number!" Warner was frantic. "I want my business back, Doug. How long is it going to take me to get my company back?"

Doug Hawkins shrugged his shoulders. "What do you want me to say, Rob?" The lawyer shook his head and grimaced. "I'll be honest with you. The St. Paul law firm that set this thing up for Helen did one hell of a job. They have crossed all the Ts and they didn't do all this in just two weeks while you were out of town. You have been blindsided, my man royally blindsided; and it looks as if we are going to have to fight just to get back half of your joint equity."

151

An extremely well-dressed man carrying a briefcase walked by their table, then turned around and came back.

"Excuse me, sir, but aren't you Robert Warner, of Warner Chemical?" he asked with a smile, offering his hand to Rob.

"Why yes, I am." Warner was taken back, but extended his hand politely. "And you are?" he asked, leaning forward.

"A process server," the man said as he placed a manila envelope in Robert's outstretched hand. "You have been served, sir. Have a good day." He was gone before Rob could speak.

Warner tore the envelope open and shrieked at Hawkins. "That crazy bitch has filed to divorce me and she has now acquired a restraining order preventing me from going within 100 feet of her," he was shaking his head in disbelief.

Doug Hawkins was impressed with the process server. "My God, Rob, did you notice that? That process server was wearing a $1,000 suit. Unbelievable! Those boys at Grant, Davidson and Carter do it up right. Impressive." The lawyer stared back at his client and shook his head. "Rob, we need to get in the game as soon as we possibly can. If I can just find where your wife is, I'd serve a suit on her tomorrow and ask the assigned judge to expedite the trial date for us. That brings up the main question of the day, Rob. "

The lawyer paused and studied his client for several seconds over his plate of scrambled eggs. "The question is: where did she go and where is she hiding? Do you want to make a guess?"

Warner shook his head. "I have no idea. Her closest friend in town told me that she was going south to get out of the

152

cold weather, but she had no idea where. If she told anybody, she would have told this person. Helen is an only child. Since her mother passed away two years ago, she has no living relatives that I know of."

"What about good friends?" Hawkins asked.

"She has quite a few good friends. I don't know where we should start. She is close to her college roommate; they swam in the Olympics together. I think she lives in Palm Beach. She could have gone to visit her. I have no idea." Robert Warner hung his head dejectedly.

"I doubt that she would go to see anyone that you know. She has been way too smart and organized at this stage to let us find her by leaving bread crumbs along her trail." Hawkins was thinking out loud about his options. "How about travel plans? Which companies do you use for company travel services?"

Warner picked his head up. "Joyce Hunter's company, Bon Voyage," he said excitedly. "Helen is close to Joyce and Bon Voyage does all of our travel. Joyce would know where she is, because she arranged it." Again, the attorney shook his head. "If that is true, I doubt that Miss Hunter will tell us anything, Rob. If she booked the travel, she has to be in on the plan. However, she may not be in on all of it, so it wouldn't hurt to call her and see how she reacts. What you could do instead of asking her for Helen's location is just act as if you assume that she knows where she is, but she left without signing some papers that have to be filed this coming week and can she get them to her for signature. If she says yes, then we will have a viable source to work with."

After Doug Hawkins left for his office, Rob Warner went back to his room and used the phone to call Bon Voyage

Travel Agency. They prided themselves on their 24/7 service, so he was certain someone would answer the call.

"Good Morning, Bon Voyage!" a cheery voice answered.

"Hi, this is Robert Warner. Would Joyce Hunter happen to be in the office this morning, please?"

"I'm sorry, Mr. Warner; Joyce is out of the office for the rest of the month; may I help you in some way?"

"Where is she?" he blurted out abruptly before quickly backing off. "I mean, is she somewhere that I may be able to reach by phone?" His voice was pleading.

"No sir, she and her husband are gone for the whole month." The woman on the phone sensed the urgency in his voice. "They have chartered a sailboat and are making a bare boat cruise with another couple in the Caribbean. Joyce tries to check in with us every Friday if she is in port somewhere. May I give her a message when she calls?" She was trying to be helpful.

"Well, maybe you can help me." Why not use a little sugar? Warner thought to himself. What did he have to lose by asking someone who was trying to be helpful? "Joyce arranged a trip for my wife, Helen Warner, last week and Helen forgot to sign some legal documents before she left that we must file with the government this week, so I needed an address so that I could overnight them to her and get them right back in two days."

"Just a minute, sir, and I will pull the file." She was gone and was replaced by music on the line. Warner was holding his breath. If only she would come back with a location that would provide him immediate contact with his wife.

"Hello, Mr. Warner; your company is Warner Chemical, right?

"Yes, yes," Robert said excitedly.

"Sir, we have nothing pending for your company right now. The last work order is for round trip tickets for you to Dallas and a room at ...."

"That is the last booking you have?" Warner interrupted. He sounded disbelieving. "You don't show any travel arrangement for my wife, Helen Warner?"

"No sir, they weren't made from this office."

"Do you ever work with other agencies in town to book trips and tours together?"

"Yes sir, on occasion we refer clients to Twin City Travel, as they do business a little differently than we do."

"How is that?" Robert asked.

"Oh, they do a lot of private charters. You know, outback stuff and mountain climbing expeditions, etc. In fact, this trip that Joyce is on at the moment was arranged by TCT."

"Do you have a number for their office?" Robert Warner picked up the hotel pen and shifted the complementary note pad over in front of him in preparation to write.

****

Chapter 15
Recovery

The act, process, duration, or an instance of recovering; A return to a normal condition; something gained or restored in recovering; the act of obtaining usable substances from unusable sources.

Andrews' corner hotel room faced southwest and had a beautiful view of the water on two sides. He opened the drapes, unpacked his bags, and changed into a pair of black swim trunks and a bright red and white aloha shirt. He slipped his bare feet into his tennis shoes before remembering that he should run a couple of miles around the airstrip to make up for his lost exercise regimen of the past three days. He pulled on a pair of wool athletic socks and laced the tennis shoes tightly.

On his way back through the lobby, he stopped in the hotel's duty-free gift shop to investigate the latest newspapers. They were all the same editions he had seen that morning in Freeport. There was nothing new. He was standing inside the glass wall that overlooked the pool area, leafing through an older edition of Sports Illustrated, when he saw her.

She walked slowly out of the corridor that led to the rooms of the hotel with a little Yorkie terrier on a leash. Her wide, dark sunglasses and enormous straw hat hid much of her face, and except for a pair of shapely legs, her body was completely covered by a black sarong. Still, there was something about the regal way she carried herself that caught Andrews' attention. The woman glanced neither left nor right but, with definite purpose, crossed the pool deck to a corner table.

Andrews turned his body back towards a magazine rack, but found it hard to take his eyes off the stranger. The woman removed her hat and sunglasses and took off her sarong. Andrews guessed that she was in her mid-forties, but he was startled by the wonderful shape and condition of her body. Her bathing suit, which was a simple one-piece black nylon tank suit, was not stylish at all. And although it was modest indeed compared to some of the two piece swimsuit standards, the tank suit accentuated this woman's long waist and figure perfectly.

As he watched her through the window, she took a bathing cap and a pair of thin black swim goggles out of her large straw bag and, after carefully putting them on, slid slowly into the blue filtered salt water and set out to swim laps. Her strokes were measured and strong, knifing her long body through the water. Watching her do a side-turn in the shallow end and a quick, perfect flip-turn back in the deep end of the pool, Andrews decided immediately that she was, or had been, some type of competitive swimmer.

"Don't even think about it," a voice said behind him. Turning around, Jack saw his friend Bart Keener, the fish spotter, smiling at him. "Believe me; I have already had my hair set on fire by that lovely Dragon Lady. She is beautiful, but she is hiding from somebody and wants to be alone."

Jack smiled and stuck out his hand to grip his friend's hand firmly. "Is that so?" Andrews smiled. "Well then, she and I could have a lot more in common than I imagined. So, I take it that you have already introduced yourself to

Gertrude Ederle?" He chuckled at Bart's "Dragon Lady" description.

"Who in the hell is Gertrude Ederle?" Bart asked. "Maybe that was my problem. Cookie told me her name is Helen Warner. I was my friendly self, but she would not even look my way."

"Gertrude Ederle was the first woman to swim the English Channel. She was an American," Jack said as he glanced back in the direction of the pool. Helen Warner did another quick flip turn in the deep end and pushed off on a long underwater glide towards the other end of the pool. Andrews shook his head. "She is obviously some sort of competitive swimmer; she is a fish in the water."

"Well, you are forewarned. She is a cold fish, I promise you." Bart picked up a tube of sun block. "I never ever even got a smile from her or a chance to introduce myself." He checked Jack over. "What's going on with you? Are you here to do a little bill fishing by yourself?"

"Absolutely," Jack responded. "Cookie showed me your new ride. How is it, flying the Beech Baron?"

"Great, until I have to put gas in it." Bart shook his head. "And it's only a little faster - and I'm not sure that it is one bit safer - than my Cherokee Six. You are still flying yours, right?"

"Yes sir, I came here in it and I'm planning on hanging on to it as long as I can pass my flight physical. So you traded up on me, you rascal," Jack smiled at his friend.

"Oh, I still have mine, but it is in a thousand pieces in my dad's hanger in Ocala. He is doing a total rebuild for me. It is going to take him forever, I know."

"Are you here working a tournament now?"

"No, nothing's happening until February. But I have a pretty good rate here. I ferry around the islands for them in exchange for room and board. They cover my gas tab, plus this gal Kate is a lot of fun. How long are you around?"

"Just a couple of days, or maybe the rest of my life," Andrews said, and both men laughed.

"I hear that," Bart said as he backed away. "I'm working on my plane today, but keep me in mind for a fishing buddy tomorrow or the next day."

"Will do, my man." Jack gave him a wave. He glanced back out the window at the form cutting through the pool. He thought for a second that there was something familiar about her and he found himself wondering if this attractive woman was, in fact, part of the newlyweds from Orlando that had been staying in their room for days, which was why she was so cool to Bart. If so, would she or her husband know him? He returned the magazine to the rack and slowly made his way back through the lobby to the registration desk. Kate Judson glanced up from her work.

"Yes sir?" she inquired with a smile.

"Kate, I didn't mention this to you when I checked in, but I am sort of taking a sabbatical from my work for a few days and I don't want to take any calls while I'm here. There are only a few people who know that I am here, but even if they call, I would prefer that you just tell them I am off the island and take a message so I can call them back at my leisure."

"No problem, sir," she said efficiently. She wrote something quickly on a note pad and, taking a red tag out of a desk drawer, she hung it over his message box on the wall behind her. He noticed immediately that there was one other red tag hanging down in front of another box next to his, and he smiled.

"Does that red tag put me in the 'do not disturb' category with your newlyweds?" he asked smiling broadly. She glanced at the other red tag and smiled back at him. "No, that's for another guest who doesn't want to take any outside calls either. She's been with us for several days now." She was about to add something and then hesitated.

"Oh, by the way," he said as an afterthought. "How old would you guess the honeymooners from Orlando are?"

"I would say early twenties," she said with a grin. "Their last name is Bolton. I think they're both still in college. Do you think you know them?"

"No, I don't think I do," he said, shaking his head.

"Is everything all right with your room?"

"Yes, fine ... thank you. It's nice." He turned away.

"Doctor Andrews?"

"Yes." He turned back.

"If there is anything I can do for you while you are here, to make your stay more enjoyable, just let me know." She smiled and he smiled back politely.

"Thanks, Kate, I will; and you can begin by calling me Jack."

"Yes sir ... I mean, Jack."

As he crossed the pool deck toward the path leading down to the marina, he noticed that the woman he had seen from the duty free shop window had stopped swimming now. She was standing in the shallow end of the pool adjusting the strap on her swim goggles. As he walked by her she glanced up at him.

"Hi," he said, smiling.

She said nothing but flashed a beautiful smile. *Good* he thought to himself, *she was just another pretty woman who wanted to be alone and needed privacy;*. They should have an easy time avoiding each other; plus her smile put him way ahead of Bart Keener. He walked quickly across the pool deck and down the path toward the marina. He didn't look back, but he sensed that he was being watched. He broke into a run.

****

Chapter 16
Secrets

Secrets serve a purpose. They protect the innocent as well as the guilty and once they are exposed, like smoke or a vapor, they cease to exist, leaving in their wake only the possible damage caused by their unmasking.

The marina was empty. Jack Andrews stood on the seawall and stared out over the empty boat slips. It was strange to see so few boats in the Walkers Marina. During his trips there in past summers, with Jill and the Wadleys, it was not uncommon to see dozens of boats crowded into the little sheltered cove, with many of them rafted together overnight in the same slips.

In fact, Jack had found it a strange phenomenon that so many boaters could be assembled together in one place over night and yet when most of them motored out of the pass in the morning for a day of fishing or diving, the vast ocean of blue water swallowed them up. It was not uncommon to leave the crowded little marina at dawn and spend an entire day fishing and diving without seeing another boat. His friend, Sam Wadley, called it the Walkers Phenomenon, and attributed it to the fact that Walkers Cay was so far removed from any of the other islands that there was no cross traffic.

"When you see a boat out here in this part of the ocean, it had to come from Walkers," he told Andrews one day as the two men sat in the bridge of Wadley's big Hatteras watching their baits skip along in the white foam behind them. "And there is one hell of a lot of water out here to absorb us all."

On those summer evenings, the marina would come alive with activity. Cookers of all shapes and sizes smoked and flared along the docks as people grilled part of their day's catch. Boaters called back and forth to each other as they washed the salt off their boats and equipment. Some wandered around the docks, inspecting other boats, telling fish stories, and listening for tips as to where the action could be had the following day.

During these times, the hotel was always full. Rooms were at a premium, handling the visitors who overflowed off the boats. It was not uncommon to see a boat, that slept four or six, go out in the morning with eight to ten people on board, the extra passengers having been quartered at the hotel.

This collection of boaters always brought together a strange menagerie of class types. Other than the boating families who functioned together with Mom, Dad and the kids as a unit, there were the affluent, who preferred the amenities of the hotel and let their captains and crew stay on board their boats. Then there were the younger, more daring types who had crossed the treacherous gulf stream in 15-foot Boston Whalers by running behind and in the immediate wake of the larger boats that were making the crossing. These young people slept in the bottom of their skiffs under tarps and never ventured up the hill to the hotel, but instead used The Marina Bar, next to the laundry room, as a social meeting spot.

Quite a few of the larger sport fishing boats that stayed overnight in Walkers belonged to what Sam Wadley called "the mid-life crisis crowd." These were the forty- and fifty-year-old guys. Their main reason for having a boat was the cover it provided for their extramarital affairs. The flying bridges and sport fishing outriggers on their boats just made the ruse more complete. Sam always claimed that the mid-life crisis guys were easy to spot. "They never stay long in any one port and they always keep to themselves when docked, and they never talked about their fishing," he would say, laughing.

And, of course, there were always a few sailboat owners; noticed and admired by the power boat (stink pot) owners for their skills and self-sufficiency. They slipped quietly in and out of the marina with owners who preferred to live aboard. These sailors gave the hotel little business except for an occasional drink at the pool bar.

This afternoon there were less than a half dozen boats moored in the marina and three of them he recognized immediately as belonging to the hotel. The largest of these was a 42-foot Whiticar Sports Fisherman with the name "Bewitched" painted on her transom. She was a wonderful wooden boat made in Stuart, Florida by the Whiticars, an old line boat building family with a reputation for impeccable craftsmanship. Her deep V-shaped bottom drew more water than some other sport fishing vessels and required a skipper to use more caution when working in shallow water. But out in the deep ocean, a Whiticar boat would cut through rough seas much as a sharp knife. Andrews had fished from the Bewitched on many occasions and she would no doubt be the rig that he and Cookie would use tomorrow.

He recognized the hotel's other sport fishing boat: it was a 38-foot Hatteras named "Summer Star." She was a workhorse, and because she had 2 feet less draft than the

Whiticar boat, she was used for fishing and diving trips around the waters closer to the island. She had the big twin diesels in her and could really step out if you were in a hurry to go somewhere.

Andrews recognized another barge-like boat about 35 feet long with a canvas canopy covering twenty or more seats in its bow, the "Bahama Mamma." It was used to ferry employees to and from Grand Cay, the nearest Bahamian community just south of Walkers. Most of the Walkers Resort staff lived there and commuted daily back and forth.

Now, as Andrews stared out over the empty docks, he thought about all of those boaters. He thought about all of the activity and all of the wonderful experiences he had enjoyed there in the little cove. There had been some wonderful times with his friends, the Evans and the Wadley's ... and Jill. His wife had loved the little island as much as he did. He experienced a twinge of the old ache. Where had they gone so wrong in their relationship? Was her affair his fault? Had he not been attentive enough? Had he not been a loving and understanding husband? Surely, it could not have been a lack of sex drive. He had always been the initiator, and his efforts to be romantic had often been rebuffed during the last several years.

He wondered if he would feel different if her lover had not been Phillip Cowans. He sought to think of someone who would have been worse. He couldn't.

"Mister Jack!" He heard a voice call behind him. Turning around, he saw a familiar face peering at him from over the top of a high wooden fence that screened off one of the fish cleaning areas from the docks.

"Hey, Eddie!" he said, walking around the fence. "How are you, buddy?" A powerfully built black man wearing a long bib apron, was busy filleting a mammoth grouper that was stretched out on the long wooden table. Andrews patted his friend on the shoulder. "Wow, that's a nice looking grouper, Eddie; is he going up to the hotel?"

"Yes sa, he there. You won't go wrong if you order grouper tonight."

"Oh, I won't go wrong." Andrews smiled at his friend. "Cookie told me you didn't recognize my plane and he got you for a few bucks."

"Yes sa, I didn't think you be here dis time of year. Know what I mean? Cuz, I is way ahead of Cookie." Eddie washed off a thick filet and laid it in a dented metal pan. "How long is you gonna be here?"

"Just for a couple of days. Can you go fishing with us in the morning?"

"I gots a charter flying in tomorrow for de Summer Star, but I go with you Tuesday."

"Where's your charter coming from, tomorrow?" Andrews asked, trying to be watchful.

"Miss Kate say dey come from Minnesota, but dey is in Freeport for a few days gamlin before dey come here."

Andrews had been stretching his legs out by touching his palms on the pavement in front of him. Eddie laughed at Jack's flexibility. "You's still running 25 miles erry day or whatever it was?"

Andrews laughed at the question. "That was back in my marathon days, Eddie. I sure couldn't do that now. I just try to run three or four miles a few times a week; that's all. I've been doing it so long, I'm afraid to quit." Andrews

166

touched his palms on the ground once again. "I'm going to run around the ole airstrip a couple of times. Are you going to be around this evening?"

"Yes sa, I is waiting tables in de hotel dining room tonight. Axe for Eddie if you want da good service." He smiled. "I is the only waiter tonight."

"You are a waiter now?" Andrews was surprised, as usually the dock employees didn't work with the hotel employees.

"Yes sa, Miss Kate said I could do it when fishing and diving was slow. I likes it a lot."

"Good for you. You'll be good at it, I know. I'll be sure to ask for one of your tables." They both laughed.

"Is there any of the regulars here fishing now that I would know?" Andrews asked, as if it were an afterthought.

"No sa, ain't nobody bin fishing here all dis week 'cept Wednesday, me and Cookie took a charter out. But all dem folks left over de weekend. In fact, dere ain't nobody here right now Doc dat wants to fish, 'cept you and maybe a young just married couple and the swimming lady."

"The swimming lady?"

"Yes sa, she bin here since Friday. She told Cookie when she got here dat she want to fish sometime; but so far, all she do all day long is swim back and forth in de big pool. Dat's all she do all day long. Sally and Anna, in de gift shop, say they gets tired by just watching her."

"Does she have a little dog with her?" Andrews asked.

"Yes sa, she has a little bitty dog."

167

Jack smiled and told Eddie that he would see him that night in the dining room and trotted up the side path from the marina towards the air strip. On the way he spotted Bart Keener's Beech Baron.

Bart had been a wild man in his earlier years. He once purchased a beautifully restored 2 place WWII Messerschmitt ME-109. It was painted the original olive green and came complete with wing and fuselage swastikas, a siren, and CO2 gas guns on the wings in place of the German 30 Calibers. The gas guns were louder than the original equipment.

Bart had flown the plane into Orlando's Executive Airport and phoned Jack to go for a ride with him. Keener bought a pair of the old German leather helmets and built a new intercom system in them for the pilot and passenger to communicate with each other. He let Andrews fly the plane. It was a dream, as Jack put it through its paces. It wasn't until they had left the Orlando airspace with Keener back in control and headed for the military's bombing range at Avon Park in the middle of the state that Andrews became concerned. And that concern doubled when Jack found out that his friend planned to enter the restricted area with the hope of jumping a Navy jet while it was making a bombing run.

"Keener, are you shitting me?" he had yelled at Bart on his intercom. "You're going to get us both arrested and lose your license and this plane before you're through.

"Come on, Jack. You know yourself that those jet boys will love it," Bart said. "We'll only get one chance to make a pass at them, but we can come in out of the sun with our guns blazing."

To Andrews's great relief, there were no practice sorties taking place that day, and they were forced to head back to

Orlando without bagging a Navy jet. However, over the town of Lake Wales, Bart Keener had spotted a festive gathering taking place on someone's large estate below. Bright colorful tents and awnings had been set up for the guests and several hundred well-dressed people were apparently having cocktails on the lawn overlooking a lake. Before Jack could protest, Bart did a wingover and, pointing the nose of the 109 toward the middle of the lake, he let the air speed double before he leveled off about 50 feet above the surface of the water. With the Messerschmitt's siren wailing and gas guns blazing, the ME 109 roared in on the gathering. People were running in all directions. Bart pulled the stick back, clearing the house by a good fifty feet, and did a double roll out to the right.

"God damn it, Bart, you're an idiot!" Jack was ready to fight him. "You had better hide this plane as quickly as you can before the FAA takes it away from you."

"Ease up, Jackson!" Bart had said. "We just livened up what otherwise was a dull party. We should send them a bill for entertainment."

"Please leave my name off of it," Jack growled into the intercom.

Andrews never flew with Keener again after that day, until Bart became a spotter pilot for bill fishing tournaments. They both bought their Piper Cherokee Sixes together. Jack had always thought that he was one of Bart Keener's closest friends. And Bart was definitely a friend that would help him move a body.

As Andrews now studied his friend's Beech Baron, he thought Bart had acquired a beautiful ride to go to work in. It seemed to be in great shape with what Andrews thought was a brand new paint job. The cowling was off the left engine, and an open box of tools sat under the left wing. Andrews checked around for the pilot and then opened the door. He stuck his head inside and was admiring how neatly the inside of the plane was maintained, for a working plane. The plane held six passengers comfortably with the club seating four chairs facing each other with a table between them. Now the rear two seats were collapsed down and two 20-gallon bladder fuel tanks took their place.

"Want to buy some bladder fuel tanks?" a voice said behind him. Jack pulled his head out of the plane and turned around to see Keener walking down the path from the hotel.

"Congratulations on this plane, Bart!" Jack said enthusiastically. "This baby looks to be in great shape. What's wrong with the bladder tanks?"

"Not a damn thing." Bart picked up a wrench from his tool box. "They just aren't big enough for me to fly the distance I need to cover now. This ship will burn through both of them in four hours, so even though I am flying faster, I am limited in how long I can keep working for my clients. I've ordered two 40-gallon units to take their place. They have been delivered to Marsh Harbor and I just need to fly over there tomorrow to pick them up."

"No, I don't think that I have any use for them," Andrews said. "But if I were you, I would just hang on to them until you get back on the mainland. You'll have a much better chance of getting something for them there."

"No doubt, that is good advice."

"Cookie and I are going out off the shelf in the morning. Want to join us?" Jack asked his friend, sticking his head back inside the plane to look at the bladder tanks.

"I'm going to fly to Marsh Harbor later today," Bart said. "Don't wait on me in case I have some complications picking up my new tanks in the morning, but if I can get back in time, sure thing."

"Great!" Andrews gave his friend a thumbs up sign and trotted on down the runway.

****

Chapter 17
The Meeting
A coming together of two or more people, by chance or arrangement.

Back in his room, Jack cranked off his age in pushups (47) and took a long, warm shower. He toweled off, collapsed on the bed nude, and stared at the ceiling. His options were few. Maybe he would just stay there at Walkers. He could sell everything he owned, buy a good size boat, and live on it. Maybe he could even find something that he could charter out. His veterinary practice wasn't salable, particularly if he lost his license - which, under the present circumstances, was certainly a possibility. He closed his eyes. He was exhausted. He hadn't slept much the last several days and the exercise and shower had relieved just enough of his tension that he relaxed. He fell asleep.

He wasn't sure how long he had been sleeping when he was awakened by a knock at the door. He quickly wrapped a towel around his waist and opened the door slightly to look out into hall. Eddie, in his waiter's uniform, was standing with his back to the door looking back up the hallway.

"Thanks for the wakeup call, Eddie. I could have slept for days if you hadn't stopped by. What's up?" He opened the door to let him enter the room, if he wished. Eddie remained standing in the hall.

"Sorry to bother you, Mister Jack. But Miss Kate says I needs to check with you to make sure it's all right about tomorrow." Eddie was uneasy.

"What about tomorrow?"

"Too many folks want to go fishing with us now and Miss Kate says dat we gots to put some folks together tomorrow, so ya all gets a chance. She want me to take de Star with four peoples coming from Miami in de morning and has already signed up for group charter. But we had two other guests dat asked for private charters before you came. So, Cookie is going to take de three of you out together, if dat be okay with you?"

"Sure, Eddie. The good news is it sounds as if it could be a third of the price." Andrews could see the relief on Eddie's face.

"We sorry, Mister Jack. Cookie and me, we's looking to going with just you. We told Miss Kate dat you was our number one man, but she say to axe you if you'd mind da others."

"No problem whatsoever." Andrews shook his head. "And maybe you, Cookie, and I can go later in the week. Who are the other people going with Eddie?"

Eddie smiled, showing his one gold tooth. "Well, dem just-married folks are supposed to go, but nobody seen dem de whole week dey been here, so dey may not show up. Miss Kate say she gonna charge dem anyway if dey don't show and she told dem so. And den dat swimming lady, she said she would only go out if de charter was her own, so she

173

may not want to go when she finds out dat dere's other folks going."

"So, it looks as if it could be just Cookie and me after all?" Andrews smiled.

"Yes sa; could be dat. On de other hand, you may have to spend de day with a pair of lovebirds and a seasick moody lady." Eddie stepped away from the doorway. "Let me gets down to da dining room now, befo dey start serving."

"I'll be down to eat with you in an hour or so, Eddie. I'm looking forward to that grouper." Andrews waved his hand and pulled his door closed.

****

There was only one other party, of two couples, in the dining room when he arrived for dinner. The sound of a piano playing Tom Jobim's beautiful "Black Orpheus" came faintly from the ceiling speakers and the tables were garnished with fresh hibiscus blossoms from the flower garden just below the pool deck. Eddie emerged from the kitchen doors. Andrews took a corner table and ordered a glass of freshly squeezed grapefruit juice and the broiled grouper. He told Eddie that he would be right back and slipped down the hallway to the front desk to see if he had had any messages.

Kate Judson smiled and said no, there had been no calls for him, but a lady who was staying in the hotel had become concerned about the health of her little dog and Kate had inadvertently told her that a famous veterinarian had just arrived on the island that afternoon. She grimaced. "I hope that was all right with you?" she asked.

He nodded to assure her that it was fine. "And would that lady be the one Eddie calls "the swimming lady"?" he asked.

"Why, yes," Kate acknowledged. "She's a lovely person and has been most generous with our staff ..." Kate caught herself in midsentence, considering that she was perhaps providing more information about a guest than was necessary.

"Kate, I think anyone who stays in this hotel for a week needs to be well off, right?" Andrews said, attempting to put her at ease. "I may have been well off before I came over here this week." He laughed and she smiled.

"You're right," she said. "And with all the big boats that we have in and out of this marina, it takes a lot to impress Cookie and Eddie, but when she flew in here in that Learjet from Minneapolis with just her little dog, it was a first."

"A Learjet landed here?" asked Andrews, trying to hide his astonishment.

"Yes sir, the first one to ever put wheels down on the island, according to Cookie. The pilot told Ronnie Lee that he was in the Navy and he had landed on carriers that were twice as long as our strip. He was traveling so light when he left here that he had just enough fuel to clear customs in West Palm Beach."

"Yeah, he topped off his tanks there to go home," Jack said.

Kate admired Jack Andrews' understanding and appreciation for the little island's landing and takeoff challenges for visiting aircraft.

"Landing is one thing," Jack said, shaking his head in disbelief, "but taking off is another." Andrews had turned to walk away when a thought occurred to him.

"Kate, what is the swimming lady's name, if I may ask, just in case she seeks my professional services."

"Her name is Helen Warner," Kate said instantly. "And her little Yorkie is named Bentley." She smiled.

"Thanks. I've ordered Eddie's grouper for dinner, so I'm going back to the dining room and check it out."

"I've already had it," she gushed. "It's wonderful!"

He was on his way back to his table in the dining room when he caught sight of her out of the corner of his eye. She was seated at the corner table opposite from his with her back to the wall. They were the only two people in the dining room now. She was wearing a white linen dress and had her long black hair pulled back into a tight bun. What seemed to be a Bloody Mary cocktail, with a stalk of celery coming out of the top of it, was placed in front of her. Andrews recognized her immediately as the woman he had spoken to at the pool that afternoon. The swimming lady was staring at him. When he nodded towards her, she responded with a bright smile and a wave of her hand. Andrews thought her strikingly beautiful in an exotic sort of way and he found himself not only smiling back at her, but walking directly towards her table.

"Pardon me," he heard himself say. "But are you the lady with the sick Yorkie?"

"Why, yes," she said, smiling. "Are you the famous veterinarian from Florida that Kate told me about?"

"It's infamous, not famous," he said with a smile, "but I'm happy to be at your service. My name is Jack. What seems to be Bentley's problem?"

Now she flashed a dazzling smile at the sound of her Yorkie's name. Andrews was taken aback by her pale blue eyes. "Bentley has had an upset stomach and has eaten little since we got here last week. I have been worrying about him."

"How old is he, and is he drinking water?" Andrews asked.

"He is five, and water is about all he is taking in."

"That's all good news. Dogs are similar to humans in that they experience motion and stress sickness just like we do. You can treat their upset stomachs just as we treat our own. I have something in my bag that I'm certain will settle his stomach and I would be more than happy to take a look at him for you."

Eddie was by his side. "Mister Jack, your dinner is on your table, sa."

There was an awkward silence before he said, "Thanks Eddie, I'll be right there."

"Look, Miss, "he hesitated, intentionally not wanting to show that he already was aware of her name.

"Helen. Helen Warner." She flashed another broad smile at him now. *Cool*, Andrews thought ... *You know her dog's name, but you don't know her name. She's wondering what kind of a fruit cake is this guy?*

"Look, Helen, although there is a rumor that there are a pair of newlyweds also staying here, as far as I can see, you and I are the only two people staying in this hotel tonight.

Won't you please be kind enough to join me at my table for dinner?"

She hesitated just long enough to convince him that she was considering it. "But your dinner is already waiting for you," she said. "Why don't you go ahead and eat it?"

"Nonsense." He had taken the bit in his teeth now. "My main man Eddie, here, will set another place at my table and we will eat my dinner as the first course for the two of us. And if it is as good as I think it will be, we'll eat your order as our second course." He picked up her cocktail and walked around behind her to pull out her chair.

He was impressed with his own aggressiveness. Only Eddie was moving faster than he was. The waiter had quickly crossed the dining room and commandeered another silverware place setting from a nearby table and set it up next to Andrews' chair so that both parties were looking out into the dining room.

"My, that sounds promising. What are we eating?" Helen asked, smiling and rising up out of her chair. She followed Jack across the dining room to where Eddie held a chair for her.

"We're eating Eddie's grouper," Andrews offered, giving Eddie a wink as he took the chair-holding duty from him. "He caught it this afternoon and I watched him filet it down at the marina with my own eyes. It looked fantastic, but now you can be the judge."

Andrews seated himself and quickly divided his dinner onto another plate that Eddie produced for him. He recommended to Helen that she try it first with only a little lemon juice squeezed on it.

The fish was, in fact, remarkable. "Heavenly! Just heavenly!" she purred, and they ordered his same dinner for her with two hearts of palm salads.

She had a second cocktail ("Virgin Mary, not Bloody," she said to Eddie emphatically. "No vodka!") and Andrews held up his glass and ordered another of "The same." When she asked what his drink was, he explained, in a matter of fact manner, that it was fresh grapefruit juice brought over from the Grand Cay every morning. "Here at the hotel they call Grand Cay 'The Big Island' and it is where all these folks who work here live."

Helen smiled and nodded her understanding. There was a long pause before either of them spoke again. Andrews was mulling things over in his mind. Two strangers trying to be social but both drinking fruit juice, and she had been so emphatic about no alcohol in her drink. He decided to take a chance and go all in.

"Hi, my name is Jack, and I'm an alcoholic," he said softly, offering the standard AA meeting greeting.

Helen's eyes widened in surprise. "Hello, Jack," she said, using the standard AA response. They both smiled knowingly. After a long pause, with eyes locked on each other, she broke the silence.

"Hi, my name is Helen, and I'm an alcoholic."

"Hello, Helen," Jack said.

The two sat in silence, staring at each other for a full minute, each refusing to speak for fear of breaking the magic of the moment. *God Almighty*, Andrews thought to himself. This woman was absolutely gorgeous! Her expressive blue eyes never blinked as she studied him. She had high cheekbones, but a soft chin, and the corners of her wide, beautiful, full-lipped mouth turned up slightly, producing the first hint of a smile. She was sizing him up, and apparently so far approved of what she saw. Their drinks arrived and Andrews spoke.

"To The Twelve Steps," he said, holding his glass out to her.

"To The Twelve Steps," she said, smiling and touching his glass with hers.

Andrews was slightly intoxicated by her presence. She was beautiful, smart, unpretentious and charming. A fascinating woman, he thought.

"Is this your first time here to Walkers Cay, Helen?" he asked, hoping not to appear nosy.

"Yes, my first time," she offered. "But I can tell from all the staff here that you are a regular."

"You've got me there," he grinned. "This is one of my favorite places on earth."

"When I was at the front desk this afternoon, Kate Judson told me that your unexpected arrival had caused such a great commotion among the staff that Cookie and Eddie were like two little kids before Christmas, arguing over who was going to take you fishing."

"I think Cookie won that argument, as he is the senior man at the marina," he said; and then, making an effort to keep her as the subject of their conversation, he asked, "Where are you from, Helen?"

"Minneapolis," she smiled. "It's a good place to be from this time of year, don't you think?" she added.

He smiled and nodded several times. "For sure. How did you hear about Walkers Cay?"

"A friend of mine, who owns a travel agency, told me about it. I wanted to more or less get away from it all and she said Walkers Cay, in the off season, would be the perfect place." She paused and asked, "I guess you're here to fish, though, right?"

He smiled and nodded a yes, but added, "Not just to fish. I'm here to billfish. Those are the big boys with bills on them such as sailfish, swordfish and the king of all fish, the blue marlin. But you could also say that I'm doing a little 'getting away from it all' myself. Have you ever been bill-fishing, Helen?"

"I have only been ice fishing, Jack, so I can't tell you if I enjoy what you do or not. But I'm looking forward to trying it out and have signed up to go out with the group tomorrow." She took a sip from her drink. "Where do you live in Florida, Jack?"

"I lived in Orlando." The past tense just somehow slipped out.

She didn't pick up on it or acknowledge it, if she did. She was keeping the discussion centered on him. "Do you have a family back in Orlando?"

"No children. I have a wife, but right now that is part of my wanting to 'get away from it all.' How about you? Any children?" He pushed the subject back to her.

"No, I'm afraid not," she said - a little sadly, he thought. She wore no wedding ring, which prompted his next question.

"Is there a Mr. Warner back in Minneapolis?"

"Yes there is ..." She paused and then added, "... for the moment, anyway. But we don't want to go there. I saw you running this afternoon. Eddie says you run around the air strip 20 times, but surely that was an exaggeration."

"Totally. I try to do whatever it takes to get in about four to five miles. I usually start slow and then taper off. But I did see that Johnny Weissmuller Tarzan stroke of yours in the pool this afternoon. How far do you swim?"

"I try to get in about two to three miles a day," she offered. "That's 250 laps down and back in this pool here."

Andrews let out a soft whistle. "Wow! That's impressive," he said. They finished their dinner in silence before Andrews motioned Eddie to their table. "Eddie, my man. Can we have two dishes of that mango ice cream for dessert, please?"

"Yes sa, Mister Jack," Eddie said as he cleared away their plates. "Two mango ice creams coming right up."

"Just wait until you taste this stuff," Andrews told Helen. "They use an old fashion crank churn and make it when the mangoes come into season. They run the mangoes lightly through a blender and then add the fruit to an old fashion frozen custard recipe. I've helped them crank out gallons of it in the summers when I'm here."

"Can't wait," she smiled. Her black hair was mesmerizing with her pale blue eyes.

There was an awkward silence before Jack Andrews spoke. "Okay, let's recap what we know about each other so far. We are two alcoholics ..."

"Recovering alcoholics!" she interrupted him with a smirk.

"Recovering alcoholics," he corrected himself. "I'm from Orlando and love to fish. You're from Minneapolis and have never fished. Sorry, ice fishing doesn't count. Both of us would be considered 'exercise-nut cases' by most ordinary active people. Neither of us have children, but both of us have spouses that we are currently unhappy with and we both have situations back at home that are so difficult as to have us, may I say, 'hiding out' in an empty hotel on a little island far out in the Bahamas. What have I left out?" he asked.

Helen burst into laughter. "Makes a pretty corny script, doesn't it? So, tell me, Jack, what is so bad back there in Orlando that you can't tell a perfect stranger, who is totally removed from the situation, about it? Maybe what you need is an outsider's opinion; or to at least talk about it and air it out. I'm a good listener." She flashed her broad smile at him once more and cocked her head to one side.

"No, Helen, I already admire you way too much to ever burden you with my problems," he said. "But you tell me more about yourself. What made you want to get away from it all in Minneapolis, other than the weather?"

"Isn't the weather enough?" she asked, but her smile disappeared abruptly and she shook her head. "Let's not talk about either of our problems," she said. "My problems have to be worse than yours because they are so complicated and mixed up that they are unsolvable."

Eddie emerged from the kitchen with a tray and placed a bowl with mango ice cream in front of each of them. Helen took a taste. "Oh my God, this is heavenly!" she exclaimed.

"Told you so," he grinned, and the two ate their desserts in silence.

For the next hour they enjoyed each other's company in the dining room. They talked about everything except each other's recent pasts. She had grown up in the Twin City area, went to Michigan on a swimming scholarship, majored in finance, and was also a yoga instructor. He had graduated from Florida with a degree in biology and, faced with the draft, had gone into the Marine Corps to fly jets. After Vietnam he attended Auburn University and got his degree in veterinary medicine. She asked about his vet practice and he explained that he no longer had a small animal clinic, but worked out of his home doing consulting for thoroughbred horse breeders.

He attempted to get some information from her on her Learjet ride down to Walkers. Was it leased, or did she own it? She never answered the question, but instead asked him if he often came to Walkers Cay by himself. Both he and she noticed that whenever the conversation shifted closer to current happenings and a question was asked too close to recent events, it slowed conversation and dulled the mood for both of them. When the dining room closed, they relocated to the chairs on the patio, at poolside.

There they discovered that they both loved classical music and jazz. She played piano. He played guitar. He was also into country music, while she was more of an opera fan. Both agreed that, as with beer and black coffee, those two tastes had to be acquired. They both loved to read fiction, she more than he. They both loved to cook, he more than she. He told her all about the Florida in which he had grown up and she told him all about the Minnesota of her roots that had helped to form her midwestern values.

When he talked about his Marine Corps flight training, she mentioned that she understood all about the Marine Corps, as her husband had been one. He had also done a tour duty in Vietnam.

"Once a Marine, always a Marine, right?" She showed him her dazzling smile again.

"Right!" Andrews said. "Once you have served, you could be called a "Former Marine" but never an "Ex-Marine."

They both admitted that they were considered "heath nuts" by their close friends. He was into running and calisthenics; she into swimming and her yoga. She had little knowledge about Walkers Cay and the other Bahaman islands. After flying over and sailing around them for years, Andrews was an authority, and he promised that he would help her catch a big billfish before she left the island.

It was past midnight when Andrews walked her back to her room and then went to his own room to retrieve his medical bag to take a look at the Yorkie. When he returned to her room and knocked on her door, it took a few seconds for her to open it. She was still dressed in the same white linen but she had let her hair down and it was now on her shoulders. He brushed past her as he entered into the room and was aroused by her fresh, clean, soapy smell.

"Where is Mr. Bentley?" he asked, looking around the room.

"Mr. Bentley is in his bed," she said, pointing to the bathroom. "He must have known that you were coming, as he just ate a small can of his food and drank a bowl of water, so I think he is on the mend."

Jack pushed the bathroom door open and peered in at the little dog who, upon hearing a strange voice, was now standing up in his elaborate wooden kennel, wagging his tail. Helen quickly unfastened two snaps at the top of the kennel and both sides slid down into the base of the kennel, leaving the little dog free to hop out of his bed. "Hey, Bentley boy," Andrews said, reaching for the Yorkie and lifting the little dog up to his chest. He carried him into the bedroom and placed him on the table in a corner of the room. Slowly he probed the little dog with his fingers from his head to his tail.

"No temperature; no swollen glands; you must be feeling a little more chipper?" he asked the Yorkie. He opened his bag and took out a bottle of small tablets and counted six of them out on the table. Andrews picked up one of the tablets and, opening Bentley mouth with this left hand, he quickly pushed the tablet down the Yorkie's throat with the index finger of his right hand.

"Wow, you have quick hands." Helen said. "I'm not sure I can do that."

"I don't think you will need to right away," he smiled at her. "Those extra ones are for when you leave the island, and only if the air travel gets him stressed again. It is the equivalent to you or me taking a small dose of Pepto-Bismol. He has basically already corrected himself and should be fine in the morning."

Bentley walked back into the bathroom and gazed up at his kennel. Andrews followed him into the bathroom and studied the kennel. The base was made out of several different types of wood, inlaid to form intricate beautiful patterns in the high base platform and on the two ends. The woven wire side panels and top panels were hinged together and rode in tracks, which allowed them to be dropped down on the outside of the wooden base so that the dog was free to move in and out of his bed.

"Wow, this is the most beautiful dog kennel I have ever seen," he said, working the sides up and down. The pieces slid along their tracks, interlocking and rotating over the top to come together to produce a self-enclosing cage that fastened with four locking catches at the top. Two of the catches also connected to make a handle, which allowed the kennel to be carried with one hand. He stooped down and picked up the little dog, placing him back in his blanket bed.

"Bentley, you sleep in a real palace, buddy, but I'm sure that you deserve it." He scratched the little dog gently behind its ears and smiled at his owner. "He is a real cutie." The Doctor K training was never too far away from him, he thought.

Helen beamed at his comments. "A friend, who does woodworking and is also a clock maker, made it for me," Helen offered, pointing to the kennel. "I've had dozens of people want to buy it and ask where they can get one."

"It is one of a kind all right," Andrews said as he walked out of the bathroom and smiled back at the little Yorkie. "I think he is going to be fine, but give me a call in Room 224 if you think he is having any more problems."

The two of them stood close together, staring at each other.

"Let me pay you something for the medicine and your services," she offered.

"Don't be silly. I owe Bentley a lot," he said. "If not for him, we may never have met. I have enjoyed the evening, Helen."

"Me too, Jack," she smiled.

He wanted to take her in his arms and kiss her beautiful mouth, but he was constrained. He enjoyed this fascinating woman. But they had just met each other. She had no idea that he was perhaps a fleeing felon, facing assault charges and maybe even prison. He reached out and took her hand. He held it.

"It was fun tonight, Helen. Thanks for keeping me company. I am looking forward to helping you catch a billfish while you are here on Walkers."

"Thank you, Jack," she said. "I'm so glad we met each other."

Andrews released her hand, turned, and walked out the door and down the hall towards his room. He had reached the end of the long hallway before he heard the door to her room close softly behind him.

****

Chapter 18
Consummation
The action of making a marriage or relationship complete by having sexual intercourse

The ringing phone on the bedside table woke him. "Hello," he half-croaked as he sat up on an elbow.

"Good morning, Sunshine!" Bill Evans sang in his ear. Jack Andrews glanced at his watch which showed that he was just minutes away from his normal seven o'clock reveille. Billy had always been too much of a morning person, Andrews remembered. "How's the fishing, Jackson?"

"Haven't been yet," Andrews mumbled into his phone.

"Jack, I've been trying to reach you since yesterday afternoon."

"Yeah, phone service here has been iffy," he lied.

"How are you holding up, Jackie boy?" his friend asked.

"Okay, I guess. I'm not drinking, Billy, if that's what you and Sam are so concerned about. Sam told me yesterday that you two were going to go by the Cowans' house. Did you see him?"

"As a matter of fact, we did. He was in his pajamas and bathrobe. Sam thought he was pale and rather subdued, but the son-of-a-bitch seemed fine to me. Sam talked me out of greeting him with a "How are you hanging, Congressman?" Billy roared with laughter. "However," he continued, "I did notice that his voice is much higher than it used to be, and he told us that his biggest problem these days is fighting off the overwhelming urge to go shopping." Billy barely got out the word, "shopping" before letting out a peal of laughter. Neither Andrews nor his two friends had any use for their congressman, but Billy Evans had hated Cowans with a passion since the night he and his wife had retrieved and befriended the young college student, soaked to the skin by lawn sprinklers, from Cowans' front yard.

"I must be honest with you, Jack; that last line is Sam's. He gets all the credit for it. Look, I know you are hurting over Jill and all, and Sam and I don't mean to be flippant about your situation, but Cowans is such an asshole. He is so lucky you didn't kill him. Sam and I think that you showed amazing restraint in that situation."

"What did Cowans say? What did you talk about?"

"We just talked about freeze damage, Jack. All of us with citrus may be totally out of business. We were there to encourage the congressman to work on some legislation to help out the Florida growers. He just sat in a chair and listened. He let me do most of the talking, while Sam just studied him. Sam now thinks that Cowans is going to keep this thing a big secret and is going to pretend that whole deal never happened. I kind of agree with Sam, as it is the type of secret that would end his political career if the word got out."

Andrews sat up on the edge of the bed. "Billy, I don't think I'm coming back to Orlando today. I haven't called Jill since

I left Friday, but I think I am going to spend some more time here at Walkers and see what shakes out before I fly back. Check with Sam for me and see if he thinks it is okay for me to stay here for a few more days."

"Roger that, but I'm sure he will agree that you can stay as long as you want. Everyone thinks that you were long gone Friday when these events happened. If Sam and I understand the facts correctly, neither Jill nor Cowans ever saw you in your house Friday night; nor did any of your neighbors, isn't that right?"

"That's right. I carried Jill to our guest room, but neither she nor Cowans ever regained consciousness while I was there."

Billy lowered his voice and spoke so softly that Andrews could barely hear him.

"Jack, Sam and I think you should just pretend that you never went back to the house. When you talk to Jill, try to act as normal as you possibly can. She is the one who is going to be on the defensive. Just tell her that the fishing is great right now at Walkers, and you flew there from Freeport to take advantage of it."

"That wouldn't be far from the truth." Andrews quipped.

"What's happening there on island?" Billy asked.

"Not much at all; there are only ten or twelve other guests here in the hotel right now and just a few local boats in the marina. They have a fishing charter flying in this morning from Freeport to go out on the Hatteras with Eddie. I'm going out in the deep water with Cookie this morning, so maybe we will catch a big blue marlin. The boys here say that they are out here right now, just off the shelf."

"Okay, buddy. Have some fun and I'll call you if I hear anything." Billy hung up.

After hanging up his phone, Jack headed to the bathroom. He brushed his teeth and shaved and was about to step into the shower when the house phone by the bed rang. He grabbed it up on the second ring.

"Yep," he said quickly.

"Hello, Jack?" He recognized the soft, but deep, voice immediately.

"Good morning, Ms. Warner. Yes, this is Captain Jack, your fishing guide for the day. I hope you had a good night's sleep because you could just be fighting a big blue marlin before the day is over."

"Oh, good morning to you, Captain Jack." Her voice became cheery. "I was just wondering if I had time to swim a few laps before we embark today.'

"Well, the management here says that it is now just going to be the two of us going out there on the high seas today with our boat captain, Cookie. So we can shove off whenever you wish. There are two things that you will need to know to help you make your decision."

"Okay, what are they?" she asked.

"First, the sooner we get our baits out behind our boat, the sooner we could catch a big marlin."

'Point taken; what is the second thing I should know?" She asked gaily.

"The second thing you should know is that I don't care if you would rather swim than fish with me, and I will

192

certainly understand your decision to do something you love to do verses spending time with me sitting in a boat and breathing diesel fumes all day. But if you want to come, I would love to have you join me."

After a long silence she said, with great sincerity, "If you wouldn't mind my tagging along, I would rather do that than anything else."

What a woman this gal is, he thought to himself, but he still sensed the need to clear the air.

"Look, Helen, we had a great time together last night. I think we enjoy each other a lot; but as I said at dinner, it is pretty obvious that we are both running from some things in our recent past. You seem to feel that your situation is somehow much worse than mine and all I can say is 'God help you if that is the case.' You don't want to talk about it and I fully understand, as I certainly don't want to talk about my situation. But I do know this: there is absolutely nothing you can do for me that would help my cause. And let me just say this: if there was something you could do for me that would help my situation, I would not hesitate to let you do it. I know that you are sincere and I totally trust you. On the other hand, if I can help you in any way, all you have to do is ask. I have an airplane and I know these islands better than most of the folks who live here. If you need to go to Nassau, Freeport, Treasure Cay, or any place, I'm happy to take you any time you want to go. I'll be your 'new best friend;' one that you can count on. That's a promise I can make to you."

Helen was silent. Then, after a long pause, she spoke. "Thank you, Jackson Andrews, that's the nicest thing anybody has said to me in a long time and I can't begin to tell you how much I appreciate your support. Now, I have a favor to ask of my new best friend."

"Your wish is my command," he said, laughing.

"Do you think that my new best friend could also become my lover?"

Andrews held his breath. He felt the muscles in the back of his neck tighten. But the question stunned and shocked him into silence. Helen filled the void.

"Will you be my lover, too, Jack?"

When he caught his breath, he attempted to hide the excitement in his voice by speaking slowly in a whisper, "Why, of course, Helen. I'll be your lover. That's easy! The hard part is being a great friend through thick and thin."

"Room 224 is located where, Jack?" There was a serious tone in her voice now.

"It's on the second floor, up the stairs and all the way to the end of the hallway and...."

"Click." The connection was broken and after a second or two, a dial tone was all he heard.

He turned the shower on as hot as he could stand it and let the water run on the back of his neck. He was just reaching for a towel when he heard a knock at the door. Thinking it was Cookie wanting to give him the lowdown on the fishing reports; he quickly dried himself and wrapped the towel around his midsection. He turned the dead bolt and opened the door. She was standing there in the same black sarong he had seen her wearing the day before at the pool. Her hair was down and she was smiling that mischievous smile he had seen so often the night before each time she had sought to coax some information from him about his past.

"May I come in, Captain Jack?" Helen asked as she brushed by him, placing a hand on his shoulder. He let the door close and pulled her to him. Their mouths rushed together in a frantic kiss and then her free hand quickly pulled the towel from his body and then undid and dropped her sarong to reveal that she had no tank suit on this morning. They fell onto the bed, groping and fondling each other. Andrews' excitement overcame him as she pulled him to her and guided him into her. He nearly ejaculated, but fought off the orgasm just in time and froze in place.

"Don't move," he whispered to her, and she was still. After a few seconds of silence, she panted in his ear: "What's happening?"

"That was going to be a runaway train," he whispered. "I've got to slow myself down so I can be not just your lover, but your most excellent lover." She smiled up at him. "Whatever you say, Captain Jack."

After several minutes of letting their bodies lie together motionless, he continued to move again; extremely slow at first but then, as she became more aroused, he quickened his movements. Then he remained motionless for several minutes. "Don't move, Helen," he said again, smiling down at her.

"What is going on now?" she asked.

"When I was a young man I had a problem with premature ejaculation and I learned a little trick to compensate for it," he whispered. "If I can just have about a 30 percent orgasm, it desensitizes me enough that I can then run a marathon with you."

"A marathon. I'm impressed," she cooed.

"It's a little tricky to do," he offered, "because a 31 percent, orgasm does in fact have the same effect as a 100 percent orgasm."

They laughed together.

"And so you are telling me that you just had a 30 percent orgasm, is that right?"

"Yes, more or less; that's a fact, My Lady."

"And... because it was just 30% and not 31%, it desensitized you so that you now can stay erect and continue to make love to me, is that correct?"

"By God, I think she's got it," he said as he began moving again, slowly rocking himself gently back and forth as he slid in and out of her. He kissed her again on the mouth; softly at first and then with great passion. For almost an hour they made love to each other before ending in a straining crescendo that collapsed them both. For several minutes they lay wet with sweat, motionless and exhausted, in each other's arms. Helen spoke.

"Wow, you weren't kidding! Can all men do that?" she asked.

"I have no idea about other men. I would guess that answer is no just because it involves work on the man's part to focus on the lady. A lot of guys wouldn't make that effort."

"But, you Captain Jack, always make the effort and focus on your ladies, right?" she said in her deepest voice.

"Well, certainly during the courtship stage," he laughed. "They say that you only get one chance to make a first impression. How did I do?"

"More, I want more!" she cried at the ceiling.

They laughed together, then Andrews spoke. "I was just thinking that here we are, Jack and Helen, two people who came to a little island running from their depressing pasts. I think it is safe to say that two days ago neither of us had much positive going on in our lives; we certainly weren't carefree and laughing. Yet, look at us today. Thank God for lust, huh?"

"You just speak for yourself, Captain Jack," she cried, hitting him playfully with a pillow. "I think we have a lot more going for our relationship than just lust."

"What is wrong with lust?" he questioned. "We know nothing about each other except that you're from Minnesota and I'm from Florida and we are both alcoholics."

"Not true," she protested. "We both love to exercise, eat good food; we both love animals and are kind to them. We both love art and music and we both love people and people love us. We both love to laugh and...."

He cut her off with another hard kiss on her mouth.

"Cancel the fucking fishing trip!" she cried out when they came up for air.

"You're special, Helen," he whispered.

"I couldn't sleep last night after you left me," she confided to him. "I couldn't believe that after our wonderful dinner, the intimate conversation, and a magical evening, you just walked away from me."

"I didn't feel that I had the right to push us further under my present circumstances," he said.

"Tell me about those present circumstances." she smiled.

He rose and pulled her up off the bed. "Not right now, My Lady. Let's take a shower and then maybe we can have a serious talk." Exhausted and covered with sweat, they retired to the bathroom shower together. They washed each other's backs in silence; and then, between kisses, they took turns drying each other. Before he could pull on the cargo shorts that he planned to wear on the boat, she pushed him back to the bed and fell on top of him.

"Help," he laughed. "I've become the sex slave to a driven nymphomaniac queen."

She laughed with him. "Tell your own Delilah, Samson," she said. "What makes you so big and strong? And what is that bad thing in your past that makes you so sad and serious?"

Andrews stared at her for some time before propping himself up on an elbow. "I assaulted a man on Friday night and I could have to go to prison for it."

Helen blinked several times. "Wow! Why did you do that?" she asked. "You must have had a good reason."

"He was having an affair with my wife."

"See, I thought there had to be a good reason. Surely you don't go to prison for beating up somebody that is having an affair with your spouse."

"No, but I didn't beat him up."

"What did you do to him then?"

"I castrated him."

"You did *what?*" she gasped, staring into his eyes.

"That's right, I gelded him. I surgically removed his testicles."

"Oh my god, is he still alive?"

"Yes, it's a simple operation once you control the bleeding. He is, in fact, a United States Congressman."

Helen opened her mouth as if to scream, but made no sound. She whispered, "Oh my god, Jack! Is the FBI looking for you?"

"Not yet; the congressman doesn't know that it was me. And I have two good friends in Orlando, my AA buddies, who have been by to see the guy and they say he is doing fine and it looks as if he could let the whole thing go by without comment. If he goes public with it, it will undoubtedly end his political career, for certain. He is presently running for the U.S. Senate. Of course, my AA friends are fearful that I will start drinking again."

"Damn, I don't blame them. *They* could start drinking again, with that pressure on them. These are your best friends, right?" She was concerned.

"Lots of people have friends that will help them move, Helen. A great friend is one that will help you move a body. Sam and Billy would help me move a body, I am certain."

"Would you help me move a body, Jack?" she asked.

"Of course," he smiled.

"Have you got one that I need to move?" he asked with a grin.

"What does ... what does your wife say about all this?" Helen was struggling to keep her matter of fact composure.

"I'm not certain that she even knows about his surgery; and even if she does, she doesn't know that it was me, either..."

Andrews continued to explain in detail all the events of Friday night, including his falling off the wagon, his just about committing a double homicide, and how in fact it all ended with his flying to Freeport early Saturday morning, giving his lecture to the Thoroughbred Breeders Convention and then coming to Walkers Cay to wait and see what would develop. There was a long silence when he was finished and then he gazed at her and smiled. In his best Bogey voice, he said: "There you have it, sweetheart; do you still want me to be your lover?"

"More than ever," was her reply as she pulled him down and attempted to kiss his mouth again, before he pulled away.

"Now, its Mrs. Warner's turn!" He pointed his index finger at her. "Let's hear it. What's with all this mystery about you, and what are you running from?"

Helen studied him for several seconds. "Well, I guess you could say that I am sort of similar to you in that I assaulted my husband. Not physically, but certainly financially. As in your case, I found out that he was unfaithful to me and when he was away on one of his two week trips with his girlfriend, I liquidated all of our assets. I sold our house, furniture, cars, artwork, boats, and our company for cash and converted it into bearer bonds and offshore trust accounts. When he came home this weekend he found out that nothing was as he'd left it. This week my lawyers are filing for my divorce and asking for a restraining order to keep him away from me until our affairs are settled."

"Wow, how did you do all that in just two weeks?" Andrews was looking at her in disbelief.

"Oh, I have been working on it for over a year. The hardest part was playing the good wife and acting as if I had no idea what was going on." She smiled at him. "Plus, I had a lot of good help from one of the best law firms in St. Paul. They did all of the heavy lifting. I had run our chemical business for the past five years, so the employees were loyal to me. I got a fair price for the business, as I own part of the new one that bought it, but I had to take a steep discount on the house to make the sale for cash."

"How could you do all that without your husband's signature and approval?"

"I had his full power of attorney, which I had him sign on several different occasions to make me the sole decision maker. It wasn't that difficult to arrange, but the two week timing limitations to make it all work were stressful."

"Remind me not to screw around with you," Jack said, shaking his head.

"You just did," she laughed. "Plus, at least I didn't castrate him."

Jack grimaced. "So, then, how do bearer bonds work?" he asked. "I understand that the interest is paid to the bond bearer on a coupon that is attached to the certificates, but do they have titled ownership? In other words, are they Helen Warner's bonds?"

"No, they are issued without title. The advantage they have is that they are easily transferable, easily negotiable, and anonymous. They have some disadvantages in that they have been used in the past to cover up criminal activity and avoid income taxes, so they are no longer issued in the United States. There are still a few US Bearer Bonds around, but you have to look hard to find them. My law firm found some for me and they were much easier to buy on the international market. But if your issuer is strong and solvent and you are making all of your transactions on the up and up and with the full knowledge of the IRS, they are great. But you do need to treat them as if they are cash. If they are transferred or stolen, then there is a new bearer cashing in those coupons. For that reason, they are hard to trace," she smiled broadly. "Just as I hope to be hard to trace."

"So, your husband has no recourse. You converted all of your joint assets into cash and the cash has just disappeared with you. Correct?"

"That's right, Captain Jack. Bentley and I are the only ones who know where the bearer bonds and my trust documents are located, and we're not telling anybody."

"That is a good secret to keep between the two of you." He glanced over at Bentley and smiled. "Now, what are your plans; are you going back to Minnesota?"

"Definitely not," she replied. "I have a good friend from college that has a house in Palm Beach. She wants me to live with her for as long as I want, but my husband knows all about her and will look there first."

"Who knows that you are here on Walkers Cay?" he asked.

"Only one person, and she is a good friend who owns the travel agency in Minneapolis. She arranged the private charter to fly me in here under an assumed name. Only when I came through customs here did I have to show my real passport and identity. But Kate and her staff understand that I want privacy above all else."

"Wow." Andrews shook his head. "Helen, I don't think that you have any problems. Even if your husband somehow finds you, the best he can hope for is that you give him half of your bearer bonds."

Helen studied him closely.

"Jack, we have only known each other for just a day; but you told me earlier this morning that you feel I am sincere. You said you trusted me and that you would be a best friend that I could count on. Did you mean all that, or were you just talking to my vagina?" She fought to keep a straight face even when she saw his shocked expression, but her laughing eyes gave her away.

Andrews struggled to suppress his own smile, but drew back his head with an overly mocked-up look of shock. "I beg your pudding, Madam," he whispered softly, as if others may have heard her. "Ms. Warner, please!" They stared at each other for a second or two and then both burst into laughter. He kissed her softly again on her lips.

The house phone by the bed rang, startling both of them. "Saved by the bell," Andrews said, looking at his watch. "God almighty, girl, it's 10 O'clock. We were supposed to meet Cookie on the docks hours ago."

She smiled and reached out for him. "Time flies when you're having fun." He reached across her nude body and grabbed the receiver. It was Kate.

"Jack, Cookie said to tell you that he has the boat ready and he is all set to go fishing whenever you and Mrs. Warner want to go, sir."

"Thanks, Kate; tell Cookie we are on our way." He hung up and grinned at Helen. "Well, the staff here has figured out that we are definitely an item."

She smiled back at him. "You don't mind, do you?" she asked, tilting her head to one side.

"Of course not," he said. "Let's go fishing."

****

Chapter 19
"Boss Fish"
The name seasoned saltwater anglers give the big blue marlin

The day was bright and sunny, yet the 18-mile-an-hour wind was cool enough that everyone was wearing jackets or sweaters. Andrews had warned Helen that the breeze off the deep water would be much cooler than the one around their little island. He was carrying a navy pea coat in addition to wearing his windbreaker. She was wearing a sweatshirt with the word 'Michigan' printed on the front of it in large letters. She also carried a fleece-lined poncho coat. Helen had brushed her hair back into a ponytail and pulled it through a navy blue ball cap and was wearing her wide sunglasses. She wore no makeup and her natural beauty was amazing. Andrews couldn't take his eyes off of her and, apparently, neither could Bart Keener.

"Here come the movie stars," he cried from the stern of the Bewitched, where he was working on one of the outriggers. He had made it back from Marsh Harbor with his new bladder fuel tanks and was already onboard helping Cookie get ready to make way. He gave a mischievous grin at Jack and Helen as they stepped onboard.

"Is this the famous Gertrude Ederle?" Bart asked Jack, putting him on the spot.

Before Andrews could think of an answer, Helen smiled at Bart and said, "No sir, but I thank you for the compliment. My name is Helen Warner, and I have met "Trudy" Ederle, and she has certainly been an inspiration to me and all women who swim competitively." Bart smiled at her quick response and recovered quickly.

"Hi, Helen Warner, my name is Bart Keener - and welcome aboard the Bewitched," he said happily. "You've picked a great day to go to deep water. I just feel lucky today. Do you feel lucky, Jack?" He smiled broadly at Jack.

"Jack and I have already been lucky today," Helen said gaily. "We're still on a roll, so you just hang on..."

Keener stopped what he was doing and made a disbelieving face at Jack.

"You heard the lady," Andrews said, smiling. "Let's get this show on the road."

As Eddie's Miami fishing party charter had cancelled, he jumped aboard as they were pulling away from the fuel dock.

"I is gonna to work de lines and bring you some good luck today, Mister Jack," he said, smiling at Andrews and Helen.

"That's great, Eddie. I have promised My Lady here that I was going to help her catch a big blue today," Andrews said, putting his arm around Helen's shoulders. She beamed at his gallantry. "So, I am going to need all the help I can get." He glanced up at Cookie and Bart on the flying bridge. "As we all know this requires a total team effort."

206

They both smiled back and Bart gave him a thumbs up gesture.

Running at about 24 knots, the forty-two foot Whiticar cut through the choppy waves and was out over deep water within 30 minutes. Jack kept his eyes on Helen for any sign of sea sickness. He gave her a rice cracker to nibble on and explained how important it was for her to keep her eyes on the horizon when they got into rougher seas. When Cookie cut the engines, Bart and Eddie went to work tying on the Spanish mackerel baits and letting out the lines. Jack seated Helen into the lone fighting chair and explained in great detail what was about to happen.

"Okay, Helen; while we are setting up the baits and lines, I want to tell you a little bit about what we are going to try to do." He handed her a pair of soft leather gloves. "See if these fit comfortably."

"Kiss me for good luck, Captain Jack," she said, pulling on the gloves.

"Yes, My Lady." He smiled at her seriousness and kissed her on the mouth, and then he continued on with his instruction. "Similar to flying an airplane, marlin fishing has been described as 90 percent boredom and 10 percent sheer terror. There is no question that of all the sport fishes, the blue marlin are the "Boss Fish." All of these competitive deep sea fishing tournaments that you read about are all built around blue marlin fishing. Now, we could catch a wahoo or a yellowfin tuna on these same baits; but they will be secondary to what we are after. Even if we get a white marlin or sailfish, which can be a lot of fun, it's just not the same thing as a big blue. "

"Go, Blue!" Helen cried, pointing to the Michigan letters on her sweatshirt.

"Right, dear." Jack was focused. "You're sitting in this chair because your rod has the longest bait on it. It is called the "center rigger" and it's the one that Eddie is setting right now with that little fish called a Spanish mackerel. He is running that bait out to about 160 feet from the boat and connecting it to that outrigger that sticks straight back from the top of the flying bridge over our heads, here. That line will snap right out of that clamp when we get a fish on it." Eddie handed the rod and big Penn reel to Jack and turned to set the two side baits.

Jack put the rod between Helen's legs into a cup built into her chair. "Put this rod between your legs into your gimble mount," he whispered to her.

"I love it," she whispered back, gripping the rod with both hands and smiling at him.

Jack shook his head, smiling, and glanced around to see if anyone had heard them before continuing his lecture. "The baits Eddie and Bart are setting now on each side will come from those two rod holders here on the left and right side of the transom. They are called the left and right "long riggers." Next to your "center rigger," they are the longest lines, and you can see that Bart is running his out now, all the way to the tip of the outrigger. Eddie has already run his out on the other side on the thing we call a "roller-troller."

"And so we have three lines with bait?" Helen asked.

"We are going to drag five, today. The guys are going to set two more rods up in those rod holders on each side of us." Jack pointed to the side gunnels. "They will be our shortest lines, and we call them "tag lines." We will run those lines out only halfway on the outriggers. I know it sounds complicated, but what it does is spread our bait out both

208

horizontally and vertically and allow us to steer the boat in fairly tight turns without tangling the bait lines."

"Okay, let me see if I've got it now," Helen said. "My line is called the "center rigger" and it is the longest. Those two rods on each side of mine are call "long riggers" and they are not as long as my "center rigger" and we extend them all the way out to the far side on each outrigger to keep them apart. These lines coming off the side rods are short and set only half way out on the outriggers. We call them "tag lines" because I guess they just tag along."

Jack smiled and flashed her two thumbs up, then turned and gave one thumb up to the bridge. Cookie added a few RPMs to the diesel engines and the boat speed increased slightly.

"How will I know when I have a blue marlin on the line, and what do I do?" Helen was getting excited.

"Believe me, honey; you're going to know when it happens. That line will snap right out of the outrigger clamp and your reel will begin to scream as the fish runs out with the line. Normally I would not have that rod in your hands yet, and we would just let it ride in the rod holder there in the middle of the transom. We don't know which bait we're going to get a strike on, but if he doesn't take yours, and he does another one, we will grab the rod with the load on it and exchange it for that one you are holding on to now. I just wanted you to get a feel for the position, and I'm going to coach you a little bit on how to play the fish once we have him hooked." He patted her on her shoulder and bent closer to her.

"Here's how this is going to go down. When we get a strike, you will hear Cookie yell, 'Big fish on.' If it is your bait, you're going to know it before he calls out. If it isn't your bait, I am going to take your rod away and Bart or Eddie will bring you the rod with the fish on it. See these clips on your fighting chair? Once the loaded rod is placed in your fighting chair's gimble mount, we will attach these clips to the eyelets on top of the big Penn reel. Cookie is not going to slow the boat down until we reach that stage. Once you are locked in a comfortable position, he will begin to slow the boat. "

"Now, you are going to have to work. Just take your time and start reeling in the fish by pulling up on the rod and reeling as you let the rod back down. The most important thing is to keep the line tight. You do that by always keeping your rod bent."

Because we release these big fish after we catch them, there are no barbs on our hooks. It's called a J hook because it is just a piece of metal in the shape of the letter J and the only thing that keeps the big fish on is tension on the J hook. If the line goes slack, the fish can give a good head shake and he gets off. Cookie is going to keep the boat moving to help you keep your rod bent, which means the line is tight. If he sees you are able to reel fast enough to keep the rod bent yourself, he will slow the boat and let you work the fish. However, if the fish swims toward us and your rod is not staying bent to keep the slack out, he will speed the boat up to keep it tight. Sometimes it may seem as if you are fighting with Cookie and not the fish. But he is trying to help you."

"Also, Helen," Bart chimed in. "From time to time a big fish may just decide to make a run for it again and run off with another 200 feet of your line. It can be disheartening when it happens, but it's no big deal. Expect it. Each time he does it; just remember when it happens that his swimming against your drag will make it easier to reel him in when he stops."

"As soon as we have a strike, Helen, the three of us are going to reel in all our other lines to get them out of the way." Jack continued on with his instruction. "Now, once we do that and Cookie sees that you can keep your rod bent yourself, by reeling, he will begin to slowly back the boat up and let you reel the fish in. When you get him under the stern of the boat is when the real hard work starts."

"Honey, they say the last 45 feet are the toughest because you are now pulling his weight up from directly below you and you have to "pump and reel." It takes lots of little short stokes. You will only be able to lift the rod about 20 degrees at a time, which will give you about one turn only on that Penn reel when you drop it back down." Jack smiled at the strained look on Helen's face.

"Helen, you know that you can bail out on pulling him in anytime you want. You've got both Bart and me right here; either of us will jump at a chance to bring him in that last 50 feet for you. We just want to get him close enough for our wireman, Eddie, here, to handle the leader line, pull him alongside the boat, take his picture, release the hook, then let him go. So, just say "help" when you need it."

"If I can get him under the boat, I will get him up here," she said, and the three men saw the determination in her eyes and the jaw set of the competitive distance swimmer. Jack Andrews also saw why Robert Warner never had a chance.

"Yes ma'am, you can!" Eddie said.

They trolled for two hours without a strike and then something ripped the bait right off the center rigger. Eddie had no sooner re-baited and reset the line when Bart caught a yellow fin tuna on one of the tag lines. The fish was a good size, and after fighting it standing up for 15 minutes before Eddie could bring it into the boat, Keener sat down on the cooler.

"Cookie," Jack called up to the bridge. "Let's make a slow turn around and go back over that area where Bart caught that tuna and something took our bait."

"Yes sa, Mister Jack,' Cookie said, turning the wheel and bringing the bow of the boat around is a slow turn.

Bart opened their lunch basket. "Tea time!" he called out to the others.

"What's on the menu?" Andrews asked.

Bart peered into the basket for a closer look. "It looks as if we've got lots of sandwiches, fresh turkey, ham and Swiss cheese, tuna salad, you-peel-'em shrimp, hardboiled eggs, dill pickles, apples and bananas. And here are two pimento and cheese sandwiches with a note on them that says, 'Captain Cookie.' Have you got someone sweet on you in the kitchen, Cookie?"

"Yes sa, Mister Bart. Dey's looking out for me." Cookie laughed as Bart pitched him the baggie with the two sandwiches in it.

"How about you, Helen, what would you want?" Bart asked. "We have plenty of each kind."

"I think I'll have a turkey sandwich and an apple, please," she smiled at him.

"Coming up," he said, handing her another baggie and a large red apple.

"How about you, Jackson, what sounds good?"

"I'll have a turkey, if you have plenty, and an apple." Jack answered.

Bart glanced at the two of them as they smiled at each other. "Eddie, you can have anything you want. There is another turkey in here."

"Yes sa, I would take de ham and cheese, if dere's plenny."

"We have plenty," Bart shot back. "Do you want an apple?"

"No thanks, sa, just de sandwich be fine."

Bart handed him a sandwich and opened the lid on the cooler.

"Okay, and now for drinks. We have in this cooler everything under the sun. I am going to have a beer, but we have all kinds of soda, bottled water, and..." He was stopped in midsentence by the loud snap of the center rigger line being ripped out of the outrigger. The big Penn 80 reel on Helen's rod screamed as its line rushed out.

"Big fish on!" Cookie cried out with a mouth full of sandwich.

Andrews was already moving to Helen's chair. "Hang on, babe," he whispered. "I'm going to snap these chair clips into your reel so we don't lose a couple thousand dollars' worth of fishing tackle when we get a chance to slow this fish down." He spoke to her softly, with great calmness in his voice. "When this line stops running, honey, you reel him in as if your hair is on fire. Keep that rod bent at all times. You've got you a Boss Fish on the line, and he's talking to you." He smiled at her and winked.

Bart and Eddie were reeling in the other lines and stowing them as fast as they could. Both long riggers were in and they were now working on the tag lines. Helen's big Penn reel stopped screaming and three male voices said in union, "Reel, reel, reel." And reel Helen did, with the veins standing out in her neck she reeled as fast as she could to keep her rod bent. Cookie had slowed the boat and was watching her rod closely. After watching how hard she was bending it, he eased the boat into reverse and moved towards the fish."

"Has anyone seen it jump yet?" Andrews asked his shipmates.

"No, it hasn't surfaced yet," Bart told him.

"It damn near ran off with all our line," Andrews said, shaking his head. "How are you doing?" he asked Helen.

"Piece of cake," she said. "He doesn't know it yet, but he is mine."

"That's my gal!" Jack said, nodding his head and smiling at Bart, who just shook his head and smiled.

With Cookie backing the boat slowly towards the big fish, Helen had recaptured most of the line that the fish had taken out against the drag, when all at once the reel screamed again. "Here is that run I was telling you about, Helen," Bart said. "He is a fighter and is using a lot of energy each time he swims against the drag."

"Thanks, Bart, I was expecting it, after what you told me. Jackson, would you hold my rod for a second while he is running? I need to get this sweatshirt off."

"Got it," Andrews snapped as he grabbed the rod carefully, avoiding the running line. Helen ripped her sweatshirt over her head, exposing her muscular arms. In just the 20 minutes she had been fighting the big fish, her T-shirt had

214

been soaked through with sweat. She grabbed the rod back from Andrews. "Thanks, Captain Jack," she smiled at him. The line stopped running.

"Go get 'em, Tiger," he said to her. "Reel him back in!"

And she did. For the next 40 minutes she reeled when Cookie backed the boat, rested for a few seconds when he pulled it forward, and then reeled again when he backed up. After playing cat and mouse for over an hour, the big fish made its first appearance, leaping high out of the water several hundred feet behind the boat.

All four men on the boat were speechless. Only Helen thought it would be as big as it was. "He's a beauty!" she cried.

"Jesus, that's a trophy blue marlin there, Helen!" Bart Keener yelled. He was stunned at the size of the big fish. "Jack, that's a thousand pound fucking fish there," he said, looking at Andrews. "What do you think, Cookie?" he called out, looking up at the bridge.

"He de biggest I seen," Cookie answered back. He was backing the boat up slowly now, trying to close the distance to the big marlin while Helen pulled and reeled with all of her strength.

"He de biggest I ever seen," Eddie added, looking over the side. "There he is now, Mister Jack. He is right below us." He pointed in the water just to the right of the stern.

"Watch that he doesn't go under the boat on us, Cookie," Andrews called out as he leaned over to put his mouth near Helen's ear. "All right darling, this is the last 45 feet. He has worn himself out with those two long runs. Let's see if we can pump and reel him to the surface."

Helen struggled to pull up on the bent rod. It just bent a little bit further, but it allowed her to get a half turn in on the reel when she dropped it back down. She grunted as she attempted to pull it back up. It didn't come.

"That's all right," Jack said. "You got a half a turn on him. Now let's see if you can get another half turn."

She did, and then she moved into her own rhythm of pull hard, reel; pull hard, reel; pull hard, reel. Sometimes there was no gain on the reel at all, and then on the next hard pull, she would be able to get a full turn. She got another half turn, then another full turn. Helen was working so hard that Jack Andrews' heart went out to her. He was overcome with admiration for this woman he had only known a few days. It was hard to believe she was real.

Eddie had his gloved hands on her line now, and was looking down under the right side of the boat's transom, waiting to see the leader wire. Helen was still pumping and reeling a little bit at a time. "I sees it!" Eddie shouted, and leaning out of the boat, he caught the leader wire with his right hand. "Lord God, he is a big blue, Mister Jack!" Eddie shouted as he grabbed the big fish's giant bill with his left hand and guided him on his side along the back transom.

"Congratulations on the catch, Helen," Jack smiled at her. "In tournament fishing, once your wire man touches the leader wire, it is considered a catch." He unhooked the Penn reel from the chair clips and took the rod from her. He offered her his hand to bring her out of the chair. "Come see your fish."

She staggered slightly as she made her way to the transom and peered down at her marlin. The fish's eye stared back up at her. "You are so beautiful and majestic," she whispered to the fish.

"Keep that leader tight, Eddie," Bart cried. "And look out for him to dump on you and make another run."

"Yes sa, Mister Bart," Eddie responded. "But I tink Boss Fish here is through fighting for dis day."

Bart had unhooked the gaff pole and was now swiveling the wench arm over the side of the boat.

"What are you doing?" Andrews asked.

"We're going to bring him in the boat, right?" Bart was dumbfounded. "I guarantee you, Jack, this fish is well over 1,000 pounds. I make my living working with these fish. The world record for a blue marlin is 1,400 pounds; the Florida record is 1,040 pounds. I think that this fish is bigger than the Florida record."

"No, we're not taking him back." Helen's voice was loud and definite. She sat back down in the fighting chair, trying to catch her breath.

Bart was stunned. "Helen, please. You worked so hard. You deserve to have your picture taken with this fantastic fish and be in the record books. You'll be famous." His voice was pleading.

Helen smiled at Andrews. "What do you think, Captain Jack; do we want to have our picture go into the record books and become famous?" He shook his head and smiled back at her.

"Jack, please can you do something?" Bart was desperate.

"No, Bart. You heard Helen. She caught it. She says set it free. Eddie, you want to do the honors?"

"Wait a minute. Don't you even want to take a picture of him?" Bart couldn't believe what he was witnessing. Jack nodded at Helen. She shook her head. "No pictures, Bart. He fought a great fight and I will never forget him. I think that he would be embarrassed that he got caught. Set him free, Eddie ... please."

"Yes, ma'am," Eddie said as he held the big fish's bill and pushed slack into the leader wire, jiggling it until the J hook came free. Then, pushing the bill out away from the transom, Eddie pulled the big marlin around to one side of the boat. There, with his other hand, Eddie helped the big fish to right itself as Cookie idled the boat forward to force water through its gills. After a minute of this dragging, the marlin began moving its tail from side to side; and as it seemed to grow stronger, Eddie released the bill. They all watched it slowly swim away.

They were silent for several minutes before Andrews picked up his pea coat. "That's a wrap, guys," he said. "Today is one of the shortest days of the year, so it will be getting dark by the time we get home. Eddie, please take care of Bart's yellowfin. Tuna is for dinner tonight, right?"

"Yes sa, Mister Jack," Eddie said.

"Is my Boss Fish going to be all right, Jack?" Helen was shocked at how slowly the giant fish had left it captors and slowly swam away from the boat.

"More than likely," he said. "He has to stay away from sharks until he get his strength back. He gave you his all. His strength is his speed, and right now he doesn't have any. Speaking of strength, you never ate your turkey sandwich. Do you want it now?" He pulled a baggie out of his pea coat pocket and handed it to her with a smile.

"I certainly would. I'm famished," she said with a slight British clip, taking the sandwich from him.

"Is 'famished' anything similar to 'the hongries?'" he asked.

"Hongries? What on earth is that?"

"See what you missed by being an opera fan? You've never heard Buck Owen's country song, 'I've got the hongries for your love and I'm waiting in your welfare line?'"

Helen threw back her head and howled. "Are you serious?"

"Well, it was never that big a hit, and you could be right. Buck should have used 'Famished' instead of 'Hongries.'"

"I don't think that would have helped sales much," she said, laughing.

Cookie pointed the bow of the Bewitched in the direction of Walkers Cay and pushed both throttles forward. When the boat leveled out, he eased them back to 2800 RPMs to conserve fuel. The sun was turning into a large red ball as it dropped toward the horizon.

Helen had put her Michigan sweatshirt back on soon after she left the fighting chair. Now she pulled on her poncho and followed Jack, wearing his pea coat, up onto the bridge. Andrews sat down in the captain's chair next to Cookie's and Helen sat in Jack's lap with his arms around her.

Andrews put a hand on the big man's shoulder and, smiling, he asked, "That was some fish, wasn't it, Cookie?"

Cookie shook his head and laughed. "If I hadn't seen it with my own eyes, Mister Jack, I would not believe it; and Miss

Helen, Eddie and me, we is thanking you for letting him stay in de water." Helen smiled at him.

"We're chasing the sun," Jack whispered in her ear. "You've had quite a day for yourself, Mrs. Warner."

She squeezed his arms hard against her. "Yes, I have, and I don't want it to ever end. It's one I'll always remember," she sighed.

****

Book III
Chapter 20
Test of Friendship

When they returned to Walkers on the Bewitched on Monday evening, Helen, Jack and Bart had an early dinner together in the dining room. Eddie had dressed out Bart's yellowfin tuna and delivered it to the kitchen before returning to help Cookie clean the salt off the Whiticar boat. Sally had been their waitress and all agreed that the dinner was wonderful. The big event of the evening in the dining room was the appearance of the newlyweds for the first time. Bart, who had flown them down to Spanish Cay and back the day they first arrived, initiated the clapping when they became visible in the doorway of the dining room. And after Jack and Helen joined in, so did the foursome at another table across the room.

"They remind me of a cute story," Bart said, smiling and waving at them as they sat in a corner table. "A couple of honeymooners were in New York City, staying at an expensive hotel and their reservation included a pair of theatre tickets for a Broadway show; but they never came out of their hotel room the whole time they were there. On the last day, the concierge knocked on their door, and when the husband answered, the man asked, "Sir, your stay here includes a set of theatre tickets that you have never used. Would you care to use them this evening?"

"What is the play?" the husband asked.

"Sir, I believe tonight it is Oliver Twist." The husband turns and calls out to his wife, who is in the bathroom, "Honey, do you want to see Oliver Twist?" and she yells back, "You show me one more trick with that thing and I'm going back home to my mother."

They had all laughed and watched the young couple across the dining room, holding hands with their heads together. Helen said, "I don't think that she is going back home to Mother."

During dinner Helen had noticed Jack talking to Sally at her service station as he was returning from a trip to the restroom. But it wasn't until she was leaving the dining room after dinner, when Jack and Bart went to the office to check for messages, that Sally had approached her. Jack had asked Sally to move Helen from her room to his room that night. Sally was more than ready to do it, but wanted to make sure that it was all right with Helen.

"What do you think, Sally?" Helen asked with a smile, pressing something into Sally's hand. "He's a great guy, and he helped me catch a record blue marlin today. Should I move in with him?"

Sally giggled at the prospect that Mrs. Warner would not want to move in with Mister Jack. But as she later told Chef Walter, in the kitchen, "When she put dat hundred dollar bill in my hand and whispered, 'We is gun go sit out by da pool,' she want to keep her own room key so she can act surprised. When she do dat, de little dog was gone to a new home."

Bart joined them for about an hour on the pool deck. He entertained them with stories about his flying exploits. He had been a chopper pilot in Alaska for three years after Vietnam and before coming back to Florida to work as a crop duster. Jack had heard many of the stories before, but he laughed at each of them again and continued to encourage Bart to tell another. Bart had been drinking Heinekens ("Dutch Pops," he called them) before and during dinner, and after having two more on the pool deck, he had become relaxed. He could no longer contain his curiosity.

"Be honest with me, now." He studied Jack and then Helen. "You two didn't know each other before you came here last weekend?"

"No, we had never even seen each other." Helen was quick with her answer.

"I've just got to say this to you guys. I've known Jackson Andrews here for 20 years, and a finer man I have never known. I consider him today to be one of my best friends."

"Would he help you move a body, Bart?" Helen asked, smiling at Jack.

"Move a body?" Bart was confused.

"Yes, Jack is always saying that a lot of friends will help you move, but only your best friends will help you move a body."

"Why hell, yes, he would help me move a body and I would help him move one. I'm trying to remember if we have ever moved one together." Keener paused. "I don't think we have yet, have we, Jack?"

Andrews laughed, "No, not yet, Bart, but we could be close to moving one here soon."

Bart gazed into Helen eyes. "I've just got to say this to you, Helen. I just met you today, but tonight I feel as if I have known you for years. You let our big fish go today, but I love you for it now and I know that Boss Fish loves you for it. I love Jackson Andrews here as if he was the brother I never had, and I just hope you two can hang together, because you make one hell of a couple." Keener pulled himself up out of his chair. "And now, my friends, I am tired after watching you work so hard today, Helen. I will say goodnight."

Helen sprang up out of her chair and kissed Bart on the cheek. "Thanks, Bart, for all your help today. We couldn't have done it without you; and the fact that you and I both feel the same way about this guy, here," (She gazed lovingly at Jack) "binds us together as special friends."

After Bart had wandered away, Helen took Jack's hand. "I need to feed Bentley. I had Anna walk him around noon when we were gone, but he will be wondering where I am. Are we spending the night in my room or your room?"

"You choose." He smiled.

"Well, let's go to my room first and I will feed Bentley and then pick up my toothbrush and something to wear after I take a shower in your room."

"Sounds like a good plan," he said, rising and pulling her back up out of her chair.

When they arrived at her room, she fumbled with her key and opened the door to find the room empty of all her luggage. Bentley and his kennel were nowhere in sight. She pretended to be concerned. "What happened here?" she asked as she glanced around the bathroom. "I think I've been evicted!" The room was ready for a new tenant.

"I think Mister Bentley has decided to move you to my room," Jack said with a grin. He held up his key. Helen smiled back at him. "What if I said that I think the view from this room is better?" she teased.

"Then I'll stay here with you, but I would point out that until we decide to open the drapes, the view in either room is pretty much the same."

She laughed and fell into his arms.

****

Chapter 21
Housekeeping
Management and maintenance of the property of an institution or organization.

It had been raining hard Tuesday morning when they awoke, so they just stayed in bed together, talking and making love until noon. Helen told Jack about losing her young son to a motorcycle accident and her trying to hold it all together, but losing to alcohol. Jack told Helen about his drinking days and the techniques that he'd developed for helping himself and other alcoholics beat the curse.

"What most people, including many drinkers, don't know or understand is that alcohol is a biological problem every bit as much as it is a mental problem. If a drunk wants me to work with him, I come in heavy," he explained.

"Most alcoholics live in total denial. We love to think that we are just social drinkers and could do without it anytime we want to. To those people I just say, 'Maybe you are; so just prove it to me and yourself, that you are. Refrain from drinking alcohol of any kind for six months or just give it up for Lent; but go without it for at least several months and I will confer the title of 'social drinker' on you, for what that's worth. A smoker who goes from a pack a day to just one or two cigarettes is still a smoker, but with alcohol the effects of the one or two is much worse because of the drunk's metabolic reactions."

"To those people who want my help, if you want me to spend my valuable time helping you to beat alcoholism, the first thing you have to do is call yourself a drunk in front of me. If you can't do that, I'm not interested in wasting time with you. You and I are drunks, Helen! It stings when you say it to yourself, doesn't it? But if you can't accept that fact to yourself - if you can't look in the mirror and call yourself a drunk - then, my sweet girl, you are going to drink again one day. So the first thing you have to do to get my help is admit that you are a drunk. Once you do that, I'm your main man," he smiled at her.

"Oh, I'm definitely a drunk, Doctor Andrews," she smiled back at him.

Andrews couldn't help but laugh at her frankness. He continued. "Now, what drunks need to understand is that they don't process alcohol like other normal people. That's what makes them a drunk. The best simplified example I can give you (and this is a simplified example) is that all of our body cells convert glucose and other sugars to at least nine different forms of alcohol dehydrogenase; each with slightly different properties. That's right, our bodies make alcohol for cell functioning. I always make the analogy of visualizing these cells working away to make the required alcohol for their functioning and all of a sudden there are alcohol molecules floating right by the cell in the blood stream. 'Whoa,' they say, 'Why not just absorb some of these molecules and stop working so hard at making my own.' And that is exactly what they do. They stop working."

"Once you understand this concept, you can see that an alcoholic's whole body chemistry is now different. That is why just one drink can make a difference. Once those cells have been on easy street, having the alcohol furnished to them instead of making their own, they don't want to go back to work. If a drunk goes on a long bender and makes them totally dependent, they could even refuse to go back to work; hence, the body just shuts down momentarily and the drunk now suffers severe withdrawal and delirium tremens."

"To put it in its proper perspective, I always say that alcohol is to a drunk what kryptonite is to Superman. He not only loses his great strength, but it makes him so weak that it brings him to his knees. Alcohol does the same thing to a drunk. The big difference is that "The Man of Steel" is fiction and a drunk is real."

"You make it sound so easy," Helen said. "I will never drink again," she said with great conviction.

"It's never easy, girl," he said, looking at her with an unblinking gaze. "We never say 'never' and that is why we always say 'One day at a time.'"

They had a late lunch of fresh conch salad and conch fritters in the dining room. Helen had never eaten conch before and thought it was delicious. The day was still cool with a light rain falling, when they returned to their room.

"Nap or exercise," Helen called to him from the bathroom. Jack was changing into his running togs when she came back into the bedroom. "Oh, surprise! I should have known that my main man was going to go with exercise." She went back into the bathroom and pulled her tank suit off the towel rack where it had dried. "That's okay; I need to swim a couple miles in the pool just to work out my body kinks. Between Boss Fish, and Captain Jack, I am feeling quite physically abused," she joked. "I'm not complaining, mind you; I love it. Must be masochistic, huh?"

"Oh, you're definitely masochistic," he said jokingly. He finished double tying the bow knots on his running shoes. "I just thought that you were going to swim, and I would feel guilty if I didn't run in the rain."

"You shouldn't at all," Helen said pulling on her tank suit. "When I'm swimming, I'm already wet and don't even feel the rain. That is a lot different than running in it. Besides, if you're worried that you could melt, come join me in the pool..." she grinned at him. "I can teach you some tricks that will make it worth your while, Captain Jack." She lowered her tank suit to her waist and laughed at his raised eyebrows and mock-shocked expression as he grabbed his fleece shirt and rushed out of the room, closing the door behind him.

****

Chapter 22
Planning
The act or process of making or carrying out plans

Jack ran five times around the airstrip, which he estimated to be about four miles. On his way back to the hotel, he saw Bart Keener up under his Beech Baron, out of the rain, working on the plane's landing gear.

"What's up?" Andrews asked the pilot.

"Hey, man," Bart glanced over at him. "This gear doesn't close in all the way sometimes. Another pilot spotted it this morning when I was flying down to Spanish Cay. Listen, thanks for dinner last night; and I hope that I didn't make an ass out of myself with you and Helen." Keener stepped out from under the wing, wiping his hands on a towel.

"Not at all," Jack retorted. "You were your charming self all night. You said some nice things about both Helen and me."

"Wow! She is such a peach, Jack. Those looks and that 'can do' attitude of hers are too much to put together in one female. I noticed that she is also one of your non-drinkers."

"Yep, she is the same as most of us, I guess." Andrews stared down the runway. "She has had her share of tough times. She lost her only child to a motorcycle accident and had a hard time dealing with it."

"Who wouldn't?" Bart said, and shook his head. "What are your plans now, if I may ask? Or do you even have any? Please don't just tell me that you are going back to Orlando and that the Lear is coming to take Helen back to Minneapolis. I won't believe that."

"Well, I think it safe to say that she is not going back to Minneapolis anytime soon, and I'm not going back to Orlando either. I've got some things that I need to tell you and bring you into my confidence, as I may need your help, ole buddy."

"I'm at your service, man, you know that," Bart said. Jack nodded his head.

Andrews spent the next half hour bringing his friend up to date on the happenings in his life during the last five days. With regard to himself, he left nothing out. Bart set his jaw and stared at the ground as Jack gave him all the details.

"Bart, only Helen, Billy, Sam, and now you know about all these facts. Jill, my wife, and Philip Cowans, have no idea that I was even in Orlando when this event occurred or that I even know about their affair, at this stage. Both Billy and Sam think that the congressman is going to stay mute on the subject, rather than end his political career."

Bart was friendly with both Sam and Billy and nodded his head in understanding. "Jack, what are you thinking that you need to do now?" he asked.

"Well, I am not running from anybody at this stage. I am not going back to my vet practice and I'm not going back home to my wife. So, I am free to make any move I want. Helen's situation is a little more complicated." Andrews went on to explain how Helen had caught and trapped her philandering husband by selling their company, house, cars, and all other joint assets while he was on a vacation with his girlfriend, before converting the cash into bearer bonds and disappearing. "We're talking about millions of dollars here, Bart."

"Jesus," said Bart. "That guy certainly stepped on his dick, didn't he?"

"You could say that. He will be looking for her and will come once he finds out where she is. She must have a great legal team working for her, as they have already served the husband with divorce papers and a restraining order. While he has no idea where she is now, we know that he is looking for her." The rain picked up and Andrews stepped in under the plane wing with Bart to get out of the drizzle as he continued to talk.

"I've thought about different places I could take Helen, and I think living on a boat would be the best move for us right at this moment. It gives us privacy and the flexibility to move instantly. Maybe even something that I could run charters out on. Are there any big boats over there at Spanish Cay?"

Bart shook his head. "No, the great boats that you'd want to live on, like a fifty or sixty foot Cheoy Lee, are in Bermuda, Jack; not here in the Bahamas. That's where you need to go right now. Once you're there, you can rent a place and take your time looking around for something that fits. If money is no problem, you could buy two boats, such as a Cheoy Lee to live on and a smaller Hatteras similar to our Summer Star, here, to charter out. I have some pretty good friends in Bermuda who would help you for sure."

"Well, I appreciate your help - and I need to buy your bladder tanks now and get you to help me install them, just so I have the extra range capability."

"Consider them yours; I want to give them to you as a present. If it stops raining, I will install them for you this afternoon in less than an hour. As your lady friend says, 'It's a piece of cake!' And Jack, we always have room for a good pilot in our fish spotting business any time you want it. Those are contracts that I can lay in your lap, buddy. Just say the word."

"Thanks, man; now let me see if I can get my Gertrude Ederle out of the pool," Andrews said with a grin.

"Wait one and I'll walk up the hill with you," Bart said, dropping his hand towel into his tool box and closing the lid. "Chef wants me to take a look at the compressor unit on his walk-in cooler."

Helen Warner Ederle was still churning up a large wake in the pool when Jack and Bart found her. She saw them standing on the side of the pool as she glided out of a flip turn and stopped in the shallow end to stand up and pull her goggles up on her head.

"Come on in, guys; the water is a wonderful temperature today."

On a whim, and feeling silly, Jack pulled off his running shoes and socks and, taking off his fleece shirt, he did a perfect "Little Abner" dive into the water off the one meter board.

Helen was giggling when he came back to the surface. "I score that a two," she shouted at him. Jack lay out on his back and pulled his knees up to his chest with just his feet sticking up out of the water about three feet from his head, then he kicked them violently. From Helen's perspective down on the water surface, he appeared to be a three foot midget swimming on his back.

She roared with laughter. "Can you swim, or do you just do tricks?"

Jack swam towards her. "You bet I can swim, baby. Just because you were a me-she-gang swimmer doesn't mean you can out swim me. I'm a Florida Gator. Did you ever see a Gator go after something in the water? We're bullets. Bang, we're there! No way does a Wolverine out swim a Gator. I'm going to prove it! You and me! We're going down and back for the championship."

"Freestyle?" she asked, laughing at his antics.

"Free style, cat style, dog style - any style you want, baby. Gators don't care." He mimicked practicing a dog paddle from one side of the pool to the other in the shallow end. Helen and Bart howled with laughter as his head went under water and he acted as if he was drowning. When he stood back up, Jack noticed that they had drawn an audience in the duty free shop. Helen and Bart's laughter had brought both Anna and Sally to the window of the shop and now some of other hotel guests had joined them.

"All right, big mouth," Helen said, her smile disappearing, and Andrews saw that same glint in her eye that he had seen when she was talking about the blue marlin being under the boat. "What's the prize for the winner?" she asked.

"The loser has to give the winner a full body massage," Jack said.

"Oh goody; a happy ending massage?" Helen asked.

"Is there any other kind?" he smiled. "Hold on to the wall and Bart will start us off."

They each put a hand on the wall and Bart called, "Swimmers to your mark ... get set..."

Jack kicked off the wall before Bart called out "go." Helen, anticipating his move, was right behind him. Both swimmers raced the length of the pool. Andrews had not been kidding about being a powerful swimmer, and he covered the 75 feet and touched the wall a fraction of a second ahead of Helen, but her perfect flip turn and long glide out from the wall left him in a cloud of bubbles.

Damn, Andrews thought to himself, *she must have catapults for legs.* But from the turn on he was steadily losing ground to her, and in desperation he reached out and grabbed her ankle. He could hear her screams under water as he pulled himself past her and then, just as he was swimming again, he felt her arms and legs wrap around him and their two forms sank slowly to the bottom of the pool. Helen was squeezing him so tightly, holding his arms into his sides and with her powerful legs wrapped around his body, that he was helpless.

He turned and kissed her on the mouth. She kissed him back. Nothing changed, and then it dawned on him that she must have filled her lungs with air before she wrapped herself around him. He was starting to miss his air and she was smiling at him as if she was Esther Williams with an air hose nearby. As Andrews struggled to free himself, Helen dramatically increased her squeezing clamp on him. *Damn*, he thought to himself, *this is getting serious.* In total desperation he was able to pinch a tiny part of her skin high on her inner thigh between two of his finger nails, and she released him instantly.

Free at last, he extended his legs against the bottom of the pool and shot for surface, his lungs bursting. Only when he was just about to the surface did he feel Helen's fingers on each side of his baggy running shorts; and then it was too late. With one quick movement, Helen ripped the shorts and their liner down off his body. He had to gasp for air at the surface for several seconds before he could shout at her.

"God damn it, Helen! You beg me to swim with you and then you try to drown me. Give me back my skivvies."

"You cheat, Jack!" She was laughing and holding up his shorts. "I am going to take these to Kate and tell her that I found them in the pool. Maybe she can hang them up in the office and the owner can stop by and claim them." Bart was laughing so hard, he had to sit down in a chair.

"No, come on, Helen." Jack was still trying to catch his breath. "I'm sorry I grabbed your ankle, honey, but I thought you were having a cramp or something. I seriously thought you were in trouble."

"Jackson, you are such a liar. And you are not getting these shorts back either, until you say that 'Wolverines are faster in the water than Gators.' Let's hear it... let's hear you say, 'Wolverines are faster in the water than Gators.'"

Andrews filled his mouth full of water and said, "Wolvrn fast in wawa thn gaor."

"That doesn't cut it, Andrews," Helen shouted at him. And then both she and Bart screamed with laughter as the daylight sensor turned the pool lights on.

"Okay, okay, Wolverines are faster in the water than Gators," Jack cried. "They are much faster. Oh God, are they fast! Helen, please honey ..." He was now huddled over by a side ladder facing the wall. The duty free shop spectators were all laughing on the other side of the window.

Holding his running shorts out in front of her, she slowly swam to him just using her legs. "Here you go, Captain Jack," she said as she pushed the shorts to him. "Don't let your Oliver Twist."

When they were walking back to their room to change for dinner, Andrews said, "Helen, you don't know your own strength. I thought you were going to drown me down there on the bottom of the pool. I was totally out of air."

"I'm sorry, Jack; I didn't realize that you were that short of air until you stuck that pin in me. Where did you get that, anyway?"

"That wasn't a pin; I just pinched your inner thigh skin with my fingernails. Have you never heard of that?" he asked.

"No," she said. "I thought it was a needle. It hurt me, Jack!" Helen punched his shoulder.

"That's a basic self-defense move. Remember it! The skin on your inner thigh is sensitive because it is not exposed to outside contact. So when you pinch hard there, it hurts." He put his arm around her and gave her a hug. "I'm sorry, Helen. I will make it up to you. I'll kiss it and make it well."

She smiled and hugged him back. They walked on in silence.

****

Chapter 23
Moving to the Dark Side
The negative and often hidden aspect of someone or something.

Robert Warner paid his cab driver, crossed the sidewalk, and walked in the front door at Antonio's Café Exceptional. He pushed by the line of people waiting for a table and made his way to the velvet ropes that kept patrons out of the dining room. The handsome maître d' greeted him warmly.

"Hello, Mr. Warner; nice to see you, sir. Would you prefer to sit in the fountain room with Manny today?" He unhooked the barrier.

Warner gave the man a wan smile. "Not today, Pauli, I am meeting Joe Bruno here for lunch."

Pauli stepped back to usher Warner inside the dining room and then quickly added, "Yes sir, we are holding Mr. Bruno's regular table. Let me go ahead and seat you, as you are the first of his guests to arrive."

Warner followed Pauli to the back of the restaurant where the maître d' pulled a chair out from a corner four top, for him to be seated. It was not yet noon, and the Monday lunch crowd was just starting to build.

"May we bring you something to drink while you wait, Mr. Warner?" Pauli ran a tight ship and was amazingly efficient.

"Yes, just coffee, please, with cream."

"Yes, sir." And with a snap of his fingers and a quick point of his index finger, he assigned the table to one of the three waiters standing by the lone brick wall. "Coffee, cream, and hold the menus till Mister B is here," Warner heard him say softly; and he was gone.

When Joe Bruno arrived, he was accompanied by two tough-looking characters dressed in high collar, dark colored shirts and dark silk suits that were too tight on them. Mafia costumes, Warner thought to himself.

"Mikey, you and Vinnie sit there," Bruno said as he pointed to a corner table that was adjacent to where Robert Warner was waiting and then, staring at Warner, he added, "Sorry I'm late, Robert, we had to stop to fix a problem on the way from the office." Bruno pulled back the chair next to Warner and sat down on his right side. He stared out into the restaurant. "I sit here, Robert, 'cause I don't hear so good out of my right ear anymore, you know what I mean?"

"I know what you mean, Joe," Robert agreed. "I don't hear as well as I used to, either. Thanks for meeting with me so soon."

The waiter brought menus to the table. Bruno waved his hand to take them away.

"Let me order for us, Robert. The parmigiana here is the best in town." Without waiting for Warner's reply, he smiled at the waiter.

"Hi, Johnny, bring us two string bean salads and the eggplant parmigiana with risotto with your meat sauce on the side."

"Yes sir, Mister Bruno," the waiter nodded, and was gone.

Bruno glanced over at Warner and whispered, "I cook a great eggplant parmigiana at home, but here they work a miracle with it. My wife says it is because they cut it on a mandolin slicer. I told her, 'Whatever; then get us one and I will cook it at home.' She said, 'No way; then you would never take me out to dinner.'" He unfolded his napkin and tucked it into his shirt to protect his silk tie.

"I told my brother Tony when I was leaving the office just now to come here. 'I'm going to meet Robert Warner for lunch today, Tony. Do you remember him from high school?' My brother says he remembers you as the guy who blew up the chemistry lab when we was in school. Is that true?"

Warner nodded and smiled. "Yep, that was me. I got in a lot of trouble for that; they almost kicked me out of school."

"Well, from your phone call this morning, it sounds as if maybe you're in a lot of trouble today." Bruno stared at Warner with deep-set, coal black eyes. He was a short but powerfully built man, and Robert thought at that moment how much he resembled an Edward G. Robinson character. Joe and Tony Bruno, two Italian toughs when he was in high school with them, had been successful in business. Their company, Bruno Waste Management (BWM), was the major contractor for both Minneapolis and St. Paul and had been for years. While competitors came and went, not one could ever get enough of the market away from the brothers to stay in business.

240

"I don't understand, Robert. I read in the papers where you have become a successful businessman. Warner Chemical is your company, right?" Warner nodded. "But I don't hear nothing from you for twenty years, not even a Christmas card, other than to just wave and say hello at Viking games, right?" Warner nodded. "Now, you think you have an emergency that Joe Bruno can help you out with, right?" Warner nodded again. "So okay, Robert, what can I do for you?"

Robert took a deep breath and commenced to tell his sorry story. Over lunch Warner told Bruno everything he could think of about his situation; from his discovery Friday that his wife had taken all of their joint assets from him and left him nothing; to his lawyer Doug Hawkins' opinion that his business was gone forever. At best, Hawkins was expecting that he would legally be able to reclaim 50 percent of the total equity value. But it could take months and maybe even years to go through the legal process. After he became silent, Bruno spoke.

"How much money are we talking about, Robert, in these bearer bonds? "

"Somewhere between eighteen and twenty million dollars."

"And so you want me to help you get these bearer bonds back from your wife, is that it?" Bruno pretended to be annoyed.

"If you can," Robert nodded in agreement.

"What makes you think that I can do something for you that Doug Hawkins can't?"

"Look, Joe, I don't know that you can do anything. I'm just hoping that you can. Doug has got to work through the system. I am just hoping that you know some shortcuts around the system to get the bonds back before the trail to them goes cold."

"To tell you the truth, Robert, BWM don't do strong arm stuff anymore. Tony and I stopped that shit years ago. Now, I do know a guy who knows a guy - you know how that is. Tell me what is in this for BWM." Joe Bruno smiled for the first time since he sat down at the table.

****

Chapter 24
Storm Warnings
Any sign of approaching trouble

Jack Andrews was awakened by the wind noise outside the hotel room. He had opened the drapes the night before to show Helen that his room did have the best view in the hotel, and the dawn was just beginning to silhouette the swaying palms and sea grapes off his balcony. He sat up on the side of the bed and checked around him in the dim light. It was Wednesday morning.

Helen was sleeping quietly next to him and Bentley was curled up in the back of his kennel, which was sitting on a table across the room. Andrews eased off the bed and quickly pulled on his cargo shorts and his fleece warmup shirt. He slipped his feet into his boating moccasins, crossed the room, quietly turned the night bolt, and opened the door into the long hall that led to the hotel lobby. Before he could step through the door, he heard a voice behind him.

"Calling Captain Jack," Helen's deep voice said softly. "Report back to your duty station immediately." Andrews turned to face the bed. Helen, giggling, threw the covers off her nude body and reached out both arms for him. He smiled back at her then closed and relocked the door.

"I cry foul," he said, crossing the room. "You are using unfair tactics. I was just going to walk down to the air strip. Bart was going to install his old bladder tanks in my plane if the rain stopped. It's clear this morning, so I wanted to see if he did it; or maybe if he needed my help to do so."

"Okay, would you want me to go with you?" she asked.

"Of course," he grinned. "We can take my buddy, Mister Bentley, for a walk and let him run a little bit."

Helen leaped out of bed and was brushing her teeth before Jack had fitted the lead on Bentley and was taking him out the door. "Bentley and I are going to be hanging out in the duty free shop looking at their boating magazines," he called to her. "Come as soon as you can."

The phone on the bed stand rang. Andrews picked it up. "Hi," he said.

"Good morning, Jack. It's Kate. I'm sorry to bother you, but Helen has a call from a lady who says that she needs to get in touch with her right away, and that it is an emergency. She has been ringing through to Helen's old room and nobody answers. She says that it is urgent that she speak with her. Would you want me to put her through?"

"Yeah, Kate, I think Helen had better chat with her." Andrews motioned Helen out of the bathroom with his index finger and handed her the phone. Helen quickly wrapped a bath towel around her and came to the phone. Andrews watched her out of the corner of his eye as he took her place in the bathroom to shave.

"Hello, this is Helen," she said.

"Yes Stella, sure, I know who you are." Helen stiffened.

244

"When did this happen?" she asked.

"Oh my ... Oh my ... Yes, I've moved to a different room. I'm so sorry; I should have checked in with you." Helen sat down on the side of the bed. "Yes, I understand, and I appreciate the trouble you've been going through to reach me. Please thank Joyce for me and tell her not to worry. And tell her that I love her." She put the phone back in its cradle and stared at Jack, who was lathering his face.

"That was a girl who works for my travel agent friend, Joyce Hunter. Their agency didn't arrange my trip down here. To protect me, Joyce jobbed it out to another agency that they do a lot of business with. That agency was broken into Monday night, but they haven't been able to find anything missing, except that they think somebody may have pulled and copied my travel file. They think this happened because the last sheet was left in the copier, and when they went to file it, my file had been returned to the wrong drawer. Stella called Joyce, who is living on a sailboat somewhere down here now, and she told her to contact me immediately and get a message to me that 'we had been compromised and that I should get out!'"

Jack continued to lather soap on his face, "There is always somebody fucking up paradise," he said, shaking his head. "It may be about time to think about moving on."

"You're going to take me away with you, aren't you, Captain Jack?"

"Absolutely," he grinned. "With all your money, do you think I would leave you behind?"

Helen stuck her lower lip out. "Do you just want to be my friend for my money, Jack?"

"No, darling; right now I kind of wish that you didn't have so much of it so that we could just relax and hang out here for a month or so."

"So, let's do that, then. Let's just stay here and handle whatever shows up," she said. "What is the worst that can happen? They can't arrest me for anything I've done."

"Helen, you told me that your husband has a bright lawyer friend. There is a chance that he could get a judge that he knows well to issue a bench warrant for your arrest just to have you come before him and answer questions about your actions. If they send a Federal Marshal down here to serve it, he could take you back to Minneapolis. I'm not certain about that and will have to check it out with my friend, Sam Wadley."

"Jack, if I have to, I will just tell them that Robert's stocks and bonds are back in Minneapolis."

"Are they?"

"Yes," she said. "So I could swear to it, but if they take me back to Minneapolis, I am going to leave Bentley here with you. Please take good care of him for me." She was serious.

"Helen, I can assure you that I am not going to let anybody take you anywhere you don't want to go." He set his jaw and she could see that he meant it. "Plus, please don't worry about Bentley; I promise that I won't let anything happen to him."

"Well, that is comforting, but it would be more important that you never let anything happen to his kennel." She smiled at his puzzled look.

Then, walking over to the now empty dog kennel sitting on the desk table, she removed the blanket from its floor and pushed down with her thumbs on the two front inlaid pieces of dark wood that were set in all four corners of the kennel floor. With a loud clicking sound the floor popped loose from the kennel base and became the lid on a box built into the floor of the kennel. In the box lay several manila envelopes and a legal folder.

Andrews had come out of the bathroom with soap still on half his face and had followed her over to the table. He stood there speechless for several seconds. "Whoa, please don't tell me that those are all your securities?" he whispered.

Helen shook her head. "Just a few." She held up a separate legal folder. "These are my trust documents. When I sold all of Robert's and my holdings, including the business and our home, we had a little over $22 million dollars. A good portion of that equity today is invested in Helena Chemical stock, which I did to facilitate their purchase. My lawyers suggested that I split that stock evenly with Robert, so he couldn't argue that I had benefited over him with the sale. I agreed to that and I also split the cash, about $14 million, equally between us."

 "My lawyers had also suggested that I buy tax free bonds for Robert with his cash, so that he would have it safely invested with some income without additional tax consequences. I did just that and so today Robert has his share of our combined estate liquidation available to him.

"My law firm is holding it in escrow for him with written instructions from me to disperse it all to him as soon as he signs a release, along with a non-compete declaration for Helena Chemical and our divorce papers. But in the meantime, he had better start being nicer to me. And if he sends some U.S. Marshall, or any of his goon friends, down here after me, it is going to cost him big bucks."

Jack smiled at her. "So, Helen, when does your husband find out that he is not penniless?"

"When he sits down with my attorney at the divorce hearing and our settlement offer is read to him," she smiled back at him.

"He doesn't have too much wiggle room, does he?"

"None, I hope ..." Helen said, and her smile vanished.

Andrews was stupefied. He had to ask himself again, what had he found? This woman that he had known for less than a week, this beautiful lady who had recently become the focal point of his life, was absolutely amazing in her planning and control. She was beyond belief! Helen picked up a manila envelope from out of the box and, undoing a string tie, pulled a sheaf of papers out. She handed them to Jack for his inspection. "There are two bearer bonds here, but most of my money is held in an offshore trust in Bermuda."

Andrews had put down his razor and was examining the base of the dog kennel and the tight tolerances of the floor locking system. He snapped it closed and attempted to open it again by pushing on the two dark wooden corners that Helen had used to open it. They clicked, but nothing happened.

She laughed at his attempt to open the floor of the kennel. "That won't open for you, Jack, unless you know the sequence."

He gazed up at her. "You're kidding me! There's a sequence?" he asked.

"Yes, my friend who built it for me is a clock maker. Push on the right one first until it clicks, then push the left one

248

down until it clicks, then push the left down again until it clicks - it needs to click twice - and then push both of them together at the same time. And don't rush it."

Jack did as instructed and there was another loud click as the floor opened. "Unbelievable," Andrews whispered as he shook his head. He smiled as he glanced back up at her. "Why is your trust in Bermuda?"

"I just wanted to get as far away from Robert as possible. And my lawyers said that if I placed money offshore, it was important to deal with a country that follows and adheres to international law; a country where you can get legal consideration and service. Countries such as Panama, Hong Kong, and Singapore are all good, but Bermuda is closer and I already had a good connection with someone there to help me."

"So I assume that you are the trustee of your offshore trust, right?"

"No, there are no Americans named in my trust, but my title rights are enforced by a trustee who acts as my person of last resort. My friend in Palm Beach, who invited me to come live with her, is Canadian and she has a twin sister living in Bermuda. Her twin is a lawyer and is now my trustee; but her appointment is at my pleasure and I could replace her at any time if it were necessary because of her health or if she thought it was just too much responsibility."

"Are you the beneficiary of the trust?"

"Well of course; but indirectly, as my name is not even in the trust documents."

"Amazing!" he said. "Who is Helena Chemical and why is its stock so valuable?"

"It is a private LLC corporation that has most of its assets invested in real estate and manufacturing plants and equipment; in addition to quite a lot of inventory."

"Let me guess," Andrews smiled. "You and Robert are the sole stock holders of Helena Corporation."

"No; Robert and I are now minority stock holders. My former Warner Chemical employees own about 60 percent of Helena stock. Our company is in the chemical business. We have the same assets and customers and make the same products that Warner Chemical made, but we now also hold some additional assets and I think we have a much more motivated work force."

"It is a little complicated and I'm sure that Robert thinks that all of the money I got from liquidating our assets is invested in bearer bonds, but that is hardly the case." She took the sheaf of papers back from him and removed one document. "Here is one bearer bond certificate with a coupon that was due last month. I need to turn it in and have the funds deposited in my account."

Andrews studied the coupon, which had required a payment of $128,000 twenty days earlier. "All right," he said, handing it back to her. "Now, how do you cash this?"

"I have an account with the investment firm of Credit Suisse. They are out of Boston, but I know that they have an office in Bermuda. They will handle the transaction for me."

Jack picked up his razor and went back into the bathroom. "It seems as if we have a plan. Now we just need to execute it correctly," he said.

The phone by the bed rang again, Jack pointed to the phone from the bathroom, and Helen, who was sitting on the bed, picked it up. It was Kate.

"Hi Helen, is Jack available?"

"He's shaving right now, Kate, but he's almost finished. What's up?"

"His wife is on the line. She has called twice this morning and I just wanted to see if he wanted to talk to her."

"Just a second, Kate," Helen said, and then, covering the receiver with her palm, she called to Jack, who was bent over splashing water on his face. "When it rains, it pours. Your wife is on the phone. Kate wants to know if you'd want the call put through." Andrews was drying his face with a towel. "Sure, put her through," he snapped.

"It is fine, Kate, please put her through." Helen laid the phone on the bed and got up. "Do you want me to leave and take Bentley for the walk?" she asked Andrews.

"Absolutely not," Jack said sternly. "I want you to hear what I say to her." Jack pulled on his running shorts and grabbed a pair of socks and his running shoes as he walked over to the side of the bed. He sat down, tucked the phone under his chin, pulled on the socks and began lacing up the shoes.

"Hello," he said.

"Hello, Jill. Yep, it is the real me."

"Yes, I flew over here Sunday. I should have called, but I'm glad Sam told you that he had talked to me."

"It is quiet here right now. They expect it to pick up next month, but there are only about a dozen people staying in the hotel at present."

"No, the only person you would know here now is Bart Keener. He is here."

"He seems to be doing great. He loves what he does. He went fishing with me Monday. Yes, we did. We caught a huge blue marlin." He winked at Helen.

While Jack was on the phone, Helen had pulled on her tank suit, wrapped her sarong around herself, picked up Bentley, and seated herself in the desk chair across the room, watching him and listening to the conversation.

"Home? I'm not coming back home, Jill. The house is yours."

"That's what I'm saying. I'm not coming back to Orlando. I'm staying here in the Bahamas and I want you to give me a divorce. I will give you until the end of this month to file and then Sam Wadley will file a petition with the Orange County Court on my behalf."

"You tell me why, Jill. We just ran out of gas. It happens to couples all the time."

"Jill, Jill, listen to me. You will find somebody else to take my place, if you haven't already."

Helen's eyes flashed at Jack from across the room and she shook her head. Damn, it was hard for him to stay away from the truth. To tell Jill he was aware of her affair with Cowans, would instantly set him free emotionally, but it would also incriminate him.

"Yes, Jill, I'm sure this is quite a shock. It came as quite a shock to me, also. But there is nothing more for us to talk about."

"No, Jill, I won't go to counseling."

"No, Jill. All that is for people who want to try to save their marriages."

"No, I don't!"

"Our marriage is broken irrevocably, to my mind, and I want to end it as soon as possible and move on with my life." Andrews had been staring at the floor, but now he glanced over to Helen, who was watching him closely.

"I know, Jill. I am sorry; but you will be fine. Jill, Jill, it's all over, girl. I'm not going to try to put anything back together again. And that is the point; I don't want to be in your life anymore."

Now Jack smiled slightly at Helen.

"Yes, Jill, as a matter of fact, I have just met someone. We've only known each other a few days, but she is a special person. She has given me a whole new outlook on life. She has transformed me back into someone who loves life." Jack nodded his head towards Helen.

"Do I love her? Let me think about that." Jack stared at Helen and smiled. "I must love her, although now that I think about it, I don't think that I have ever told her that I do. Hopefully, I have shown her that I love her. If that sounds crazy, it is because we have only known each other for four short days. Let me just say that I am absolutely crazy about her and I don't want to ever be more than 100 feet away from her if I can help it."

"I'm going to sign off now, Jill, but Sam has my power of attorney and we will take good care of you financially. Anything you need, he will provide. I will give him good instructions."

"Goodbye, Jill." Andrews stared at the phone for several seconds after he hung it up. Helen put Bentley down, walked over to the bed, sat down beside him, and put her arm around his neck. Her blue eyes were wet with tears. He studied her intensely for several seconds before speaking softly.

"How in the hell did you live with your husband for over a year knowing all the time that there was no trust in your relationship?" he asked her. "I lost it just then when Jill was trying to lay some heavy guilt on me."

"You just have to be strong and keep your eyes on the big picture," Helen sighed. "Sometimes it is hard for us drunks to do that." She was smiling at him.

"Hot damn, you're special, Helen," he said, laughing.

"Hot damn, you're special, Jack." She kissed him gently. "It has always amazed me how we never appreciate what we have until we don't have it anymore," she said. "When friends come to me wringing their hands and talking about how bad their situations are, I just tell them: 'You're not going to believe this, and it won't make you happy, but these are the trying times that we will refer to tomorrow as the 'good old days' - and most of the time it's true.

"I don't know your wife, Jack, but I feel sorry for her, for what she has just lost. I've never known another man with all your attributes. You are just about too good to be true. I've been looking for your flaws and so far they are damn hard to find. I never dreamed that there was anybody out there available for me. I'm pretty tough and I think I can take a punch, but to tell the truth, if you now told me the things that you just told Jill, I would be devastated."

Andrews patted her knee and glanced over at Bentley, who had relocated back by the door and was lying there patiently looking at him. "My little bud, Mister Bentley, says, 'Did you say it is "talk time" or "walk time?"' They both smiled as the little Yorkie wagged his tail at the sound of "walk time."

"Let's do it, then!" she replied.

****

Chapter 25
The Plan
A set of actions that have been thought of as a way to do or achieve something. : something that a person intends to

The call from Helen's travel agent informing her that their offices had been broken into and that it was assumed that her location on Walkers Cay had been compromised put Jack Andrews on high alert. He walked a few minutes with Helen and Bentley until Helen wanted to visit with Kate in the hotel lobby. He excused himself and immediately went in search of his friend, Bart Keener. He found the pilot just finishing the installation of the bladder fuel tanks in his Cherokee Six.

"You're all hooked up, Jackson. I've put about 5 gallons in each tank so you can test them out. What you need to do now is make a little test run and switch back and forth between the two bladders and your main tank just to make sure the switching goes smoothly."

"Thanks a million, Bart." Jack patted him on shoulder. "Now I have another favor to ask of you. I am going to fly to Spanish Cay tomorrow and gas up. I don't want anyone to know that I can take on 124 gallons of fuel at one time, so if it's all right with you, I would use your credit card and reimburse you with cash."

"Fine," Bart smiled. "Sounds as if you are working on a plan."

Andrews explained that they had just been informed an hour earlier that there was a great probability that Helen's husband was now aware of where she was; and if he was taking the chance of committing felonies to acquire such information, there was no telling what he would do when he found her. "I don't want to take any chances. I want to fly Helen out of here this week," he told Bart. "And now, with the help of your bladder tanks, I think I can reach Bermuda without any problems. What do you think?"

"Oh, hell yes," Bart agreed. "I think it is less than 900 miles from here. So then, when you get to Bermuda, you guys will buy a boat and go to sea, right? So even when they follow your flight plan to Bermuda, your trail will go cold."

"If we can do it, I would prefer that the trail to go cold right off this island," Jack said.

"How do you do that?" Bart asked, cocking his head to one side.

"Bart, have you been watching the weather? There is a huge cold front coming down into Florida from the northwest. When it hits our warm air, we are going to have a major winter storm. That could be a big help."

"Yeah, I've been keeping an eye on it, as it looks as if the storm center could come right across the state; but I don't think it comes this far, as the Gulf Stream should turn it north. How does the storm help you?"

257

"Well, if the weather gets piss poor around Fort Pierce and Palm Beach, I could file an IFR flight plan from here to Ft. Pierce and then get lost in the storm."

"Wait a minute, Jackson; you are going to fly into the storm in your Cherokee Six?"

"Not into it, just up to it. Then turn my transponder off and drop down on the deck and run for Bermuda. Once I get about half way there, I will regain altitude, reset my transponder, and begin broadcasting my new identity."

Bart stared at him thoughtfully for several seconds. "That just might work," he said. "What new identity are you going to use?"

"Well, I could make up one, but the perfect one for me to use is yours."

"Mine?" Bart was caught off guard.

"Yes, didn't you tell me that your Cherokee Six was in a thousand pieces in your dad's hanger in Ocala somewhere?"

"Yes, I did; and it is! Sure, of course, you are welcome to use it. The call sign is N2427FR. So, you are also going to file a VFR plan from here to Bermuda so they will be expecting you, right?" Bart was nodding his head.

"Exactly," said Jack. "But I think I will file the VFR plan from Spanish Cay, so there won't be any question about it being a different aircraft. But that is why I am concerned about fuel, as I am not flying from here to Bermuda, but from here to Ft. Piece and then from Ft. Pierce to Bermuda. That could be about 1200 miles."

"That is a brilliant plan, Jackson." Bart grinned at his friend. "I can't think why it won't work. So you are just going to disappear as my friend Jack Andrews? What is your new name going to be?"

"Andrew Jackson has a nice ring to it," Andrews quipped. "He was always one of my favorites."

"Who else are you going to tell about this?" Bart became serious.

"Absolutely no one." Jack was squinting hard and staring directly at his friend. "Absolutely no one. That is the most important factor in being successful. We could bring Cookie into our confidence, just to make certain his paint job on my plane stays a secret. What I need to do right now is to get Cookie to repaint my plane with your ID numbers, so there will be no question when we land at L.F. Wade International Airport in Bermuda that we match up with my flight plan." Jack handed Bart an envelope with hundred dollar bills in it.

Bart took out the cash and put his credit card in the envelope and then, finding a pencil in his tool kit, wrote his pin and billing zip on the envelope before returning it to Andrews.

"Wait one minute here," he said as he counted out the bills. "There is no way you can put $2000 worth of fuel in your plane."

"Please take it," Jack implored his friend. "It gives you something for the tanks and for helping me figure this whole thing out. I wouldn't be doing this without you, Bart."

Bart Keener smiled, "I'll keep it if I can come see you guys in Bermuda whenever I get there."

259

"You'd better. We are going to be friendless for a little while. All we'll have is each other, if we can pull this off."

"That's a hell of hand to draw to," Bart grinned. "And you, of all people, can pull this thing off." Bart bear hugged his friend.

"Helen and I can't thank you enough for your friendship, Bart."

****

After he left Bart at his plane, Andrews stopped by the marina repair shop. Cookie was already shaking up some white paint, trying to match the color of the Cherokee Six base coat to cover over the current ID insignia. Jack furnished him with the new ID numbers and letters and Cookie opened his large box of stencils.

"Mister Jack, I knowd you wanted dark blue lettering, but we don't have no blue here on hand. Can we use dis green instead? It's called "British Racing Green.""

Andrews studied the sample color on the paint can's label. "Yeah, that will get the job done for us. Cookie, I need to count on you to keep a secret about this ID change. No one should ever know anything about it, under any circumstances. Do you understand?"

"Yes sa, Mister Jack, I ain't gonna tell nobody. It'll be our secret."

"Bart knows about it too; so it will be a secret for the three of us."

260

"Yes sa, Mister Jack, for just the three of us," Cookie repeated back with pride.

****

On his way back to the hotel, Jack met Helen coming down the winding walkway with Bentley trotting alongside her. "Hey, beautiful lady, where are you going?" he asked, reaching out to pull her into his arms.

"I was looking for a handsome pilot to fly me away from pending danger," she said, kissing him gently.

"Here I is," he said with a grin.

"Did you find Bart?"

"Yes I did," he smiled at her. "And we now have bladder tanks installed in our aircraft which will allow us to fly all the way to Bermuda without refueling. And tomorrow we will make a little test run over to Spanish Cay and fuel up; then just come back here and keep a close eye on the weather.

"Shouldn't we leave Bentley here if we're only going to be away for a couple of hours?" Helen asked.

"No, I think we should take him with us to try to get him more accustomed to flying. It's a short trip and if he is riding in his kennel with us, he should not get too distressed. Our flight to Bermuda will be 7 or 8 hours and if we are ducking around bad weather in the early part of it, that could be stressful on all of us. I want to get him at least a little bit used to being bounced around."

261

They walked slowly back to their room, holding hands. While Helen was in the shower, Jack opened up his medical bag and emptied all its contents on the bed. He lifted the thick leather case out of the bottom of the bag and, unzipping it, retrieved his 1911 Browning 45 and the flat box of cartridges. He had originally purchased the gun to protect his drug supplies, when he used to carry large supplies of painkillers and steroids. Dropping the magazine, he loaded eight of the Federal 45 Caliber Hydra shock rounds into it and inserted it back into the pistol. He hesitated momentarily, considering whether to chamber a round, and then thought better of it. He put the gun in his waist pack and hung it on the desk chair, and then stretched out on the bed.

"Your turn," Helen said, coming out of the bathroom with a towel wrapped around her and diving onto the bed next to him. "Did you and Bart talk about that storm front?"

"Yes, we did. He thinks that our warmer air will make the front stall over Florida and the Bahamas, which I agree with. The Gulf Stream should help that happen. And all we need is for the bad weather to move in to Fort Pierce." He wrapped her long black hair around his fingers.

"Why are we going to Fort Piece, again?" She wrinkled her brow and studied him sideways through the hair hanging in front of her eyes.

"Because it is the most northern airport in Florida that you can fly into and still clear customs," he said.

"That's right." She smiled. "And it is northwest of us now, right?"

"Right," he grinned. "Do you remember what our transponder is?"

"Sure, that is the instrument that beams our call sign and our altitude so the FAA can keep track of us, right?"

"Right."

Helen nodded approvingly, but then she thought of something. "As far as the FAA is concerned, they are expecting us to land in Fort Pierce because why?"

"Because we are filing a flight plan with them to go there," he said slowly.

"IFR means instrument flight rules, right?" She cocked her head sideways.

"Right. If you have no visibility, you must fly on instruments."

"And VFR means visual flight rules, right?"

Andrews nodded. "It means that you can see where you are going."

"See, I remember what you tell me."

"You are one clever gal, Helen Warner."

"Ok, don't tell me; let me see how well I know the plan. We are going to file an IFR flight plan to Ft. Pierce, right?

"No, I've changed my mind. Bart suggested that we go DVFR as that will not require as an extensive search when we go missing. They will still look for us, but if we are IFR, the Coast Guard will go to work immediately. We will wait until we are in the air and then contact Miami Flight Service and tell them that we are flying to Ft. Pierce and request them to assign us a DVFR code that we can squawk, or transmit."

263

Helen seemed confused and Jack elaborated further.

"A DVFR flight plan is just a VFR plan that allows us to penetrate US airspace. That is how the FAA protects our borders from intruders. When an aircraft files a DVFR, they are asking for permission to fly into US airspace. The FAA grants that permission by assigning the pilot a code to squawk on his transponder. That's how they will keep track of us."

"What happens if we don't ask for permission?" Helen asked, smiling.

"They will scramble jets to intercept us and we will get a good close up look at a couple of our finest pilots. They could force us down and I would lose my pilot's license for being a dumbass." Jack shrugged. "Only that."

"Gotcha. And so once they have assigned us the code, we fly into the storm at Fort Pierce and it will look as if we crashed, right?" Helen was trying to understand the sequence.

"Wrong; we are not going to fly into a storm. We will fly right up to the edge of it and then appear to go down."

"Ok, yeah, I guess that is important."

"That's important."

"So how does it appear that we go down?"

"When we start getting into bad weather, I will report to the Miami Flight Service that we are experiencing severe turbulence, which will be true, and some rime icing."

"Rime icing?" Helen's eyes widened.

"Yes, my lady, ice accumulation on an aircraft is distinguished as rime icing. If enough ice forms on the wings, it affects the plane's ability to fly. After I make that report, we will lose altitude and drop down to less than 1,000 feet as quickly as we can, and then turn our transponder off."

"So once we change course, we now are flying to Bermuda; but no one would ever guess that it would be possible for us to do that."

"Why?" he asked.

"Because without the fuel bladders we got from Bart, we would not have enough fuel onboard to go the 1200 miles from here to Ft Pierce and then on to Bermuda, right?"

"Right!" Andrews replied with a smile. "And why are we flying to Spanish Cay to have lunch tomorrow?"

"We are going to fill up our tanks and both the fuel bladders," Helen said. "No one will know how much fuel we have on board because we paid Bart cash for the fuel bladders and for letting us use his credit card to fill our tanks."

"You are correct, Madam. For your reward, you can pass Fort Pierce and go straight to Bermuda."

"You're a wizard, Captain Jack; but now explain to me why we shouldn't have any trouble landing and clearing customs in Bermuda."

"Because I am also filing a VFR flight plan for us from Spanish Cay to Bermuda using a new code number for our aircraft. I am changing the numbers on my airplane to match those on Bart's Cherokee Six. He still has his plane and it is in his dad's hanger in Ocala in a hundred pieces, being totally rebuilt. That is what Cookie was doing for me last night. He had the paint and stencils in the boat shop, and our plane is now going to be trimmed out in British racing green."

"So Bermuda will be expecting us to arrive based on your VFR flight plan, right?"

"Right," Jack nodded. "Also, once we get a couple of hundred miles out in front of the storm, we can turn our transponder back on with the new code numbers that match the new numbers on our tail and climb back up to an altitude high enough for Bermuda Center to pick us up and watch us come all the way in."

"Impressive, Captain Jack!" Helen stared at him. "I'd be in real trouble without you, babe." She grabbed his hands and held them. "You do expect someone to fly in here to try to take me back to Minneapolis, don't you?"

"Yeah, I wasn't too concerned about your husband using legal channels to come after you; that would take time and happen out in the open. But when someone goes to the trouble to track down the travel agency that arranged for you to come here, and then breaks into those offices for the information, that is alarming! It tells us that whoever is coming is not too concerned about following the rule of law or pursuing legal remedies."

Helen saw the concern on his face. "Maybe we should have left already," she said.

"We can't go until that storm is in place and I would guess that it is a day or two away from Fort Pierce right now. We will gas up tomorrow, and with any luck, Friday will be our departure day." He kissed her and stood up. "I'm going to take a hot shower and then pay off my swimming debt," he grinned.

"I'll be waiting," she smiled back at him.

****

Chapter 26
Swan Song
A farewell or final appearance, action, or work. 2. The beautiful legendary song sung only once by a swan in its lifetime, as it is dying.

Jack Andrews was nervous. He sat on the bed in his hotel room staring at the telephone on the bedside table. It was ten minutes after the hour and Sam Wadley had promised to call him at 9:00 AM sharp. He was going to have Billy Evans with him in his office so that Jack could talk to both of them at the same time on their speakerphone. Andrews had sent Helen out to walk Bentley with the promise that as soon as he took care of some unfinished business on the phone with his lawyer and friend, they would take off to Spanish Cay.

He had talked a long time with Sam the night before and had given him a list of instructions on what he wanted done in his absence. This had included picking up his Volvo, where he had left it at the airport, and explaining to some of his major clients that he was going to be out of country for some time. That session had been difficult, as Sam kept insisting on knowing what his exact plans were and where he would be able to reach Jack in the future.

"All I can tell you, Sam," Jack had said, "is that I haven't planned far enough ahead to know where I will be. The important thing is that I know where you are, and when I settle down somewhere, I will be in touch and will provide you with my contact information. In the meantime, you have my full power of attorney, and please just act as if you are me."

He had gone over the details about his relationship with his wife. "I have asked Jill to give me a divorce. Please call her and tell her that you will take service for me and that you are expecting her petition. She can keep the house. There is no mortgage on it. There will be no cash settlement, but we can pay her enough alimony so that she can live comfortably until she remarries. And Jill will definitely remarry."

"Jack, what about your practice? Are you just going to give that up?" Sam sounded concerned.

"Yes, for the time being, I will. Anyway, as you know, the income from my ownership in Briggs Farms in Ocala has been my major source of income for the past three years. Invest it however you see fit, as you have done in the past, and..."

"Jack!" Sam had interrupted him. "Just suppose we have a life or death situation and I have to get word to you. Is there anybody on Walkers who could get a message to you?"

"Yes, there is one person. Do you remember Bart Keener, the fish spotter?"

"Sure, I remember Bart; he has a Cherokee Six similar to yours."

"Not any more, Sam. He is flying a Beech Baron. Bart lives here in the hotel now, when he is not working tournaments, and provides them with an island taxi

269

service. He has been helpful to me and in case of an emergency, he should be able to get a message to ..."

Sam had interrupted once more. "Jack, how do I get money to you to live on? Your credit card bills come here now, so I guess I can just continue to pay them for you out of the Briggs Farms account, right?

"Yes, that's an affirmative for the time being. But those charges are going to slow down substantially. Believe it or not, Sam, I have a lot of problems right now; but money is not one of them. I want to talk to you and Billy together, if you can arrange to have him stop by your office and then call me back here at Walkers. I will be here for a few more days for sure."

Sam had assured him that he would call Billy as soon as they hung up and have him in his office at nine the next morning. Now it was fifteen minutes after the hour, and all was quiet. Andrews didn't know what he was going to say to his two best friends, but he didn't want to just disappear without giving them some clue that he could still be alive.

The phone rang. He picked it up before the second ring.

"Jack, Sam here, with Mister Evans."

"Sorry, Jack." It was Billy's voice. "The interstate was a real bitch this morning."

"That's all right, guys. I just wanted to talk to you both at the same time and tell you how much you mean to me. Billy, I'm sure that Sam has told you that I am not coming back to Orlando; and in fact I am not even coming back to the States any time soon."

Billy wanted to say something. "Jack, I don't know if Sam has impressed upon you enough that we are certain that the thing with our soon-to-be-elected U.S. Senator is a moot point. Not only is he not going to be forthcoming with the information, but I'm sure he would deny it emphatically if even questioned about it directly."

"That's good to know. Billy and I do appreciate you telling me this; but that is not why I am staying out of the country. I am staying away because I have a chance to help a great friend who needs to stay away. The less you know about what I am doing and where I go, the better off you will be. I don't want either one of you to have to lie for me. Just know this: regardless of what happens during the next week, one day you will see me again. That is a promise. You boys have been way too important in my life, and there is ..."

"And you in ours," Billy interrupted him with a trembling emotional voice.

"There is no way I can just take you out of it," Jack continued. "I can't wait for the day when we can all be together again and I can bring you up to date. I've got to run now, but you boys take good care of yourselves."

Andrews hung up the phone and rubbed his eyes. "Focus on what's in front of you, Jackson," he said softly under his breath.

****

Chapter 27
Uninvited Guests
If someone does something or goes somewhere uninvited, they do it or go there without being asked, often when their action or presence is not wanted.

It was 10 AM when the Cherokee Six taxied off the apron and onto the runway. It didn't go more than 100 feet before it stopped, facing north into the stiff breeze that was blowing over the island.

Jack Andrews did his run-up and checked around his cockpit to double check on his passenger. Helen had her seat belt on and was quite relaxed in her fleece-lined poncho and ball cap. She smiled at him. "Are we going to take off going this way, Captain Jack?" she asked.

"You bet, darling," he answered. "With this 20 mph headwind and little gas in our tanks, we are going to get off the ground in a hurry." He patted her leg. Bentley was lying on a blanket in his kennel, which had two seat belts holding it in place on the seats behind them. Andrews pushed the throttle forward and took his feet off the brakes. The plane roared off down the runway and he could feel it wanting to fly immediately. He let it come off the pavement, but held the nose down and stayed at low altitude as he watched the air speed build. As they crossed the end of the runway and flew out over the blue water, he let the plane climb to just a couple hundred feet and then did a sharp banking turn to fly back downwind over the hotel.

"Say goodbye to your swimming pool, darling," Jack said as he tilted her wing down for a better view.

"Oh look, there's Bart and Eddie," Helen exclaimed. Andrews dipped the wing even more to see the two figures on the pool deck, waving up at them. He waggled his wings and set a course for Spanish Cay, less than 60 miles away.

"Are you ready for your first flying lesson?" he asked, nodding for her to put her hands on her set of controls. Without saying a word, Helen gripped her control yoke.

"Not so tight, honey," he said softly. "Just barely grip it. One thing you want to always remember is the plane will fly itself if you will just leave it alone. You push the stick forward like this to go down and pull back like this to climb up. To turn to the right, step on that right pedal on the floor." He helped her and the plane skidded to the right. "See: I pushed too much. If you want to make a sharp turn, as we just did, then you need to move the yoke to your right while you push on the pedal, like so. The plane will bank and the pressure on the wings will keep it from skidding, making the plane turn. You try it."

Helen made a fairly sharp banked turn to the right and then she made another one back to the left.

"Beautiful," exclaimed Andrews. "Are you sure that you have never flown a plane before?"

"I never have, honest," she said, grinning.

"Now for the fun part." Jack put his hands in his lap. "You know how to control the aircraft, so let's see if you can fly us to Spanish Cay. We want to stay at 3,000 feet until we see the island. When you just made those turns, you lost a little altitude; see, the altimeter says we are at 2,700 feet - so pull back on the stick a little bit and climb back up to 3,000. There you go. Now we want to fly on a compass heading of 120 degrees for about 50 miles. Right now you are less than 120 degrees, so you want to turn the plane a little farther to the right. Nice turn, but you went too far, as we are now on a 129-degree heading, so come back. Perfect. But you lost some altitude again, so come on back up. There you go. Beautiful job, Helen! You go ahead and fly us to Spanish Cay while I check out our new bladder tanks and listen to the weather. You'll know it's the right island when you see the airstrip."

Helen never said a word or asked one question, but concentrated on the compass and altimeter. Andrews laughed out loud at her determination.

"Darling, you are by far the prettiest pilot that has ever flown this airplane," he told her, "and the good news is that it looks as if I can sleep all the way to Bermuda."

"Not a chance," she smiled. "I know how to keep you awake."

****

Less than 10 minutes after he and Eddie had watched Jack Andrews' Piper Cherokee disappear to the southeast, Bart Keener was in his room going over some new maps that he had just picked up in Marsh Harbor. The roar of a twin engine plane sounded as if it was coming through his room. He raced to his window and drew open the drapes to see the big King Air banking on its downwind turn while landing gear descended from the plane.

274

He found Kate eating an apple at her desk in the little office. "Kate, do you know who that is landing out here now?" he asked her.

"Not sure, Bart, but we have a charter coming from Freeport to fish with Eddie. They were supposed to be here early this morning, so it could them. Eddie just took the big golf cart and went down to meet them. Other than that, we have no other reservations at the moment."

"Can you tell me where their flight originated or who booked their rooms here?" he asked, showing concern.

"They didn't book hotel rooms, they were just coming for a day of fishing; and they have prepaid our half-day charge of $250 per person for four people with an American Express card." Kate retrieved the charge acknowledgment and studied it. "It is not an individual, and it is a business by the name of Bruno Waste Management, and their mailing address is a PO Box in Minneapolis, Minnesota."

Bart shook his head and stared at the floor.

"What's wrong?" Kate asked. "Do you know who they are, Bart?"

"No, but I have a good idea that they are not here to go fishing."

"What do you mean?"

"I think these people are after Helen and my guess is that her soon-to-be-ex-husband sent them. I will need to get word to Jack at Spanish Cay not to come back here as long as they are here."

Kate came to her feet. "I can get the Spanish Cay Hotel on our radio phone if you want me to; we book reservations for each other all the time."

"The trouble is that Jack may not go to the hotel. He is flying down there just to buy gas. There is a phone at the Spanish Cay airstrip - I know because I have used it. Can you call the hotel and get that number for me, and maybe I can talk to the old fellow that runs the air service and tell him to give Jack a message for us?" Bart picked up a sheet of the hotel's stationary and, using the desk pen, he wrote out a message while Kate attempted to reach the Spanish Cay Hotel on the radio phone.

"I've got to try to get him on my airplane radio," he said. "Here, Kate; if you get the guy that runs the Spanish airstrip, give this message to him to write down and give to the pilot of a Cherokee Six named Bart Keener."

"Named Bart Keener?" Kate gave Bart a questioning look. "I think you need to slow it down a notch," she said, grinning at him.

"Yes, Jack is there to buy gas with my credit card, so we need to keep it simple." He handed Kate his message. She studied it for several seconds.

"Bart: Uninvited guest here. Do Not Return. Bringing luggage ASAP. Suggest RON at hotel with my CC until my all clear or storm in place. Jackson."

"Jack will know what this means?" she asked incredulously.

"Yes, he will," Bart said quickly. "And go ahead and book a reservation with the hotel in my name. Jack will see what I'm doing right away. I'm going down to my plane now to see if I can raise him on the radio and I'll check these waste management guys out right now."

Kate, talking to someone on the phone, nodded and waved to him at the same time.

When he reached his plane, he turned on the radio and called Jack's call sign for a good twenty minutes; to no avail. The good news was that another weather check informed him that the oncoming winter storm had gained substantial speed and was coming ashore near Naples, traveling in a northeast direction, which would put it over Ft. Pierce before dark.

On his way back from the air strip, Bart heard the diesel engines of The Summer Star rev up and soon saw the Hatteras gliding out of the marina harbor with Eddie on the bridge and four men riding in the chairs in the back area. Getting a quick start? Could these guys be here to fish? Bart shook his head, as he had learned a long time ago not to believe in coincidences.

He walked into the pool area. There he saw two men wearing swim trunks standing in the shallow end of the pool talking to each other. He abruptly decided to visit with them and walked onto the pool deck.

"Good morning, guys," he said, trying to be as friendly as possible. "Did you fellows just come in on that King Air this morning?"

"Yes sir," the tall balding one said.

"Are you going fishing?" Bart asked.

"Not today. We're the pilots, and we weren't invited," the younger man offered, laughing.

"I saw your plane when you took the roof off here, this morning. Is that the Super King Air 350?"

"Yes sir, it is," the senior pilot said. "I'm sorry about that low pass. My young friend here was at the controls and he just couldn't believe that we were going to land out here. He was trying to scope out that short runway."

"Think nothing of it," said Bart waving his hand. "We all needed a wakeup call anyway. Yep, that runway shakes some good pilots up. It's a short one."

"I told Dan here that it reminds me of my carrier days except the ship always gave us a lot more runway with 20 knots of head wind."

"That is, if you didn't mind the ship moving around on you. Are you Navy?" Bart asked.

"Sort of. I was trained by the Navy to fly the hand-me-downs of their step-sister service, the United States Marine Corps," the pilot said with a grin.

"Wonderful!" shouted Keener. "Semper Fi! My name is Bart," he said, extending his hand. "I flew choppers. Huey Gun Ships, out of Da Nang."

The pilot beamed and shook Bart's hand. "My name is Chip Evans and this is Dan Glenn."

Bart shook Dan's hand. "Welcome to our island, fellas. This is one of the greatest places on earth.... it helps if you love to dive and fish."

"Thank you sir, we want to try both, but we'll have to do it another day, I'm afraid. Today is a work day for us."

"Well, you're flying a beautiful plane. Are you guys corporate or charter?"

"We're a charter sir, flying out of Minneapolis/St. Paul. However, we came in this morning from Freeport."

"So you guys are Viking fans, huh? Me too! That's great!" Keener enthused. "I have some good friends living in the Twin Cities; you're not by chance carrying any 3M folks on your flight with you, are you?"

"No sir, far from it. This was a spur of the moment trip for us." The senior pilot smiled at his friend. "You spent some time with these guys before we left yesterday, Danny. This is a reward trip for them, right?"

"That's what they told me. Their company is rewarding all four of them for going over their sales quotas. They gambled in Freeport last night and we are taking them back there tonight after they come in from fishing. Then, back to Minneapolis tomorrow."

"I'll try to visit with them when they come back in. I bet we know some of the same people." Keener's curiosity was peeking. "Are they all out fishing now?"

"Yes sir, the four of them went out on that charter this morning." The senior pilot smiled and shook his head, looking at his friend. "But I doubt if you and these guys know the same people, sir. They are pretty blue collar rough, if you know what I mean." Chip pushed his nose to one side with his thumb to give Bart a clearer picture.

"Are they giving you trouble?" Keener asked, as if he could have a solution.

"Nothing we can't handle, sir. But Bahamian Customs took two undeclared firearms away from them that they found

279

in their luggage when we cleared Freeport. It was a little embarrassing, as they said the guns were for when they go fishing for sharks. A little hard to believe; and then, of course, the two custom inspectors wanted to take our plane apart, piece by piece."

"Holy Cow!" Keener was alarmed and the excitement of a high alert ran through his body.

"Yes sir, we're lucky they didn't impound our plane. I had to get the owner of our company on the horn and let him plead our case. He convinced them that the passengers were just riding for a fare and had nothing to do with our company or our plane."

"So, then these guys are not staying here at the hotel at all."

"No sir. We're taking them back to Freeport this afternoon as soon as they get back from fishing. But the manager here, nice lady, has given us a room right here next to the pool to change in and told us we can have use of all the facilities."

Bart decided to ingratiate himself to the two pilots and gamble that they would not accept his offer.

"If you fellows want to fish today, there is room on my boat this morning. We are just getting ready to go out in a few minutes and you are more than welcome to join us. It would be my treat."

The pilots glanced at each other and for a second Bart thought that they would accept, before the senior man said, "Thanks for a great offer, sir, but we are at our charter's service 24/7 and if they come back in early and want to take off, we should be here."

"Thanks, though," the younger man chimed in. "That's the best offer we have had since we left the Twin Cities."

"You bet," said Keener. "What time do you fellows think you will be flying back to Freeport? Do you have any idea?"

"No sir, we don't; whenever these guys want to get back to the blackjack tables, I guess."

"Don't forget, they said we would be taking a lady back to Freeport with us," the young pilot added.

"You're picking up a lady passenger here?" Bart asked, trying to hide the excitement in his voice.

"Maybe," said the senior man. "But you can't tell what these jokers are going to do. They also said we have to fly to Nassau for them to do some banking tomorrow before we head home." He smiled at Keener. "It makes no difference to us. We're on the clock right now and they are paying for all the gas and the King Air by the hour."

"Well, I had better get my show on the road," Bart said as he turned back towards the hotel. "It was nice to see and talk with you fellows. Hope I see you again sometime."

"Yes sir, it was nice meeting you, too. Semper Fi."

Keener walked back through the glass doors and into the hotel. He headed into the duty free shop where he was relieved to see both Anna and Sally working.

"Sally, I need you to do me a great favor."

Sally smiled at him. "Mister Bart, what you need now?"

"I need you to get the pass key from Kate and go to Mister Jack's room and pack up everything in their luggage in there that belongs to him and Miss Helen and just set it outside in the hallway and make the room up as if nobody has been living in it recently. I am going to bring the golf cart around to the front and I will carry all of their gear out and load it in my plane. Will you do that for me, please?"

"Yes sa." Sally glanced at Anna. "I goin ta go right now."

****

Bart went to his room, where he packed a few clothes in a suitcase and put the special 16-ounce leather Jack Sap that he had ordered from Ontario in his jacket pocket. He found one of the smaller golf carts parked on the walkway and drove it to the bottom of the front steps. He parked the vehicle and headed for the office where he found Kate with her back to the counter. She was sitting bent over in her chair, putting a manila envelope into an antique Schwab safe that stood against the back wall of the office. Bart walked up quietly and softly said, "Hi, Kate."

She straightened with a jolt, but seeing him, she smiled, "Damn, Bart, you scared the daylights out of me. I thought you were down at your plane trying to get Jack on your radio."

"No, Kate, that turned out to be a no go," Bart said dejectedly.

"Well, I did get your message to that manager of Spanish Cay's airstrip. He said that he would be sure to give it to the pilot when he got there."

"All right, Kate!" Bart exclaimed. "That is a big plus right there. Did Sally get the key from you to make up Jack's room?"

282

"Yes, I gave it to her. What are you going to do with their luggage?"

"I'm going to fly it down to Spanish Cay right now. They won't be coming back here, so you will want to check them out right now and let me take copies of their bills."

Kate closed the safe door and spun the combination off. "I sure hate to see them go. It's been fun having them around this week. But I'm glad you're here to help them out."

Bart glanced nervously around the lobby. "Kate, I was just talking to the pilots who flew in here this morning. One of them told me that when their passengers come back in from fishing, they are picking up a lady passenger and flying back to Freeport. Do you know if that is Joe Bruno fishing?"

"No, Mr. Bruno is not with them; he just made the arrangements and is paying their bill. The only one that I've met is named Mike. He seems to be in charge and he just came in here right after you left a few minutes ago and brought me some papers that he wanted me to put in the hotel safe for safekeeping."

"What sort of papers?" Keener asked.

"I have no idea, Bart," she huffed. "He just asked if we had a fireproof safe on the premises to keep valuables in. I showed him our old antique Schwab safe right over here, but I told him that I didn't know how fireproof it was. He saw it and said that would be perfect, then gave me an envelope to put in it for safekeeping. He said he would pick it up later this evening before they flew back to Freeport. What's so important about his papers, anyway?"

Keener was beginning to connect the dots, and while he didn't want to cry "wolf" and frighten Kate Judson, he couldn't take a chance under the circumstances.

"Kate, listen to me," he said softly. "The two pilots that flew in here this morning work for a charter airline. They don't work for Bruno's company. They don't know anything about their passengers except that Bahamian Customs in Freeport took two guns away from them that they found in their luggage. Something is wrong here. Now, I know you don't know all the facts, but you do know that our friend, Helen, is trying to avoid contact with the outside world if at all possible, right?"

"Yes, all of us here know that," she quickly said, defensively.

"And I know that you have been helping her do just that. I believe these guys who flew in here this morning are after Helen and somehow they have found out that she is here. This fishing trip they are on with Eddie today is just a ruse; it's a distraction to provide them a reason to be here."

Kate Judson stood up from her chair. "Bart, this all sounds too ridiculous." She stared at him in disbelief. "Why in the world would they come after Helen?"

"Because they want something she has. And let me tell you, it is something so valuable that none of us here on this island should feel safe." He paused. "Let me ask you a question, Kate. Are you keeping anything valuable for Helen in your safe?"

She shook her head. "No, I have nothing of Helen's."

Keener glanced around the lobby once more and then leaned close to her. "Kate, why would anybody who is only going to be on the island for a few more hours - why would that person bring you anything at all to keep in your safe for him? It makes no sense at all. And to my mind, there is only one explanation; and that is: when he comes back to claim his envelope this afternoon, you will have to open the safe for him. When that happens, he will take whatever else is in it by force."

"Come on, Bart!" Kate Judson's eyes widened. "And what is he going to do then, take my petty cash? Because that is all I have in there."

"Well if that's all you have in there, he isn't going to be happy. Hopefully he will just leave the island without taking any retribution."

"Bart, I think you are being overly cautious here. What does Helen think about all this?"

"Helen doesn't know about any of it. She would be frightened if she did. Okay, let's do this: you open up the safe now and see what he gave you that is so valuable that he trusts you to keep it for him. If it is something valuable, as in money, notes, or documents of any kind, I'll back off. But if it isn't something that should go into a safe, you'll have to agree that my point has real merit."

Kate hesitated. "I think his envelope is sealed," she said.

"Open it carefully. You can reseal it."

She sat back down in her chair and worked the combination dial on the old safe. Bart went to the front doors of the lobby and checked outside, both ways. When he returned, Kate had a large brown envelope in her hand. It was held together by one small piece of scotch tape over the point of the fold down. She glanced up at Keener. "I feel as though we are the ones who are doing something wrong," she said to him.

"Open it up, Kate," he said. "Let's have a look. I am hoping that you are right and I am wrong. Then I can relax and go fishing."

Kate lifted off the piece of tape holding the envelope flap closed. She withdrew its contents and laid them out on the desk in front of her. There was a brochure entitled "Things to Do in Freeport, Bahamas" and a sport section from The Minneapolis Star Tribune, along with a single plastic sheet that had given the envelope it's stiffness. On it were pictures and diagrams of an airplane and the heading "Engine Start Procedures for the Beechcraft Super King Air 350."

"Oh my God," she whispered softly, and then, shaking her head in disbelief, she gazed up at Bart Keener; but he was already moving out the front door.

****

Chapter 28
Diversion
A feint attack designed to draw an enemy away from the main attack

When Bart landed the Beech Baron on the Spanish Cay airstrip, he had already spotted Jack Andrews' Cherokee Six sitting on the apron in his fly over. He taxied his plane right up next to it and admired his insignia, painted on the side of the plane in dark green. Cookie had done a masterful job in the paint-over.

He tied his plane down and was heading toward the little office by a parking lot when he was met by the airport manager, an elderly, nervous, skinny little man whom Bart had seen on many occasions, but whose short term memory allowed him to always greet Keener as if he had just flown in for the first time.

"Sir, are you Jack Andrews?" the man asked.

"Why yes, how did you know?" Bart asked, feigning amazement.

"Bart Keener just told me that you would be flying in here in a Beech Baron within the next 30 minutes." He glanced at his watch. "And you're right on time."

"And where is Mr. Keener now? Do you know?" Bart asked.

"He wanted to know a good place to have lunch and I sent them to the Green Turtle, down the road about 3 miles. It's the best we got on the island. We have cars for rent, but he and his misses wanted to ride bicycles, so I rented them three."

"Three of them?" Bart asked, surprised.

"Well, yes," the little man grinned. "He rented one for you too, and said for me to send you on your way when you showed up."

Bart laughed. "Fantastic; which one is mine?" he asked.

"Anyone you want, son. The uglier they look, the easier they are to pedal." He smiled.

****

Spanish Cay's Green Turtle Restaurant had quite a few vehicles parked in front of it when Bart Keener rolled to a stop. He dropped the kickstand and parked his bike next to two others that he assumed were Jack and Helen's.

He found the two sitting at a corner table with Bentley in his cage on the floor next to Helen. They smiled broadly as he approached their table, and both jumped up and hugged him as if they hadn't seen him in months. He was touched.

"Thanks for the heads up, Jack," Andrews said, smiling. "Who is the uninvited guest; anyone we should know?"

Bart took a seat and stared at Helen. "There are four of them," he said.

"Good God! Four of them!" Jack exclaimed, smiling at Helen. "Damn, that's a whole fire team, honey. They must think that you are a 'bad ass' or something."

"Or they think I am traveling with a 'bad ass'," she said, grinning at Bart.

Jack smiled at Bart and added, "A tactical mistake. I think they should have sent more men, don't you, Bart?" He winked at Keener.

"Absolutely!" Bart laughed. Then turning serious, he glanced back at Helen. "Do you know a guy from Minneapolis named Joe Bruno?"

Helen slowly shook her head.

"He has a company called Bruno Waste Management. Does BWM ring a bell?"

"Oh yes, I have heard of the company," she said. "We have a dumpster contract with them, I think. Is he one of the four men?"

"No, he isn't here, but he paid for the trip and it looks as if the four guys he sent do work for him. I talked to the charter pilots who brought them in. They are flying back to Freeport later today. They have been told that they are picking up a lady there at the hotel and taking her back to Minneapolis with them tomorrow."

Bart continued to tell the story that the pilots had told him about the guns being taken away at customs and about one of them giving Kate something to keep in the hotel safe until they get ready to leave this afternoon which, when he and Kate opened it, turned out to just be scraps of paper.

Jack and Helen listened intently and then Jack spoke. "Bart, I am worried about Kate being back there by herself when these guys want to know where we have gone."

"Oh, she won't be by herself. I am going right back now and will be there with her when this Mike comes to pick up his package." Bart was serious.

"I'm sure she won't just tell them we are on Spanish Cay willingly, but they may make her tell them, and that outcome would not be good." Jack narrowed his eyes and stared at Bart.

"I was thinking that I would go see Ronnie Lee as soon as I get back and get him to stay around the office just to keep an eye on things. It would help if he is armed," Bart said.

"Don't depend on Ronnie Lee to help you at all with this, Bart. That will be a tremendous mistake. If there is going to be gun play, he won't be around at all. I am serious..." Jack was thinking out loud.

"Now, Cookie and Eddie may be a positive influence there with Kate in the office when Mike, as you call him, comes to pick up his package."

Helen handed Bart one of the menus lying on the table. "Captain Jack and I are having the conch fritters. The waitress tells us they are better than Chef Walters. What do you think?"

"I've had them several times, and they are good. They use beer in their batter instead of milk. If that is not against your religion, it is a great choice." Bart smiled at her.

"What say ye, Captain Jack?" Helen turned to Andrews. "Is beer in the batter against our religion?"

"No, honey, the alcohol is long gone before the batter even begins to rise. We're getting ready to fly into a winter storm, so let's live dangerously and try their conch fritters."

"What other ideas do you have, Jackson?" Bart was focused on his friend's thoughts.

"OK, the first thing I would do when you get back is go see the chef."

"Chef Walter?" Bart asked.

"Yes sir, his brother is the Chief of Bahamian Police in Nassau. Bring Walter up to speed and ask him if he can get his brother to bring some help up to Walkers today, ASAP."

"The second thing I would do is go see those two pilots you made friends with. Tell them the whole story and what we think is about to go down. If they call their owner again and he finds out that a kidnapping is about to be committed using his aircraft, I'll bet ten to one he tells them to come home immediately. That would shut them down. But Bart, it also wouldn't be a bad idea to tell those pilots that I am flying Helen back to the States today. If they or their mob passengers decide to check traffic, they will see that I already filed my IFR flight plan to Fort Pierce early this morning."

"And this is the third thing." Andrews sat back in his chair, unsnapped the waist pack he was wearing, and handed it across the table to Bart. It made a heavy metal clunk sound when it hit the table. "What's this?" asked Bart.

"It's my 1911 Browning."

"Jack, you were going to try to take that through Bermuda customs with you?" Bart asked.

"Believe me; I could do it all day long. I have a hiding place for it that is so good that I'm not sure I can find it again." He glanced at Helen. "Don't I, dear?" he asked, smiling. She smiled back.

"You can give it back to Jack when you come visit us in Bermuda," Helen said, touching Bart's arm.

Jack continued on with his recommendations, "There is a box of cartridges in there, but I've already put eight in the magazine. You will want to chamber one in the pipe before you show up with it. I would stay around Kate, but stay out of sight, so no one gets the drop on you. You know the rules: never pull a gun unless you're going to use it immediately; then come up blazing. If they are showing firearms to Kate, don't risk anything while she is vulnerable. But as soon as they move away, take 'em hard. Don't worry about the Queensbury rules of gun play. Just remember the Korean War advice, "When in doubt, empty the magazine."

"One more thing, Bart." Jack had just thought of something else. "After you tie down when you get back, take a coil out of one of your plane's engines to keep it from cranking. Do this just in case one of these jokers thinks he can fly and wants to force you to fly them somewhere."

Bart nodded his head as Jack spieled off one idea after another. "I will do all those things, Jack, and that is a great point about the pilots. I brought your luggage with me and Kate booked a reservation for you in the hotel here under my name. The good news is that the storm front was starting to come across Florida this morning."

292

"I know," Jack grinned at him. "I was listening to the weather all the way down here, while Helen flew us. She did a commendable job, by the way." He patted her arm.

"Wow," Bart smiled at her. "Is there no end to your talents, Madam?" he asked.

"Tell Bart what you've learned about flying today, Helen." Andrews patted her arm, egging her on.

"Well, Captain Jack taught me that the three best things in life are a good landing, a good orgasm, and a good bowel movement. And a night carrier landing is one of the few opportunities in life where you get to experience all three at the same time."

Bart laughed out loud while Andrews beamed with pride. He spoke to Bart, "We are not going to hang around here tonight, but will make our move in a couple of hours. I figure the front will be passing over Ft. Pierce about 3 PM. If we leave here a little bit after 2 PM, it should put us right on the edge of it before 4 PM."

Bart laughed and shook his head, looking at his friends. They were getting ready to fly into a storm and then over a thousand miles of open ocean, but they acted as if they were a couple going on a great weekend adventure together without a care in the world.

"Are you nervous, Helen?" he asked her.

"No, I'm excited, but not nervous; and why should I be? I'm flying with one of the best fighter pilots in the Marine Corps and he tells me that as long as we don't have to land on a carrier, there is nothing to worry about." She grabbed Andrews' hand and locked her fingers with his.

"Well, you've got that right," Bart said, laughing. "When do you think you will reach Bermuda, Jack; around midnight?"

"Closer to 1 AM, as we gain an hour in the time zone change."

They ordered lunch, conch fritters all around, and when it came, they immediately ate in silence. Bart checked his watch and it was 1 PM.

"I'm going to fly back now and try to get all my ducks in a row. Is the Cherokee-Six unlocked so I can put your bags on board? "

"Yes, it is," said Jack, "but we are going to go back with you and double check the progress on the storm."

They pedaled the three miles back to the airstrip in just ten minutes, with the guys trying to keep up with Helen. She had the smallest bike with a huge basket on the front of it that the base of Bentley's kennel fit into; but even with her handicaps, she pedaled effortlessly away from the two men.

"My god, she has some strong legs," Bart mumbled to Jack.

"Tell me about it," Andrews puffed. "You saw her drown me in the pool the other night. I told her that she doesn't know her own strength."

Once they had relocated the luggage from the Beech Baron to the Cherokee, the three friends stood staring at each other.

"Ok, this is it," Bart said. "Good luck to you guys. I will come see you in Bermuda, I promise." They all hugged each other again and Bart climbed into his plane. Jack and

Helen watched him taxi to the end of the runway and do a short run-up. Then, going to full throttle, he sent the Beech Baron roaring down the asphalt strip and up into the sky.

"I think he's worried about us," Helen said softly.

"That makes us even, because right now I am worried about him," Jack said, shaking his head and watching his friend's plane disappear on the horizon.

****

Chapter 29
The Encounter
Unexpectedly experience or be faced with (something difficult or hostile)

After Bart Keener had tied his plane down on the Walkers Cay airstrip, he opened the engine cowling on the right engine and removed the magneto lead as per Jack Andrews' suggestion. He placed the cap under the pilot's seat and locked the aircraft. He then headed straight for the little customs house. As his luck would have it, Ronnie Lee was inside doing some paperwork when he came through the doorway.

"Say, hey, Bartman, what can I do you for?" he smiled at Bart.

"I'm here to give you a heads-up, Ronnie Lee, on something that could be going down on your watch." Keener took about 15 minutes explaining to Ronnie Lee about the King Air's visit and what he thought it meant.

"But, so far, these gentlemen have done nothing wrong, right?" Ronnie Lee was uneasy.

"Right, other than to try to bring hand guns into your country illegally and to ask Kate to keep some worthless paper in her safe so that they can have access to it later."

"Well you know, Bart, I can't arrest somebody for what I think they *could* do."

"I don't want you to arrest anybody, Ronnie Lee, until they do something wrong; but just your presence in the lobby when they leave this afternoon may be enough to keep them from doing something wrong. "

"When they do something wrong, I will arrest them," Ronnie Lee said with conviction; but then, seeming to remember something, he shook his head. "The problem is, Bart, that I have a function that I must attend on the Big Island this afternoon, so I can't be here all day. " He paused. "Do you know what I mean?"

"I know exactly what you mean, Ronnie Lee," Bart said under his breath.

When he left the little customs office, Bart walked out onto the apron to the big King Air. No one was around it, so he climbed the walkway up to the hotel. He used the kitchen service entrance and found Chef Walter peeling shrimp with Anna, who was heaping a large portion of shrimp salad onto a plate with a bed of lettuce on it.

"Feed the customer, girl, don't fatten him," Walter said, slapping at her hand.

Bart explained what he and Jack thought was going on with the new visitors and mentioned that Ronnie Lee wasn't too interested in getting involved.

"Jack told me that your brother is Chief of Police in Nassau and he thought he would appreciate a phone call from you, just to give him a heads up."

"Thomas is coming to Big Island today to spend a few days with us, anyway. I will make sure he come early," Walter said. "He do dat for me."

Bart thanked Walter and walked out of the kitchen into the dining room, where he found the two pilots having lunch at a table overlooking the pool.

"Hi guys," he said as he approached their table. "Would you mind if I sit down with you for a minute?"

"Not at all," said Chip, the senior pilot. "Dan and I saw you go off earlier in that Beech Baron. Talk about a nice plane. What do you do, Bart, if you don't mind my asking?"

"I'm a fish spotter, Chip," Bart smiled at him. "I work as a private contractor, but I do most of my business for the boat builders, Hatteras and Bertram. I work the tournaments that they sponsor. I try to locate the big fish from the air and help to get their boats there first." Bart glanced around the dining room and, leaning forward towards the two pilots, he lowered his voice and spoke almost in a whisper.

"Listen guys, I want to talk to you about something that has just come to my attention and I think you ought to know about it." For the next 30 minutes Bart spoke non-stop about the situation with Helen Warner and her husband, who it now appeared had sent men on their airplane to take her by force back to Minneapolis.

"I think these guys are about to commit a felony using your aircraft as the getaway vehicle," Bart said sternly. He then told them about Mike asking Kate to store paper scraps in her old safe just to give them quick access to it when they came back from fishing.

"I told you that these dudes were mobsters, didn't I?" Dan said to Chip, who was looking all around the dining room.

"Does this hotel have a land line phone?" he asked Bart.

"Yes, they do," Bart replied. "But it only comes through an older switchboard in the office. Kate will be glad to let you use it if you ask her." The pilot quickly rose out of his chair and, nodding to his two companions, left the table and headed towards the office.

"How long have you been a fish spotter?" Dan asked Bart.

"About 5 years," Bart replied.

"Wow, it sounds as if your work would be a lot fun."

"It is if you love to fly; but you need to know a lot about fishing to be good at it."

"Is the money pretty good in that field?" the young man asked.

'It can be if you are good at it. Most spotters work on a share basis. My contract price just covers expenses: fuel, wear and tear on the aircraft, and compensation for my flying time. I am also compensated with a share of the purse for winning tournaments. If I can find the fish for my boat and my boat can catch them, we all make money together."

"Wow," Dan said. "How many tournaments do you work a year?"

"I usually get in at least 5 to 6. One year I did 10, which is when I bought my new Baron."

Chip, running, returned to their table and gave his co-pilot a thumbs up.

"Saddle up, Danny," the senior pilot said as he glanced around the dining room. "We've been summoned home."

"Are you serious?" asked the younger pilot.

"I'm dead serious. The boss knows this Warner lady. His wife is in her yoga class. He says to take our passenger's luggage off the plane and leave it at the custom house. His last words were, "File IFR to MSP and do it now!"

He smiled at Bart. "I know a direct order when I hear one."

Bart was impressed. "Can you fly that King Air from here to Minneapolis non-stop?"

"Yes sir, we topped off in Freeport yesterday and once we clear customs in Fort Pierce, we'll have plenty of fuel left to get home." He smiled at his co-pilot. "One thing you've got to be happy about, Danny, is we're at least a thousand pounds lighter going out of here, so you won't need all 3300 feet of runway to get her off."

"That's right," Dan grinned back at both of them. "I feel better already."

The senior pilot laughed and smiled at Bart, "He's a good pilot. A little bit bold for my taste. I've told him several times that I'm old; he's bold; but there are no old, bold pilots."

"Rule number one," said Bart with a grin.

The two pilots said good bye to Bart and walked briskly out of the dining room and down the back walkway towards their plane.

Keener followed them out to the pool deck and watched the two men disappear. Off in the distance he saw the Summer Star making its way back around and through the channel markers. Eddie was bringing his fishing charter home. He couldn't help but smile at the irony of it all. "Jack and Helen would love to see this," he said softly. Just when he was wondering if the two pilots had also seen the Hatteras returning, he heard the big engines of the King Air crank up down below him. Chip and Danny would be in the air before their passengers discovered that they had lost their ride.

After a few seconds, Bart heard the run-up of the King Air's engines and was sure that the pilots had positioned the plane into a takeoff position up at the close end of the runway. Out in the marina, Eddie was easing the Summer Star into her slip and his charter crew members were throwing ropes over pilings. Then, all at once there was a huge roar as Dan had pushed the throttles all the way forward on the King Air, and she was carrying the sound away from the hotel. After 30 seconds Bart saw her rising up above the tops of the sea grape surrounding the pool deck. She set a course west by northwest and was soon just a dot on the horizon. Bart glanced around and saw Kate standing there, also watching the plane.

"Katie Girl, I don't think your man Mike is coming back to collect his important papers. He just lost his ride out of here." Bart was smiling.

"You don't think so?" she said. "What does their plane leaving mean to us now?'

"Well, they are not going to be too quick with the strong-arm stuff because they don't have a getaway vehicle. Walter said that he would call his brother, Chief of Police in Nassau, to come here today as soon as he could."

"I know," Kate said. "He has already called him and Walter told me that his brother was on his way, flying here right now with a couple of his officers. Walter also said that his brother has alerted the Royal Bahamas Defense Force, and they are flying people in, also. "

"Bart, I think what they are going to need now is someone to fly them out of here before the authorities show up. You should fly your plane off the island." Kate was worried for him.

"I can't do it, Katie, I'd be happy to help them out and I could use the money, but I'm having engine trouble." Bart smiled at her.

"Seriously," Kate was alarmed. "You honestly do have engine trouble?"

"Yeah, my starboard engine won't start. Jack Andrews told me how to fix it, though," he paused and smiled at her again, "just as he told me how I could prevent it from starting."

"Oh, I see," Kate said, shaking her head. "Are Helen and Jack ever coming back?"

"Not today or anytime soon. They are flying far, far, away and Jackson Andrews called this one perfectly."

"Jack is a smart guy, isn't he, Bart?" Kate asked.

"One of the smartest I know, that's for sure."

****

Chapter 30
Flight
The act of fleeing or running away, as from danger

Jackson Andrews and Helen Warner waited for well over an hour after watching Bart Keener fly out of Spanish Cay before they fastened their seat belts and prepared for their long flight. Jack had been wearing his headphones while checking the weather, and studying a chart. He lifted his head and smiled at Helen. "The front is right where we want it," he said.

"Where do we go from here, Captain Jack?" Helen asked, patting his arm.

"First, we will fly back to Walkers for one last look, and contact Miami Flight Service on the radio to cancel my IFR flight plan and file our new DVFR plan." Andrews was studying a chart.

"Can I fly us back to Walkers?" Helen asked.

"Look at you! I've got my own little Amelia Earhart. Do you want to take us off?"

"Will it be just as it was at Walkers?" She was hesitant, but quickly added, "Sure, if you will help me - and you will, won't you?"

"Of course, and here it is much safer than at Walkers. We have more weight now with all of our fuel and our luggage, but we have a beautiful runway twice the length of Walkers, so we can just let the plane fly itself off the ground."

"We're not going to land at Walkers, are we, Jack?" Helen was concerned.

"Not this time," Andrews shook his head. "I don't think it would be a good idea, do you?" Helen nodded. "No, but I'll miss saying goodbye to Kate and the hotel staff. They were all so good to me."

"You've been good to them, too, Helen," Andrews laughed. "Cookie has never gotten a thousand dollar tip for a day trip in his life; not even from those Hatteras Shoot-Out Tournament big spenders; and that $500 you gave to Eddie ruined him for the rest of us."

"I underpaid them both, in my book," Helen said. "I shouldn't have let you talk me out of giving Eddie the same as I did Cookie. Last Monday was a special day for me and I still feel that I need to do more for them."

Andrews studied his beautiful passenger carefully. "How much did you tip Sally for moving your room to mine?' he asked, smiling.

"Okay, I saw you ask her to move me, Jack. Sally asked me, to make sure I approved, before she did anything. But she also cleared it with Kate, as the hotel was losing the room charge."

"I told Kate yesterday that she could keep on charging me for the room. I just wanted to be near my 'main man.' She laughed and said that she didn't blame me and that there was no way she was charging me for the room after Monday. I think you could be Kate's 'main man' too, if you wanted."

Jack laughed, leaned over, and kissed her ear. "You sort of fancy that 'main man' term, don't you?"

"That's what you are to me, Jackson Andrews. You are my "Main Man.""

Andrews glanced around the cockpit, checking Helen's seat belt and the two holding Bentley's kennel in place in the back seats, then he looked all around the outside of the plane and clapped his hands together. "All right, darling, she's all yours; let's see you start her up and fly us out of here."

"How about you starting us? I'm just good at flying," she grinned at him.

"Yeah, I think Amelia had somebody to start her planes for her also." Andrews turned the fuel pump on and set the mixture to lean.

"Wait!" Helen said as she grabbed his hand. "Well, I can help you start a little bit." She glanced around the plane and in a loud voice she yelled, "Clear!"

"Nice work," Jack said smiling. He cracked the throttle and turned the ignition key. The plane's engine roared to life. "Now, do you want to taxi us over to the runway?"

"No, you can taxi us, too," Helen said.

Andrews taxied the plane off the apron and on to the beginning of the runway. He did a 360 check of the sky around them and then, with the brakes set, he did an engine run-up check.

"Put your hand on the throttle here," he said, and he laid his hand over hers. "I will move it for you, but I just want you to feel how we apply the power during a takeoff."

Gradually he pushed their hands forward and as the plane rolled forward, gaining speed, he kept moving the throttle higher and higher. As the Cherokee sped down the runway, they could feel it getting lighter.

 "Feel that?" he asked her. "She wants to fly, so now let's pull back gradually on the yoke and presto, we're flying."

"I love it," Helen squealed, laughing.

Andrews put both of his hands in his lap and laughed at her excitement.

"Okay, now it's all yours," he said. "Let's see you slowly climb to 2,000 feet and try to hold a heading of 300 to take us back to Walkers."

Helen flew with steady hands, climbing to 2,000 feet and settling in on a 300 degree heading.

"Are you sure you have never flown a plane before?" Andrews asked again.

"Never!" she said, concentrating on the plane's instruments.

"You are going to be a damn good pilot by the time we get to Bermuda," Andrews teased.

The flight to Walkers was less than 20 minutes and Jack pointed the island out to Helen as it came up on the left side of the plane's nose.

"There she is," he said. "It looks as if there are two new planes down there that weren't there when we left this morning. And where is the King Air Bart was telling us about?"

Helen stared down at the island. She saw Bart's plane parked on the apron of airstrip. Two other planes were parked right next to his Beech Baron. But there were no other aircraft parked on the apron. "Are either of those two planes next to Bart's the charter plane?" she asked Andrews.

"No," Jack grinned at her. "If Bart spoke to those two charter pilots and they called their company to update, I'll bet they were called home. Wouldn't that be something?" Jack laughed. "Let me have the controls for a second. I want to go down and take a closer look at those aircraft."

Andrews swung the plane over on its side and dropped down quickly over the runway and towards the hotel. As he passed over the parked planes, he laughed out loud and smiled at Helen.

"What's so funny, Captain Jack? Are you going to share it with your crew?"

"Do you see those black, yellow and blue insignias on the wings of those two planes?"

"Yes, I see them."

"That is the insignia of the RBDF."

"What is the RBDF?"

"The RBDF stands for Royal Bahamas Defense Force. The Bahamas do not have an Army or an Air Force, so its Navy composes the entirety of its armed forces. They protect the territorial integrity of the Bahamas by patrolling its waters, but they also work with law enforcement agencies of the Bahamas to enforce law and order. Chef Walter's brother, the Nassau Police Chief, must have called them in here for additional support." Jack chuckled, shaking his head.

"Well, that's good for Bart, Kate and the hotel staff, right?" Helen asked.

"Absolutely!" he shouted as he pulled the nose of the plane up and banked it in a sharp turn to the west. "It's more than good. It's perfect! Bruno's boys are going to be detained in Nassau for further questioning; I am certain of that."

"Okay, Amelia, you have the con once again," he said as he leveled out the plane's flight once more. "Let's set our course right now for Ft. Pierce. Try to maintain a 285 heading on the compass and let's see if we can find some bad weather." He gave her a big smile.

Helen flew the plane on her assigned heading for 30 minutes while Jack contacted Miami Flight Service and changed his earlier IFR Flight Plan to a DVFR plan with an assigned entry code to transmit.

Out on the horizon in front of them the sky emerged as a black line totally void of sunlight. Although the air around them was clear, soon the plane was beginning to bounce around as it encountered rough air.

"It looks as though we are going to fly into the night." Helen said nervously.

"Yep, but we are not going to fly too far into that night," Jack said softly as he put his hands back on the controls. "My turn to fly us now," he said; and then, just as if he had anticipated the fall, the plane dropped several hundred feet into a down draft and Helen grabbed his knee.

"Did you feel that, Amelia?" he asked, smiling at her.

"God, yes!" she exclaimed.

"That was just a little turbulence. The three most common expressions in military aviation are, 'Did you feel that?' 'Did you hear that noise?' and of course, the most popular, 'Oh shit!'"

"Well, I certainly felt that," Helen said. "And I would just as soon not hear you say those other two."

"You won't," he said, laughing, and then he studied her for several seconds before whispering in her ear, "I love you, Helen Warner."

She smiled back at him and, leaning close to him, she hugged his arm and whispered, "I love you, Jack Andrews."

Map of the Abacos

Glossary

1. **BARK BUSTER FREEZE** - Freeze damage on citrus trees occurs when the water inside the fruit, leaves, twigs and wood of a tree freezes, rupturing the cell membranes. Unlike deciduous trees, which protect themselves from cold by shedding their leaves in the fall and entering a dormant state, citrus trees continue growing year-round. Extended periods of cool weather prior to a freeze may allow a citrus tree to prepare somewhat. This is why sharp freezes following warm weather are more damaging than gradual temperature changes. However, virtually all freezes will cause damage of some kind.

2. **LIDOCAINE (Xylocaine)** – Prescription drug. Over-the-counter drug. Causes numbness or loss of feeling in an area of your body. Given before and during surgery, childbirth, or dental work. Also treats emergency heart rhythm problems. Brand names: Lidoderm, Xylocaine, Lmx4 and Recticare.

3. **EPINEPHRINE/ADRENALIN** – A vasoconstrictor drug used to slow the absorption and, therefore, prolong the action of the anesthetic agent. Due to epinephrine's vasoconstriction abilities, the use of epinephrine in localized anesthetics also helps to diminish the total blood loss the patient sustains during minor surgical procedures.

4. **JOHN PHILIP SOUSA** - (November 6, 1854 – March 6, 1932) Known as "The March King" Sousa was an American composer and conductor of the late Romantic era, known primarily for American military and patriotic marches. Sousaphone - Semper Fidelis (march) The Washington Post (march) and Stars and Stripes Forever (march)

5. **CONCH FRITTERS – Chef Walter's Ingredients (16 Units)**
   16 ounces of fresh Cracked Conch Meat (thaw if frozen)
   1 quart oil (for frying)
   $^3/_4$ cup all-purpose flour
   1 egg
   $^1/_2$ cup milk (beer is an optional replacement)
   ground cayenne pepper, to taste
   red pepper flakes, to taste
   seasoning salt, to taste
   salt, to taste (optional)
   ground coarse black pepper, to taste
   1 cup chopped conch
   $^1/_2$ onion, chopped
   $^1/_4$ green bell pepper, chopped fine
   $^1/_4$ yellow bell pepper, chopped fine
   $^1/_4$ red bell pepper, chopped fine
   2 stalks celery, chopped fine
   2 garlic cloves, chopped fine

   Dipping Sauce
   2 tablespoons ketchup
   2 tablespoons fresh lime juice, no subs
   1 tablespoon mayonnaise
   1 teaspoon Tabasco sauce, or
   1 teaspoon Pickapeppa Sauce
   salt, to taste
   fresh ground black pepper, to taste

6. **ALCOHOLICS ANONYMOUS (AA) -** Is an international fellowship of men and women who have had a drinking problem. It is nonprofessional, self-supporting, multiracial, apolitical, and available everywhere. There are no age or education requirements. Membership is open to anyone who wants to do something about his or her drinking problem.

7. **THE TWELVE STEPS OF ALCOHOLICS ANONYMOUS** 1. We admitted we were powerless over alcohol—that our lives had become unmanageable. 2. Came to believe that a Power greater than ourselves could restore us to sanity. 3. Made a decision to turn our will and our lives over to the care of God as we understood Him. 4. Made a searching and fearless moral inventory of ourselves. 5. Admitted to God, to ourselves, and to another human being the exact nature of our wrongs. 6. Were entirely ready to have God remove all these defects of character. 7. Humbly asked Him to remove our shortcomings. 8. Made a list of all persons we had harmed, and became willing to make amends to them all. 9. Made direct amends to such people wherever possible, except when to do so would injure them or others. 10. Continued to take personal inventory and when we were wrong, promptly admitted it. 11. Sought, through prayer and meditation, to improve our conscious contact with God, as we understood Him, praying only for knowledge of His will for us and the power to carry that out. 12. Having had a spiritual awakening as the result of these Steps, we attempt to carry this message to alcoholics, and to practice these principles in all our affairs.

About The Author

James Foley Smathers is a former United States Marine Corps Officer and Vietnam combat veteran. He is a graduate of the University of Florida's College of Journalism and Communications. He and his wife reside in Central Florida where he breeds, trains and raises Golden Retrievers.